I0653841

Bratwurst and Bridges

Orchard Hill Romance #5

Susan M. Baganz

Bratwurst and Bridges
COPYRIGHT 2017 by Susan M. Baganz

Contact Information: titleadmin@pelicanbookgroup.com

Quoted Scripture, unless otherwise indicated is from the English Standard Version of the Holy Bible.

Cover Art by *Nicola Martinez*

Prism is a division of Pelican Ventures, LLC
www.pelicanbookgroup.com PO Box 1738 *Aztec, NM * 87410

The Triangle prism logo is a trademark of Pelican Ventures, LLC

Publishing History
Prism Edition, 2017
Paperback Edition ISBN 978-1-943104-95-6
Electronic Edition ISBN 978-1-943104-94-9
Published in the United States of America

Dedication

To David Mundt and Ken Nabi.
You both believed in God's calling for my writing long
before anyone else.
I am grateful and blessed to have been led by you both.

Other books by Susan M. Baganz

Orchard Hill Contemporary Romances
Pesto & Potholes
Salsa & Speed Bumps
Feta & Freeways
Root Beer & Roadblocks
Bratwurst & Bridges
Doughnuts and Detours (coming soon!)

Black Diamond Christian Gothic Regencies
The Baron's Blunder (novella)
The Virtuous Viscount (coming soon)
Lord Phillip's Folly (coming soon)

Historical Christmas Novellas
Fragile Blessings
Love's Christmas Past
Gabriel's Gift (coming soon)

Short Stories
Little Bits 'O Love

PROLOGUE

Parting is all we know of heaven and all we need of hell.
Emily Dickinson

January 2013

Smoke filled the air. Dan bolted into the house dropping his keys as he rushed to the kitchen. "Sharon!" he yelled through a cough. On his mad dash to grab the flaming pan on the stove, he almost tripped over her. He opened the sliding glass door off the dining area and tossed the metal, flames and all, into the snow with a resounding *hissssssss.*

He ran back to his wife sprawled on the kitchen floor. "Sharon?" He checked for a pulse. None. Panic seized him as he fumbled for his phone and called 911 while beginning chest compressions. "Yes, my wife's not breathing. I started CPR. Send someone, please."

The phone dropped to the floor as he counted out compressions. Under his breath, he repeated the chorus to *Staying Alive* to keep a rhythm, broken only by coughing as the hovering smoke continued to assault him.

Don't be dead. Come on, sweetie. I need you. You're too young to die. Tears fell onto her cotton shirt. Minutes dragged on like hours until a paramedic pulled him off. Dan stood by in disbelief as they too failed to revive her.

The coroner arrived.

Dead on the scene.

The words spoken to dispatch by the paramedic pierced his soul. He listened to his voice answer questions, but it was as if he hovered above it all. People came and went in a haze. They covered up the body of the woman he loved and carried her away to the morgue. *The morgue?*

Unreal.

When the house was empty again a chill reminded him of the open sliding door. He went out to retrieve the pan and tossed it in the garbage outside. He shut the door behind him in a daze and collapsed on the couch.

She was gone. His wife of ten years. He grabbed his phone, dialed her parents, and broke the news. He repeated the process with his own before calling Pastor Andrew.

"Sorry to bother you so late."

"That's fine, Dan, what's up? You don't sound good."

"Sharon's dead," he choked out. "I don't know what happened. I came home from worship rehearsal and she was...dead. The paramedics, coroner, and police all just left. I tried to revive her..."

"I'm coming over," Andrew said.

"No. It's late. I just wanted you to know."

"I'm coming over. No arguments." The call disconnected.

His stomach growled. Sharon often prepared something light for him on rehearsal nights. Even if he ate earlier, he always came home hungry. He rose and headed to the kitchen. Opening the fridge, he found his favorite dessert, homemade apple pie. He stared at it, realizing it was the last act of love his wife showed him. He slammed the door shut as his gut rebelled at the thought of food.

Soon Andrew arrived along with Tony, Simon, and Nick, the members of his accountability group. They surrounded him.

The men laid hands on Dan, and Andrew prayed. "Heavenly Father, You knew Sharon's beginning and end, and You understand Dan's grief at losing his beloved wife. Wrap Your arms around him now in the wake of this loss and sustain him through the days to come. We won't pretend to understand why You've chosen to do this, Lord. But we still love You and bless Your holy name."

Dan had no more tears to cry. "Thanks. I've called our parents and now you. Can you let others know?"

"Sure. Come on. You'll stay with us tonight." Andrew pulled Dan to his feet.

He nodded. Any energy to protest went out the door with his heart. A house of memories surrounded him and he wondered if he could live through this. There was no way he could sleep here tonight.

He trudged to the bedroom and stared at the bed where they had slept together, cried together, loved. He shoved some clothing in his gym bag and hauled it back to the living room. Opening the front door, he followed his friends out and locked it.

ONE

Mourning is love with no place to go.
Anonymous

January 2014

The last box was dropped on the stack that lined the wall of the two-bedroom apartment. "Thanks, Tony."

"Call if you need anything, OK?"

Dan nodded. The door shut behind his friend and he took in the space around him. A new bed was in the bedroom with new nightstand and dresser. There was a new sofa and loveseat, kitchen table. Even the dishes, pots and pans, and silverware were new. He'd sold almost everything that reminded him of her—except for a few boxes tucked in the closet of the guest bedroom containing pictures and memories of the children they'd miscarried, her journals, and a few other items from their ten-year marriage. Her photo was on the nightstand by his bed and even looking at that was torture.

Next to his apartment door was a small office that shared a wall with the apartment across the hall. One wall of that room had the hallway on the other side, the room butting up against a similar office in a similarly designed apartment. A wall in the hallway spanned the distance between their doors which mirrored each other in the hallway. He'd make that his home office. The other two apartments on this floor were at the other end of the hall with windows facing the parking lot.

One year had passed. He stopped by the cemetery yesterday and trudged through snowdrifts in the subzero weather for the reminder that this was his reality. That was when he finally took off his wedding ring. At thirty-four, he was a widower. An unmarried pastor at a church meant he needed to be extra careful as he worked and served. He had no wedding ring to keep the more forward single women from approaching him and making suggestions.

Right. Like I'm some "catch." In reality, he'd buried part of himself in that cemetery. Hopes. Dreams. The one person who'd understood him best…

A bang on the wall adjoining his apartment to the one across the hall startled him. Then a cry. Some softer words and a shout. *Great.* His neighbor had kids. Loud kids. Well, it was probably a good thing he spent so much time at work, then…and that his bedroom was on the far side of the apartment away from that wall.

Except he was on a forced leave of absence. He might appear put together on the outside, but inside he was numb. He'd sold the house he'd shared with Sharon and was on the cusp of an unknown future. For the last year, Andrew, his boss and senior pastor, had suggested he take time off. He'd resisted.

Finally, Andrew sat him down and insisted he take time off to heal. He mentioned "unresolved grief" and the need to rest and adjust. Andrew was right. As a pastor, Dan counseled mourning families often. So why had he been so blind and resistant to his own need to process his loss? Once Sharon was in the ground, he'd buried himself under the needs of ministry and the hurts of the people coming into his office. It had seemed safer than looking inside his own heart.

The calling to ministry had grown heavy now that he'd been barred from work. He wondered, was it time to quit? Move on to what his father called "a real job?" What would he even be good at? Ever since accepting Christ at fifteen, he'd only ever wanted to be a pastor.

Bang! Bang! Crash!

Dan stood up and went to the door, opened it, and strode across the hallway. He gave the wood three firm raps.

The door swung open and a child ran headlong into him. Dan stumbled backwards, finding support against the hallway wall that ran between the two apartments. The child ran past him into his own apartment.

A young woman appeared in a snug tank top under an unbuttoned flannel shirt falling off one shoulder...and shorts and silly fuzzy pink boots. "Quinn! Get back here!"

She pulled up short at the sight of Dan. Her stormy gray eyes suddenly struck him. Red hair pulled up in a sideways ponytail with bangs *à la* Valley Girl from the 80s provided a contrast with her pale skin.

"Oh. I'm sorry," her voice was low and husky, and he took note of the piercings on her face. "My son—"

"—just ran into my apartment." Dan straightened to his full six feet in height. Instant thoughts condemning this scatterbrained mother and her unruly children raced through his brain. *Stop it. You don't even know her.* Shaking his head, he said, "Is that your only child, or should I be expecting another any minute?"

A little head framed in fuzzy orange curls and bright brown eyes, peered out from the side of the door.

The woman glanced down. "I only have the two, and she's not as prone to mischief as her brother. I'm terribly sorry. They are always a bit wild when they return from a visit with their father. May I come in and search for Quinn?"

Dan nodded. The woman picked up the little girl and straddled the child on the hips of her low-rise jean shorts. He led her into his apartment, leaving the door open.

"Quinn?" The young woman called as she started to inch around the space. She turned and shot a hand out at him. "I'm sorry. Where are my manners? I'm Skye. My son Quinn is our rabble-rouser and Meghan here is my little mouse."

"I'm Dan. I just moved in." He let his hand grip hers in a quick shake before letting it drop.

Skye turned and quickly resumed searching the apartment with Dan trailing her.

~*~

Skye took a deep breath and hoped her face hadn't turned beet red. It was a terrible look for her and she was embarrassed that this was how she managed to meet her handsome new neighbor. She'd watched him moving in and couldn't help but drool over his modelesque appearance. Blond hair, the soul patch and nerdy glasses made him even more swoon-worthy. *Hey, I might be divorced but I'm not dead.* In an empty second bedroom, she found Quinn hidden in a closet next to boxes labeled *Sharon*.

Another woman held this man's heart. Better to realize that now. But he wore no ring on his finger. A white line where the ring would have been told her there used to be one there...until recently.

She grabbed Quinn's wrist and pulled him to his feet. "That was a bad job, Quinn. Now you apologize to Mr. Dan here for trespassing in his home."

The little boy with the dark hair and blue eyes stared up at Dan. "I's sorry, Mr. Dan."

"I am terribly sorry too, for the noise and the disruption in your day." Skye half-swung, half-dragged Quinn. She noted the frown on her neighbor's face. Obviously, she failed to impress him. Without another word, the door shut behind her. She went to her own apartment, released her kids, and closed the door firmly.

The tears came unbidden. She didn't think she was unattractive, but obviously her ex, Riley, disagreed. The names he called her when he was high on drugs still bounced around her brain. She wasn't going to let any magazine model, no matter how cute, make her feel bad about herself or her parenting.

She did that well enough on her own.

"Time for naps, kids." She followed them down the hallway to their room and got them settled in their beds.

Returning to the living room, she looked at the mess Quinn left. The paints she set up to use were scattered all over. Thankfully, none spilled on the carpet. She picked up her supplies and righted her canvas and easel. She wanted to try her hand again at another painting since she'd heard from a gallery that was interested. She tried to set up before the naps to give her more time to actually paint before she needed to deal with the kids...obviously, that hadn't worked today.

Since the divorce, she'd gone on state insurance and food stamps. Her husband failed to support them even though the state garnished his wages. He often called in sick or was sent home for being hung over. She was surprised he even still held a job much less supported his drug habit. Better not to think about that though. She started to paint and dark colors mixed with red reflected her mood after meeting her grumpy neighbor.

Can you blame him? Her kids were wild and Quinn hid in his home. A single man wouldn't be used to the kind of chaos she lived with on a daily basis. This was mild compared to what she used to experience when she was married.

Never again.

Never again would she trust a man.

Especially not a good-looking one.

She painted and shushed the part of her brain that tempted her to consider the possibility.

Dan. Dang, but he sure was attractive. She'd be keeping an eye on his comings and goings.

Maybe there was a way to beg his forgiveness for their disturbance. They, whoever "they" were, always said a way to a man's heart was his stomach. She longed for him to see her as more than a falling-apart single mother.

~*~

The knock on his door that evening shocked Dan out of his somber reverie. He opened it to find a different woman than the one he'd seen earlier. She was wearing actual jeans now instead of the shorts. Her hair was down, combed, and longer than he expected. She sported black frames that highlighted her gray eyes. Eyes that looked into his, searching for something.

"Good evening, Skye. Can I help you? I don't think Quinn has returned to hide in my closet again."

"No, Dan. I brought this for you as an apology for earlier and well, to welcome you as a neighbor."

She held up a pan and the scent of warm apples and cinnamon wafted up to make him salivate. He swallowed hard as he took the plate. "Thank you."

She handed him a potholder. "It's kind of hot."

He shoved it under the pan and rushed to set it on the table. He returned to the door where she stood, with the potholder and handed it back to her. "There."

"OK." She glanced down at his naked feet.

His gaze followed hers. "I'm new here but was wondering where you go to church?"

"Church?" Skye shook her head. "I've no use for God. He's never been there for me when I needed Him."

"Really? What happened?" Dan leaned against the doorjamb. He was curious about this woman.

"Long story. But I'm OK now. The kids and I are doing better than ever." Her eyes looked at him with a new wariness. "Well, I'd better get back. Quinn is always into mischief."

"Yeah. Thanks again for the pie."

She turned and walked away, and he admired the view. He shook himself as he closed his own door and flipped the lock. He shouldn't consider the attractions of any woman. Not that there was a place in his heart for one. The scent of apple pie drew him to the table. He remembered the one Sharon baked for him before she died. He'd never been able to eat it and finally his sister tossed it away when she came to clean up for him. He'd avoided apple pie ever since.

As if baking that pie killed her? He stepped into the kitchen to grab a plate, spoon, and knife. He sliced a piece of pie and put it on the plate. He got some vanilla ice cream out of the freezer and put a scoop next to the steaming hot pie, grateful he'd gone shopping since Quinn's visit. Soon a white soup surrounded the pie. *Just the way I like it.* He sat down and broke off a piece with some ice cream. The spoon hung in midair as he contemplated taking the bite. *It is not a betrayal of Sharon to eat a piece of pie. You need to get over this.* He shoved the pie into his mouth and closed his eyes as he chewed, letting the warmth and the flavors mix. He swallowed.

Grief welled up within him, and he pushed the plate away as the tears came. *I should be done with this by now.* He disgusted himself with his weakness.

But he wasn't done, was he? *God, why couldn't Skye have baked me brownies, cherry pie, or anything else but this?* He rose so quickly the chair tipped over as he stumbled to the bedroom, collapsed on the bed, and wept.

Morning came and he struggled to prepare. He might not be working, but he longed to be at church. No one else had to know he'd been put on a leave of absence to heal. Did they? Could he bear being there? Where did a hurting pastor go to heal anyway?

He wished he knew the answer. It was Sunday and he'd start with a church worship service. But did he dare walk into Orchard Hill?

TWO

*My grief lies all within, and these external manners of
lament are merely shadows to the unseen grief that swells
with silence in the tortured soul.*
William Shakespeare

Skye stared at her painting in shock. A man in tears. A cross. The dark colors of sorrow and pain. It resembled her new neighbor. She hadn't intended to paint him. It really wasn't him. He left that morning, head down, as if defeated before the day began. What haunted him? Whatever happened to Sharon? Her artist's curiosity was getting the better of her as she imagined all kinds of reasons for his low spirits.

She pulled out her sketchbook as the kids watched their favorite videos. Her pencil flew over the page as she sketched her neighbor. Different perspectives. Exploring. As if drawing him would give her insight into the darkness within.

The buzzer rang for the outside door and she rose to go to her intercom. "Who is it?"

"Riley. I want to see you and the kids."

"You're not allowed here. Leave or I'll call the police."

"Aw, come on Skye. It's cold out here."

"Then go where you'll have a warm welcome. Leave me alone."

He buzzed again and she picked up her cell phone as she checked the locks. "Hi, Police? My ex-husband is trying to get into my apartment building. Yes, I have a restraining order. He won't leave." The outside door opened and boots stomped up the stairs causing her heart to race. She shushed the kids and rushed them to her bedroom where she closed the door and asked them to hide in the closet. It saddened her that this was a well-known game to them.

"He's entered the building," she said to the dispatcher.

"Police are on the scene. Can you buzz them in?"

"Yes." She stepped to the door and hit the buzzer.

"Come on, Skye. Let me in. You love me. I want to see my kids. You can't keep me from coming around." He pounded on the door.

The officers ran up the stairs, followed by shouts in the hallway as he fought with them.

"Ma'am. Are you OK?" the dispatcher asked.

"Scared," Skye confessed.

"They've taken him away in handcuffs but an officer needs to talk to you. Can you open your door for her?"

"You're sure he's gone?"

"Yes."

She peeked out and a female officer awaited her. Skye unlocked the door and let the officer in. "Hold on a second." She ran to the bedroom and let the kids come out. "Coast is clear. You can go back to your TV show."

The kids ran to the living room, ignoring the officer and resumed their movie.

"I'm Officer Alvarez. Can I get your statement?"

Skye nodded and gave a rundown of the events and soon the officer left.

Her entire body shook. She went to her room, closed the door, and collapsed on the bed. When would he ever leave her alone? When would she ever stop reacting like a wounded war vet every time Riley came near her?

She loved him once and used to do drugs with him. Until she got pregnant. Sometimes she wondered how her drug usage affected Quinn, who was hyperactive. But what did she know? Maybe that was normal for a four-year-old. In contrast, Meghan was quiet and withdrawn, and Skye wondered how much of that was a reaction to her mother's fear when Riley came around.

It still surprised her that she'd managed to leave him. Where had she found the courage? Riley's jail time made it easier to pack up and go without worrying about his immediate reaction. She had anticipated retaliation. The courts gave her full physical and legal custody and awarded him supervised visits. In spite of that, the kids returned home confused, and Quinn was especially wild. She wondered if Riley slipped Quinn drugs. Having the caseworker ensure the kids received no food from him didn't make a difference. Her son probably reacted to the insanity of his father.

When her heart rate returned to normal, she went to the bathroom to splash cold water on her face. She dried off and headed to the kitchen. Soon she was settled back down with a cup of tea and her sketchpad. Her drawings now took on a darker tone. Some abstract. Some so vivid it almost brought back her panic. Footsteps on the stairs made her jump to check. It was Dan, not Riley. She peered through the hole. He approached the door wearing his leather jacket, fogged-up glasses held in one hand. He stuck his key in the lock. As he turned it, he glanced at her door. Did he realize she spied on him?

A sigh of relief escaped her lips and she returned to her sketchpad. She didn't need to worry. Riley was in jail and they were fine. Energy surged so she grabbed her laundry and headed to the first floor to throw a load in. She was surprised to find Dan down there with his own.

"Hi." He said, barely glancing at her. He'd changed clothes and now wore faded denim jeans and a Packer sweatshirt. Canvas shoes covered his feet.

"Aren't the Packers done for the season?" she asked as she dumped clothes into one of the washers.

"Yeah. They lost their wild card game so they're out. Season's over."

"I don't follow that too much. Kids don't tolerate sports much less shows I might enjoy."

He gave her a small smile and a nod. "I'm sure they keep you busy."

She nodded and pushed her quarters in the machine. "Speaking of...I should go see what trouble they've gotten into while I was down here. Later, Dan."

He glanced up, his eyes wide. "My door is unlocked. You don't think…"

She grinned at his panic. "I wouldn't put it past them, but don't worry. I don't think they would do any damage." She started up the stairs with him behind her. She entered her apartment and quickly discovered both kids were in the kitchen trying to get a box of cereal down. She ran to help them, averting a disaster. She was almost disappointed that Quinn hadn't made an attempt to escape.

She managed to get her clothes in the dryer without running into her handsome neighbor but wasn't sure why she was reluctant to see him again. Maybe because she suspected he had his secrets as much as she had hers.

She got the kids down for a nap and started to paint again. She hoped the art dealer who asked for her paintings liked what he got. She'd take pictures and send them tomorrow.

~*~

Folding clothes always made him miss Sharon. She used to take care of all that for him.

Church had been OK this morning. He was greeted warmly but no one asked how he *really* was. Most probably forgot he even suffered a loss. Every day he was reminded when he woke alone. When he ate alone. When he went to bed alone. When he folded the clothes...

Most people thought he should just "get over it." But how could he? They had tried so long to have a family and had lost so many babies to miscarriage. They had been on the verge of going through the process of adoption when she died. He had no child to hold on to in the wake of his loss.

Perhaps that was a blessing. It would be a challenge to be a single dad and pastor.

Now he wondered if he should even be a pastor. Andrew suggested he visit a therapist. Or consider a grief support group. Or talk to his doctor about an anti-depressant.

How does the caregiver even begin to ask for help? It was almost too much for his fragile ego to turn around and say how hurt he still was. How he hadn't been able to move on.

The apple pie was in the fridge. He tossed the piece last night after the one bite. It tasted like Sharon's. He couldn't go there. Would he ever eat pie again?

The clothes were put away and he strolled back into his living room. Dinner. He needed to prepare dinner. It was too cold out to be firing up the grill so he headed to the kitchen to fry up some brats on the stove. It at least brought memories of time with friends and not just Sharon. The smell and taste were something he could enjoy. To be healthier he would skip the buns. Of course, the fact that he forgot to even buy them might be a factor. Sharon always remembered. He grabbed an onion to slice and sauté with the meat.

That was the problem. It always came back to Sharon. But he was a pastor. He was the one who sat with people for counseling. He was the one to lead the teams. He was the one to provide care for others.

Now he was the one hurting.

Dang it, Andrew. Why did you do this to me? The only time he experienced any peace was buried in the work in his office. Meeting volunteers, putting out fires….all of those things kept his mind from his losses at home.

He pulled out a plate and slid the cooked meat and onions onto it along with some horseradish mustard. Grabbing a fork and knife he sat down at his small table for dinner.

"Thank You, God, for this food. Thank You that even though I feel very alone right now, You are still with me. Help me figure out what I'm to do next."

He ate in silence. When he was done, he washed dishes and put them away. He flipped on the television and collapsed in a chair. Sure, there were a few more boxes to unpack but...what was he going to do these next few weeks? It was the middle of winter. Prime time for Seasonal Affective Disorder. Sure, he could work out more and get really fit. But getting a counselor? Could he really do that? Sit down, fillet his soul, and pay someone for the honor?

~*~

Working out daily at the Y kept his head above water. Wednesday morning was his regular accountability group. He showed up, but he really didn't want to be there. Nick, Simon, and Tony all waited for him.

Clarisse had been their waitress for years at the little Greek restaurant they met at in Menomonee Falls.

Dan tucked himself in a corner. Tony was next to him. "So Tony, how's it going?" Simon asked.

"Well. Renata's getting a little crazy with the pregnancy. But generally, things are going well at work and at home. Still trying to figure out what God might want me to do at church for ministry, although I don't mind helping with providing food for bigger events."

"Your food is ministry, Tony." Simon rubbed his tummy.

Nick laughed as he dug into his omelette. "I can't argue with you there, Simon. But I understand your struggle, Tony. Your primary ministry though is to your family. You help Renata and the church by managing the kids when she comes to rehearsal and sings on a Sunday morning too. That's huge. Maybe being behind-the-scenes is where God wants you to be right now."

"There might come a time when your kids are older that you could help out with the management team or something like that," Simon suggested.

"No. Don't let me deal with budgets. Can't stand that part of business and that's why I pay others to do it for me."

"I remember when you tried and almost lost Renata over that." Nick shook his head.

"A good lesson for me to stick to my strengths." Tony shoveled in some hash browns.

"And ask for help, right Dan?" Simon looked to him.

Dan nodded. "Yup."

Tony turned to him. "You're pretty quiet. You've settled into your apartment?"

"Yeah. It's a place to live."

"So what happened when you met with Andrew last week? You were concerned about that performance evaluation," Nick said.

Dan let out a deep breath. "I'm on a leave-of-absence. My work performance was good. Andrew was concerned that I'm still grieving and haven't been able to move on from Sharon."

"And you just had the one-year anniversary of her death," Nick whispered.

Dan nodded.

"What are you going to do?" Tony asked.

Dan shrugged. "I don't know. I'm at a loss." The weight of a hand rested on his shoulder.

Tony's head bent. "Lord, You know the depth of Dan's pain and You know how lost he is now without his work to hide behind. Please give him wisdom so he can heal. Not that he would ever forget the love and the memories of his time with Sharon, but help him move into a new season of life where You have good things planned. We know he hurts right now but help him get the help he needs. We love You, Jesus."

"Amen," chorused around him.

"Thanks," answered Dan.

They moved on to Nick and Simon, but Dan wasn't dialed into the conversation. *Do You love me God? Really? I know You are good. The Bible says so. But how could You be good to me when You took away the one person who loved me so well?*

When the meal was done, he paid and made his way to his car. Tony stopped him.

"Dan. I understand you miss Sharon. She was special. If Renata died, I don't know what I'd do. I'm sorry. If you want to hit the gym together tomorrow morning, I'd be glad to sweat it out with you."

"Eight o'clock?"

"I'll be there. And I'll be praying in the meantime."

"Thanks."

Dan drove home and trudged up the stairs. Bass pumped from the apartment across the hall. As he drew nearer, the lyrics to a pop tune became clearer. He hadn't been so immersed in Christian culture and music that he'd been unaware of the stuff out there. He wondered how she could even think with that pounding. And where were the kids?

As he started to open his door, hers flung open. He turned to take in the site. Her hair was bright and her eyes held dark shadows. He peeked around her, expecting a tornado of a little boy to appear.

"Dan. You're home? I never did ask what you do. I'll turn down the music."

"I'm a...or I was, a pastor at Orchard Hill

Church."

"A man of the cloth?"

"We're not Catholic. Not high church. I wear regular clothes like everyone else."

"And wear them well," she whispered.

"What?" Did she say what he thought she did?

"Oh, nothing." Her face turned an alarming shade of pink. "If you're going to be around during the day I can keep the music down."

"Don't let me disturb you. I'll tell you if it's a problem." Dan tilted his head as he took in her white smock with splotches of paint. "Did our landlord let you paint the apartment? If you need help, I could—"

"No! No, but thank you. I'm an artist and I was working on a painting. A gallery in New York has offered to sell them for me."

"Wow. Congratulations. So you're what they would call a 'starving artist?'" He folded his arms across his chest.

"Not starving, but hopefully I'll be making a better living for my kids and I. Pastors aren't wealthy either, are they? Or are you one of those TV preachers? I could see that. You have the looks of one and I'm sure when you want to, you could be charming."

One eyebrow went up and he bit back a grin. "My wife used to think I was, but no. Not that kind of pastor. I'm not wealthy, but our church has been more than fair in the salary and benefits they provide."

"Your wife?" Skye frowned.

"Yeah." He sighed as he turned away to open his door. "She died a year ago." He opened the door and shut it behind him. He didn't want to see the look of pity in her beautiful gray eyes.

There was a knock on the door and he opened it.

"I'm sorry for your loss. I didn't mean to pry. She sounds like she was a smart lady, and very lucky to find a good man to love."

"Thank you. I was the one blessed to have her in my life. We had also lost several babies over the years in our attempt to start a family, so Sharon was all I had. She's irreplaceable."

Skye nodded. "You both had something few of us mere mortals ever do—true love."

"As I discovered, there is no happily-ever-after."

"I thought you said you were a Christian?"

He nodded.

"I don't understand much about it, but I thought heaven was supposed to be your happily-ever-after."

Dan nodded. "Doesn't always take away the pain of living down here."

"Then what good is your faith?"

"What do you mean?"

"I mean, if believing in God doesn't help you live a happy life, what's the point?"

"The point is that this life is a mere blip in the timeline of eternity. Sharon, my wife, got her happily-ever-after. She's free of the pain and heartbreak of the world. Someday I'll be there too. Just because I believe in God doesn't mean that life doesn't sometimes hurt. I'm still human."

She looked him up and down and shook her head. "If I weren't looking at you with my own eyes, I would say you were photoshopped. The only thing they missed are the dark shadows under your eyes and the weariness that marks your face in your frown. I'm sorry you miss your wife. Be glad you experienced a love like that. Not all of us get those kinds of memories when the romance is over." She spun on her silly, fuzzy, booted heel and strode across the hall. She shut the door firmly behind her.

He could have sworn there'd been tears in her eyes.

THREE

There is no grief like the grief which does not speak.
Henry Wadsworth Longfellow

Skye wiped away the tears that threatened. Riley never missed her because he never loved her. He only missed her because she was his verbal punching bag. What must it be like to be loved so much that your absence would be so cruelly grieved over? She'd never know.

And this God he spoke of. She'd watched the televangelists. God wants her to be happy and wealthy? Right. She'd mistakenly thought happiness could be found in drugs and alcohol but had a cruel awaking when she almost overdosed. Then she'd discovered she was expecting a baby. The downward spiral had almost killed two people. Her husband and friends hadn't liked her stepping away to get straight. While she would never regret Quinn or Meghan…she did regret that it took her so long to get away for good.

For good? Right.

The buzzer rang. Her mother brought the kids home from their preschool program.

She opened the door as they came up the stairs, and both children rushed into her arms. She hugged their winter-cold bodies tight.

"Hi, Mom. Wanna come in?"

Her mother nodded, followed them in, and helped her get the coats and boots off the little ones.

"Your sandwiches are at the table, kids." They ran

off to eat.

"Did you get more work done?"

"Yeah. Got an offer, and I'll be packaging up two to ship out to the gallery. They have a show this weekend. They want me to be there, but there's no way I can do that."

"Why not?"

"Come on, Mom. I have two children who need me, and there is the issue of money for airfare, meals, and hotel. New York City doesn't come cheap."

"You'd probably need a fancy outfit as well."

"Probably."

"Someday. Someday you'll get your dream."

"My dreams have changed...I want to be safe and for my kids to be OK. To grow up well-loved."

"What about love for you? Anything else on the hunky neighbor front?"

Skye laughed. "The hunky neighbor happens to be a widowed and grieving pastor. There's no way I'm going to be good enough for a man like him."

"Well, that would be different, wouldn't it? To go from a bum of an addicted failure to a handsome pastor?"

"Remember I said he was grieving? He's not ready for any kind of relationship and I could tell the day he first met me he didn't approve of me. Come on. What pastor would marry a woman with piercings, a former drug user, and oh, by the way, divorced with two kids? Along with the fact that I don't believe in his God, I'm as far away from an ideal woman for him as possible." She shook her head. "He's probably regretting moving in next door."

"You believed in God once."

"I believe He exists, sure. How could I not when I

look at the two miracles sitting at the table? But that He wants a relationship with me? Pshaw. As far away from being good enough for a pastor, I'm even less so for a God."

Her mother shook her head. "I'm sorry. I failed you. Your own father wasn't anything stellar."

"I made my own mistakes, Mom. They are mine and mine alone. I was young, stupid, and high. Trying to avoid the pain of life and taking whatever affection I could get from anyone. Initially, Riley was sweet. You even liked him at first."

"True, it wasn't until after the wedding that his true colors emerged."

"As in hours after. Our honeymoon was a nightmare."

"I'm sorry, honey." Her mother enveloped her in her arms and Skye let her.

"Hey, want to see what I sent out today? I have photos."

"Sure."

Skye took her over to her computer and pulled up the paintings she had shipped out to New York.

"I hope you know what you're doing with this art dealer," her mother cautioned.

"He's got a good reputation. I've spoken to some other artists who did shows with him and they said he's fair. I need exposure. Get my name out there with something spectacular."

"This one is sure spectacular." Her mother looked at the one of the man who resembled her neighbor. "It's dark, brooding...and why do you have a cross there?"

Skye shrugged and shook her head. "I don't know. When I get in the zone, I just paint and turn off my thoughts to let whatever comes, come. That's what emerged."

Her mother quietly looked through the other prints and soon left.

Skye glanced again at the one of her neighbor. She almost hated to sell it. If she didn't need the money, she'd keep it. Something about those eyes drew her in. She could stare at it without feeling uncomfortable, which was what happened every time she met Dan's gaze.

She put the papers back in a file drawer and locked it. She stored stuff on a cloud and in other locations too…reprints could be a moneymaker if she didn't do well on the original.

Now, as for the subject…? That masterpiece was out of her price range for sure.

~*~

Thursday morning, Dan shredded the miles on the treadmill. Soon Tony was on the one next to him.

"I remember when you struggled to catch up with me. I think over this past year you've been building your stamina," Tony said.

"I was trying to run away from the grief."

"Did it work?"

Dan shook his head. "Maybe for a moment. Work was where I was able to get lost and set it all aside. There wasn't much time at the office or in meetings to sit and feel sorry for myself."

"Yeah, well, we don't do ministry for the sake of ministry though, do we?"

"What do you mean?" Dan asked.

"I thought the whole point of ministry was

helping people grow to become more like Jesus."

"It is."

"But if everyone else gets to grow, except you, the whole church loses."

Dan hopped to set his feet on the sides of the sliding fabric. "Are you saying I helped others at the expense of my own personal growth?"

Tony nodded. "If the shoe fits…"

Dan jumped back on treadmill, grabbed his water, and chugged some down.

"Don't get mad at the messenger, Dan. You guys held me to the wall with my anger and pride in the past. You didn't let me stay stuck and, although I wasn't always grateful at the time, looking back it was the most loving thing you did for me. You forced me to face myself and grow. I would have lost so much more than the life I have now with Renata, without you all pushing me forward."

"I'm not mad at you. Ticked with myself. There's something warm and comfortable about the blanket of grief I wrap around myself. I'm not sure who Dan Wink is when that's ripped away. Have I lost my own identity behind a title and role?"

Tony wiped the sweat off his brow with a towel. "It's possible, isn't it? We've tried to push you out of the hole, but you've resisted. I'm sure Andrew did as well. You kept giving up your vacation and time off to work because there was no one to spend it with. But what about you? Isn't Dan worth spending time with? I always thought so. Sharon did too. She wouldn't want you to be suffering like this."

Dan slowed his machine down. "Want to spot me some weights?"

Tony nodded. "Sure. Give me a few minutes to

cool down."

Dan walked away and almost ran into—Skye? "Oh, sorry."

"Dan? But of course you would be here. I shouldn't be surprised."

He raised an eyebrow as he folded his arms across his chest. She was wearing a respectable T-shirt that revealed far less than most women did at the gym. She tucked it into unusual lightweight cargo-type pants that made her look almost…decent. She possessed a nice figure, and he wondered why she hid it. "I'm here with a friend."

"I'm here for some Zumba. I find it's a fun way to burn off some stress."

"You like those classes?"

Skye nodded. "Yup. So much that I'm a certified instructor." She glanced at the clock. "Well, enjoy your workout. Gotta go or I'll be late!" Her ponytail bounced behind her as she headed to one of the classrooms. He'd seen those classes before.

Tony came to stand beside him. "You know her?"

"Yeah. That's my new neighbor."

"She's cute."

"She's not a Christian."

"So, you moved into a mission field."

Dan looked at his friend. "You have no idea." The music started to thump, and Skye started to motion to the participants, most of whom were also dressed in baggier T-shirts. Considering how seductive some of the moves were, he wondered at it all. Except with this class, the moves looked more like fun exercise than hyper-sexual like he expected. "Let's go." He patted Tony's sweaty back and they headed to the weights.

~*~

Dan visited a different church on Sunday. He hoped to be anonymous, but several people there knew him from times they had been at Orchard Hill in the past. And of course, the Adult Ministries pastor, Wally Hanson, had been someone he'd met with periodically to talk about ministry.

"Dan, how are you?" Wally asked as he reached out his hand.

Extending his own, Dan responded. "I'm on a leave of absence. I miss work and it makes me miss Sharon more."

Wally frowned. "I'm sorry. I can't imagine what you've been through. I can imagine, however, the challenges you face now that all the single ladies target you as potential husband material."

"How do you deal with that?"

"Very carefully. I try not to date women at the church if I can help it. Usually I can tell pretty quickly during group activities when a woman might be worth pursuing more, but you understand how it is—everyone puts their best face forward when they are on the hunt."

Dan laughed. "I never thought of myself as prey, but I guess that's what you and I both are."

"Well, as you can tell due to my single state, I obviously haven't succeeded in ending the hunt yet."

"I'm not ready for any of that."

"You and Sharon had something special," Wally said.

"Yeah. And ministry can be isolating. I wonder how she even put up with that and me. I mean, things weren't perfect and we had our share of heartache, mostly trying to have kids and suffering loss upon loss."

"When the right woman comes along, you'll know."

"Will I? I suspect God would need to whack me upside the head to even think of a relationship or even a friendship with another woman at this point."

"Remember all the wonderful things a woman brought to your life. Support, companionship, housekeeping." Wally shook his head. "No, seriously. How often did you need to do laundry or prepare your own meals when you were married?"

"There were times she even mowed the lawn or got the snow blower out because I was busy at church. She was a saint."

Wally shook his head. "She wasn't a saint. She had faults and did things that drove you crazy. Don't make her out to be something she wasn't and set a standard that no woman could fill, not even Sharon were she alive."

Dan sighed. "Yeah, well, I should get home."

"Yeah, because your books, bed, and maybe a football game await you. How's that working for you?"

"Wally, I'm a little ticked with you right now, so leaving seems the better part of valor. I wasn't given a leave of absence to find a wife. That's not the point."

"You have time on your hands and a few weeks to at least look. Don't waste it." Wally patted him on the back. "Have a good afternoon, my friend."

Dan growled as he walked away. Any woman who had him in his sights would have been running the other way at that moment. How dare Wally speak about Sharon like that? She was—

Human. Fallible. She couldn't balance a checkbook

to save her life. She hated cleaning the toilets and let them get so bad he would be forced to finally take on the task.

He'd happily scrub toilets and balance the checkbook if it meant she were by his side. He was stuck with all the chores as it was anyway.

He trudged up the stairs to his apartment. Why did he pick the second floor? Oh, yeah, because people who move at the beginning of the year, in the middle of winter have few choices available to them.

~*~

Skye witnessed a different side of Dan Thursday morning. Hot, sweaty, guard down. He looked more human to her. As she peeked out at the man coming up the stairs a few days later, she wondered why he looked so sad. She cracked open her door and when he glanced up and paused at the top of the stairs, she gathered up her courage to talk to him.

"You look sad."

He shrugged.

"I don't bite and I can be a good listener."

"Thanks, Skye." He frowned and tilted his head. "You looked good teaching your class. I was impressed. I always thought that kind of group was far more about, well, sex, than it was about fitness."

"Some of the salsa moves can be perceived that way, but I don't present them in such a manner. I do believe some things should be left for the bedroom."

An eyebrow shot up.

"I'm not propositioning the pastor. Don't worry. I'm not in the market any more than you are. I would think it would be accurate to say as a friend, I'm a safe bet."

"I'll keep that in mind. Thanks for the offer." He looked to the side as if trying to see past her. "Kids?"

"At Grandma's for the day so I can paint. They get antsy in this tiny space, and it's too cold to go outside."

"I'm glad you have support. It has to be hard being a single mom."

"You have no idea. I wouldn't trade my kids for the world though. I wish they had a decent father figure in their life. Especially for Quinn right now. It will be important for Meghan too at some point."

"That's tough."

"That's life. You church people don't like divorce, but my husband was stealing money, doing drugs, and was generally mean. I left to save myself and my children."

"Why would I condemn you for divorce?"

"Because your God is against divorce."

"You said you don't believe in the God of the Bible."

"I don't believe *in* Him."

"So why would you think I should hold you to a standard you don't buy into?"

"I don't understand."

"While it's true that divorce can have a negative impact, divorce happens even amongst Christian couples. Sin is ugly. But God does allow for divorce in some cases. Even so, why would I expect you to adhere to a biblical principle when you don't claim the faith? Why should I judge you for that?" He leaned against the wall now with his arms folded.

"I thought that's what Christians did. Condemn everyone that doesn't agree with their way of life."

"There are some things God clearly states are

wrong. Some are universal, like killing, stealing, lying...but others are unique. The fact is, Christianity isn't about a list of do's and don'ts. It's more about a relationship, one on one with the one man who died to save your life and rose again to prove His love for you."

"Jesus."

"So, you do know about the faith."

"Not much. I've listened to stuff on the television when I couldn't sleep with a baby, or just because..."

"Not all of those preachers are accurate representations of the gospel. But I doubt I am either. I'm still human and make mistakes."

"Well, Dan, there are mistakes, and then, there are *mistakes*. I'm sure your holy God could never forgive mine."

"You doubt He's big enough?" He didn't wait for an answer as he turned and unlocked his door. "Enjoy your time to paint, Skye." He closed the door behind him. The lock clicked.

She backed into her own apartment and wandered back to her blank canvas without really knowing what to think about their odd conversation. She poured all that confusion into her art.

When she was done, she stood back, shocked. This canvas was more abstract than previous attempts. There was a shadow of a cross, hidden in the midst of the color—and on her knees before it was a young woman who looked suspiciously like her.

FOUR

Suppressed grief suffocates, it rages within the breast,
and is forced to multiply its strength.
Ovid

He'd finally done it. He checked in at the clinic and sat down to wait in a crisp room with clean lines and classical music playing. A few other people waited as well. Was it a rule that no one could make eye contact with anyone else in a mental health clinic? The lady in the corner clicked a pen open and closed in time with the music, which made it less irritating than it might have been otherwise. A sullen teen slumped in his chair next to whom he assumed was his mother who hugged her purse close as if to defend herself from attacks on her parenting skills. Another man flipped through a magazine, obviously not reading anything.

Then there was Pastor Dan Wink. No. Just Dan Wink. Drop the pastor. He wasn't really sure who he was anymore anyway. He laughed at the memory of Skye thinking he was a model. It was probably the nicest compliment he'd had in a long time. Sharon used to tell him how great he looked, but she was his wife. What was interesting was that in spite of his visual appeal, Skye wasn't interested in him as anything more than a neighbor and maybe a friend.

A man couldn't be friends with a woman. It couldn't be safely done. Anyway, she didn't believe in Jesus and there was no way he'd marry someone like her.

Marry? He rolled his eyes at himself. Where'd that thought come from? Wally. Of course. As if his leave of absence was to find a wife. Sure he had needs, but he was fine. He was working out more and in the best shape of his life.

An older woman came to the lobby. "Dan?"

He rose.

"Follow me, please."

He obeyed, trailing after her down the hallway to a spacious office decorated in peach, cream, and teal.

"Sit wherever you're most comfortable."

"Really? Because it would be in that chair behind the desk counseling you."

She smiled and nodded. "I'm Shirley Moore, your therapist, Pastor Dan."

He settled into the corner of a loveseat and she sat in a chair across from him. She was probably in her early sixties, with short, snow-white hair combed back off her face. She reminded him of his grandmother when he was a young boy. Her eyes were lined with wrinkles and genuine warmth came through her smile. He allowed his body to relax.

"Just Dan."

"Who is Dan Wink?"

"That's what I'm here to find out."

For the next forty-five minutes, he told his story and she asked questions and got family history.

"Our time is up for now. The initial session might seem disappointing because we never addressed your issues, but trust me. This was necessary. Can you come back next week? We'll dig in then."

"I suppose."

"Let me pray for you before you go."

Dan bowed his head.

"Heavenly Father, You understand the depth of pain in Dan's heart and his need for Your healing touch. I thank You that You have allowed me to be part of his journey. You have great plans and a future in store for this man whom You gifted and called to tasks You have set aside especially for him. People You intend to bless through him. Glory that will be given to Your name because of his journey. Comfort him and let Him see Your hand in his life. Jesus, You alone are the bridge to healing and wholeness in this broken and sinful world, and we ask that You will be at work here when we meet."

"Amen, and thank you." Dan rose and left. Hope broke through the hardened ground in his heart like a tiny plant emerging after winter, sensing the warmth of the sun. He fought the temptation to stomp it out with the heavy boot of self-condemnation.

That only worked until he arrived back at his apartment.

Loose ends. He didn't know what to do with himself. He had time to waste, kill, or spend and no idea what to do, or even who he could do anything with. He slumped into his chair and flipped through the channels on the television. Why had he gotten cable? He flicked the television off, grabbed his guitar, and played every song he could remember off the top of his head, sometimes singing along.

The music held the demons at bay. At least for now.

The sound of glass breaking and the blast of freezing cold air coincided with a brick that landed at his feet. He jumped up and set the guitar to the side. He ran to the window to find a man in the tree wearing a hoodie and ripped jeans. On the back side of the apartment complex where his porch faced, there was an incline and several trees.

"Where is she?"

"Where is who? Who are you?" Dan dialed 911 as the man hefted another brick. Dan backed into the apartment and ran for his coat as he talked to the dispatcher. Sirens squealed. and soon police swarmed the yard. Police officers wrestled with the perpetrator, who had to be freezing cold.

An officer came to take Dan's statement. "Do you know this man?"

"Never saw him before in my life. He asked me about a woman, but I had no idea who he was referring to."

"He's the ex-husband of your neighbor, Skye O'Connell, and he's been harassing her. We think he got the wrong apartment and when he saw you he thought maybe you and her…"

Dan held up his hands. "Whoa, I've met Skye but we are not involved. I only moved in a few weeks ago. I can't believe he would do something like that, endangering his own children?"

"Drugs mess with the ability to think logically, much less with common sense. He's high. Do you want to press charges?"

Dan thought about it. If that brick had been aimed at the right apartment, the man could have killed one of his own children. It came near to doing him serious harm. He nodded. Natural consequences might help the man. "Yes. Can I come and see him after he's sobered up?"

The officer shrugged. "Sure. Try tomorrow. He's not going to be in any condition to listen right now anyway, pastor."

"Do I know you?"

The man grinned. "I've attended church a few times. I really enjoy how you lead worship."

"Nice to meet you. I'm sorry I didn't recognize you."

"It's a big church, and I've not really introduced myself before."

"Well, Officer Nelson, thank you for your quick response and help today."

"I'm glad no one was injured."

"Me too. Guess I'd better make a call and figure out how this window is going to get fixed, and fast."

"Stay warm." The officer took off and Dan shut the door, left his landlord a message, and started to pick up the shattered glass.

He supposed the blessing is that he hardly had anything in the room, so clean up would be easier. He got the glass out to the dumpster and noted that it began to snow again. *Great.* He still hadn't heard back from the landlord, so he went to his storage unit in the basement. All that it contained were broken down cardboard boxes. He grabbed the larger ones, hauled them upstairs, and left them in the hallway while he went back inside to run the vacuum over the floor. When he returned to get the boxes, Skye stood there, still in her coat, with two little people by her side.

"Hi." He grabbed a box and went back into the apartment for duct tape. Then he headed to the window. Skye stood in the doorway with the kids.

"You're not moving, are you? Wait. What happened to your window?"

"Can you come hold this for me while I tape this up?" She came over and held the cardboard in place.

The sound of taping filled the air as the kids watched in fascination. He finished taping up the window, but a cold draft still came in. "It's going to take a while for this place to warm up again," Skye noted.

"Yeah, but it will."

"You still never said what happened."

Dan looked over at the kids. "I'm not going to when there are little ears."

Skye nodded. "Do you want to come hang out at our place while yours warms up?"

"I appreciate the offer." He walked her back to the door. "It's my policy not be alone with a single woman in her apartment without another adult present."

"My kids are good chaperones."

"It's not that at all. I'm not suggesting you, or I, would do anything inappropriate. It's the appearance or suggestion of it that prevents me."

"But I was in your apartment."

"With the door wide open and only for a few minutes. Thank you for your help." He stopped her. "Wait. Your pie pan." He whipped off his gloves and tossed them in the garbage with more of the glass. The leather was torn. He grabbed the pan off the kitchen table. "I wanted to return this to you and thank you."

"Did you enjoy the pie?"

"It was as good as what my wife used to make me. Thank you."

Her face lit up at his complement. Soon the door was shut, locked, and he shivered once again in his lonely apartment. He moved his guitar to the warmer guest bedroom and closed the door. He cranked the thermostat, grateful his heat was included in the rent. It was going to be hot in the bedrooms, but hopefully the temp would even out so he could sleep here tonight.

Soon the landlord called and brought over some particle board to help keep the cold out. Arrangements were made for new sliding glass door installation in the morning.

He grabbed his keys to head to the department store. He found himself in need of a new pair of gloves.

~*~

Skye got the kids settled down for naps and tried to paint. Something in Dan's voice had warned her. Something indefinable in his eyes and the way they had searched hers, told her that the damage done in his apartment was serious indeed and not some silly prank.

The landlord came and went with boards and she hoped Dan's apartment would warm up. The kids had been quite good today and she was grateful. The phone rang.

"Skye?"

"Who is this?"

"Riley. You're my one call. Come on. You've got to bail me out here."

"What did you do now?"

"Destruction of property."

"Why?"

"I'd rather not say. Just get money to post bail for me."

"I don't have money."

"Where does my child support go?"

"What child support? You've not been working, so we get nothing."

Susan M. Baganz

"So you and that neighbor got something going?"

"What you are talking about? There are seven other apartments here and I have nothing going with any of the people who live here."

"You expect me to believe that?"

"Yeah. I do. Just because you can't keep your pants on when a pretty girl looks your way doesn't mean I'm chasing guys. And it's none of your business anyway; we're divorced."

"Don't get your undies in a bundle. I just want out. Why can't you help me?"

"You're high, and I'm not responsible for you or your actions. I will not bail you out. Please do not call me again. If this harassment continues, I'll be contacting the attorney about a no-contact order against you."

'You can't keep me from my kids."

"No. But the judge can after I contact the guardian-ad-litum."

"They are mine."

"Then act like a man who is worth looking up to and not some selfish, irresponsible teenager."

"So that neighbor is a 'man' like that, is he?"

"What are you talking about?"

"Quinn told me all about him and how you baked him a pie."

"When or who I date is, and forever will be, none of your business." She hung up the phone and missed the old days of corded phones where the actual slamming down of the receiver hurt the ears of the person on the other end.

Skye paced the apartment taking deep breaths to slow her rapidly beating heart. She stopped.

Dan was right. The appearance or even suggestion of

42

evil is powerful. She had no clue her son would mention the handsome pastor to her ex-husband, or that Riley would be so violent about it. Dan obviously suspected something about the person who broke the window or he wouldn't have been so circumspect around the kids.

Hmmm, a man with wisdom and discretion. What a novel concept.

How did this impact her choices? She was desperate for friends and connection. She'd lost all of her friends when she walked away from drugs and the lifestyle Riley lived.

She settled down at her easel and was hardly aware of time passing until she heard Meghan cry for her. She set aside her brushes, tore off her smock, and put things out of the kids' reach before checking on them.

As they came into the living room for a snack and some television, she stepped back to look at her painting. She gasped when it dawned on her what she had painted...a little church. A cross on top. The sunrise coming up behind it, diffusing the darkness all around and bathing the small building in light and all else in shadow. The cross glistened at the top. She stepped back to try to evaluate the painting from a more objective perspective...but she couldn't. Her pulse quickened and she rushed to put the painting in her bedroom to dry...away from the kids and away from her own sight.

Church. Mom suggested she find one. Dan asked her about it, and now her art was suddenly littered with religious symbols.

God, no offense but You weren't there when Riley was destroying our family. You weren't there when I cried myself to sleep at night worried over our finances or the health of my children. You weren't there when I sought help from a shelter to get free. You weren't there in court or when Riley came to try to break in here. You weren't there for any of these awful things in my life. She paused to take a deep breath.

I was there.

She looked around and ran to the door. She peered out the peephole. No one was there. She glanced at the television. No, the sound hadn't come from there. Was she hearing things now? That hadn't been too unusual when doing some of the drugs they had tried, but it had been years...so why now? Was she finally descending into madness?

FIVE

Darkness cannot drive out darkness: only light can do that.
Hate cannot drive out hate: only love can do that.
Martin Luther King, Jr.

Dan bought his new gloves. A nicer pair than the ones that he ruined cleaning up the glass. Those were a gift from his wife years ago.

Why did it always come back to her? Was every memory to be associated with Sharon? Was he ever to be free of the shackles of his marriage? Didn't the marriage vows say "until death do us part?" Well, she parted.

He paused as he sat in his car in the parking lot. Snowflakes flitted around outside and landed on any surface available. The vows had been fulfilled. They were over. So why did he live as if he were still bound?

Maybe it was his way of deluding himself that he wasn't really all alone. Except she had abandoned him for glory. Sharon was free of pain, suffering, and the grief they struggled with. The lost dreams. The dead babies. He swallowed hard. He was left behind.

You have a choice.

He looked outside but saw no one. *God?* Dan shook his head and left the warmth of the vehicle. Trudging up the icy sidewalk, he entered the building and stomped the snow off his shoes and pants. Why did he live in Wisconsin again? Was it time to consider a change? His energy faded with every step up to his apartment. He didn't meet Skye again and frowned.

He wondered how someone so sweet and pretty ended up married to a dirt bag like Riley.

Wait. Since when did he start thinking of Skye that way? Sure she was attractive, but still… He locked his apartment door and hung up his coat. The place was a sauna now and he tweaked the thermostat down to a more reasonable level. It amazed him how dark the living room was with the sliding doors boarded up. He flipped on lights and went to the bedrooms. They were steaming too, but he suspected with the draft still coming in, that it would cool off to a more comfortable temp soon.

~*~

Two days later, Dan walked into a small room at the Waukesha County Jail to meet with Riley O'Connell. He sat and waited for the man, hopefully now sober, to be brought to him.

The man who came in was unkempt and stunk. He slumped in the seat across the table and the guard remained close.

"Whatd'ya want?" Riley demanded.

"I wanted to tell you I forgive you," Dan said. His heart raced at the venom shooting from the man's eyes, but he slowed his breathing to keep calm.

"Forgive me? You'll drop the charges?"

"No. Consequences are not erased because of my choice to not seek personal justice. Riley, you don't need to live this way. Jesus loves you. God has a better plan for your life."

"Blah, blah, blah. Another goody-two-shoes. No wonder Skye's taking up with you. A shiny new toy. But she's not into religion, so don't expect her to put up with that. It won't be long before she comes running back to me."

Dan raised his eyebrows and one corner of his mouth twitched. "I can't imagine how a woman like her ever chose you to begin with."

Riley frowned as if he wasn't sure whether he had been complimented or insulted. He must have decided on the former. "Well, she knew a good thing when she had it. She'll be back."

"Why do you hate her so much?" Dan asked.

"I don't hate her. I love her."

"A man who loves a woman treats her as if she were a precious treasure. He takes care of her. He knows what she loves and what her dreams are and works to help her reach them. He delights in making her happy...not afraid. A well-loved woman would not divorce a husband who has treated her well and has invested wisely in his marriage."

Dan imagined a piece of metal inside the man across from him, twisting. Tighter and tighter. Compressed and—

The man's hand pounded on the table as he leapt to his feet and started for Dan, fists clenched. Dan forced himself to sit still. He was certain he could defend himself if he needed to but wasn't going to give Riley the satisfaction of thinking he'd been scared by this show of force. Before Dan could react, the guard stepped forward and yanked Riley back and out of the room.

Riley hadn't spoken another word, and Dan wondered at that. The man was all hot air and overinflated arrogance. So why so silent? Dan rose and left. Riley was God's responsibility, not his. Not anymore.

~*~

Skye dashed out the door the minute Dan reached the top of the stairs.

"Good afternoon," Dan said as he withdrew his keys from his pocket.

"What church?"

Dan frowned. "Excuse me?"

"What church do you work for?"

"Orchard Hill."

"If I go, what will happen?" Her fingers were wrapped up in her flannel shirt hem, twisting the material back and forth.

"I'm not sure what you're asking. Lightning isn't going to strike you for entering the building."

"I've rarely been to church. What's it like?"

Dan nodded. Interesting. "You would walk in with your children and be greeted by people who will be glad to direct you to our children's ministry. There you would check your kids into classrooms with cheerful and safe workers who had police reports run on them to be able to serve you. After that, you would go to our sanctuary, a big room with a stage and lots of seats. They will give you a bulletin telling you about what the service will be like, and what's going on at church. You would find a seat and listen to and possibly sing with the worship team, and listen to the teaching from God's word."

"And then?"

"When it's over you go get your kids. If you want to meet with people and grab a cup of coffee, you can do that too."

"With my two kids with me, it's hard to connect

with others."

Dan nodded. "You can go home when it's all done."

"I don't need to stand up and be noticed?"

"No, but we do shake hands with people around us at one point."

"I won't be asked to come down front?"

"You can after the service if you want someone to pray for you. But that's up to you."

"What time is the service?"

Dan told her the service times. "What brought this on?"

She looked at him, wide-eyed and mouth agape. "You had something to do with this, didn't you?"

"To do with what?"

She shook her head and mumbled, "Never mind." She turned on her fuzzy-booted heel, entered her apartment and slammed the door.

Dan shook his head. What an odd day. For some reason people were angry with him and he had no idea why. Locking the door to his apartment and hanging up his coat he grinned.

Just like an ordinary day in church ministry.

~*~

He made it to his next counseling appointment.

"How are you doing, Dan?" Shirley asked as he settled into the loveseat.

He shrugged. "Been working out. Had some trouble at the apartment because of a neighbor's ex-boyfriend." He explained what happened.

"How is your depression?"

Dan looked down at his fingernails. He held them

up. "My nails are growing."

"You'd been biting them?"

He nodded. "I miss Sharon. I'm angry that she left me. I'm still not sure who I am outside of work. Everything we did, we did together, other than my visits to the Y. She wasn't a gym rat."

"You can't be at the YMCA all day. What are you doing to fill your time?"

"Play my guitar. Dishes, laundry, feed myself. Journal. Still meeting with my accountability group. I've had a few run-ins with Skye."

"Skye?"

"The young woman across the hall I told you about."

"Are you attracted to her?"

He shrugged. "She's pretty in her own way. She's not someone I would ever date."

"Why not?"

"Well, she doesn't have a relationship with Christ for one. Secondly, she has piercings, probably a tattoo and dresses, well, let's just say she's not 'pastor's wife material.'"

"There's a list of qualifications to be a pastor's wife?"

"No, but I couldn't see her in that role."

"What role is that? The role Sharon filled?"

"Maybe."

"Do all pastors' wives at your church do the things Sharon did?"

"No. They're all different."

"Marriage is a blending of the lives and personalities of two different people. Is it possible Sharon lost herself in the role of being a pastor's wife?"

Dan's heart raced. "Are you saying she didn't

want to do what she did? Serving me and alongside me?"

"I didn't know her. What were her hobbies? What did she do when you weren't around?"

"Cleaned, cooked, laundry, prepared her Bible studies for her small group."

"What did she do for fun? Did she have close friends she connected with?"

"Who can be a close friend to a pastor's wife? She understood too much about the church. She had a college friend she kept in touch with, but they hadn't seen each other for years."

"Why not?"

"It would have meant her traveling out West."

"She couldn't leave you for a week to visit a friend?"

"It would have been expensive."

"She didn't hold a job?"

Dan shook his head. "We always planned for her to stay home and raise our kids."

"I see."

His head dropped back against the chair. "I'm a hypocrite."

"Why?"

"I told someone the other day that a man who loves a woman treats her as if she were a precious treasure. He takes care of her. He understands what she loves and what her dreams are and works to help her reach them. He delights in making her happy. While I treated Sharon well, did I really know of any of her other dreams besides being a mother? Did I cherish her like she deserved? She had an aneurism. I didn't even realize she was sick. The doctors said there would likely have been no symptoms and her death was quick and painless. She didn't even know what hit her."

"And you still don't have a clue what hit you and it's been slow torture."

"You got that right."

"I think you need to give yourself grace. From all you've told me, you were a wonderful husband to Sharon. Looking back now as you move forward, there are lessons to be learned. No woman is ever going to replace Sharon in your heart or memories. But by the same token, it's not wise to rule out a woman because she doesn't 'look' the part of a pastor's wife."

"She doesn't know Christ. Right there, it's a no-go."

Shirley nodded. "Have you shared with her?"

"Not directly. I've asked questions. She recently inquired about coming to church."

"You've mentioned this woman quite a bit today. What does she do?"

"She's an artist, teaches Zumba at the YMCA, and has two small children she's raising by herself."

"Sounds like you admire her."

"I suppose at some level I do."

"You find her attractive."

"I'm a man. I find many women attractive. It doesn't mean I want to date them or envision a life with them. Besides, I'm not ready for a relationship."

"I wonder if you are using Sharon as a shield to keep you from really engaging in life on your own."

"We met in college and were inseparable. I don't remember not having Sharon in my life. There's never really been a 'me' without her until..." He took a deep breath.

"So you met her when you were, what, eighteen?"

Dan nodded. "We married after graduation from seminary."

"You dated six years?"

Dan nodded.

"And stayed pure?"

"It wasn't easy, but I was so busy studying and she was too...we really didn't do much else. Not many opportunities to get into trouble."

Shirley shook her head. "So you didn't romance her."

Dan frowned. "We were in college. Sure we went out, but our dates often involved studying."

"Did you play together?"

He swallowed hard. "I don't know that we did. Crap. I was an awful husband."

"Sharon didn't complain, did she?"

"No. She never did."

"Then don't beat yourself up for that. Look back without the rose-colored glasses and realize as much as you were in love, life wasn't perfect for either of you. You both missed out on something precious."

Tears threatened and Dan's breath shuddered. "I came here so you could help me feel better, not worse."

"Understanding the past can be a bridge to a better future for you, Dan. A future where you are more than a pastor, but a man. A man who might love a woman. A man who can play. A man who has a passion for more than putting in sixty hours or more a week at church."

"How do I learn to play at my age?"

"Your neighbor has kids, right?"

"Yeah."

"Maybe you should babysit them and they could show you how."

"Me? Babysit the four-year-old terror and his shy sister?"

"You wanted to be a father for years—maybe at some point God will bring that dream to light. Consider it practice."

"As I don't plan on remarrying, I don't understand the point."

"Just because God has said, 'Not yet,' doesn't mean 'never.'"

~*~

Skye struggled with the groceries. The kids waited inside the door. She wanted to get them all upstairs in one attempt, but one of the bags split open and cans of food went rolling through the snow and into the parking lot.

Haunted dreams kept her from a good night's sleep and now this? She let the tears fall.

"Are you hurt? Can I help?" Dan strode toward her.

"I'm not hurt and yes, I would gladly accept help."

"Where are the kids?" He started to chase the cans, collect them from the parking lot, and redistribute them in other bags.

"Inside the door."

He soon had the rest of the bags in his arms and hanging from his hands. He was able to reach high enough to catch the trunk door and slam it shut. "Let's go."

She trudged to the door, which Quinn opened. The kids scampered up the staircase ahead of them and Skye followed, trailed by her beast of burden, Dan. He followed her into the apartment and set the bags on the kitchen table. He stepped back into the open doorway. One foot in the hall. "All better?"

"Thank you." She nodded. The kids had dropped their coats and she reached down to pick them up. Her phone rang. She held up a finger to Dan indicating she didn't want him to leave yet.

"Hello?"

It was the fitness director on the other line. "Claudine is sick. If you can't take her class, I'll have to cancel. You get the pay if you do it."

"What time?"

"In an hour."

"OK. I'll be there."

She set the phone down. "Picked up a Zumba class. I'll need to put the kids in the childcare while I teach. It almost doesn't make it worth it."

"I could hang with the kids while you go teach."

Skye had been putting things in her cupboard. She slowly closed the door and stood to stare at him. "Excuse me?"

"I said I can hang with the kids while you go."

"Do you have any experience?"

"I was a kid once upon a time."

Skye bit her lip. She hated dragging them out into the cold again and it would save her money to not put them in day care.

"OK. Can you be back here in twenty minutes?"

Dan nodded and left.

Skye unpacked the groceries and started water boiling on the stove to make macaroni and cheese from a box. Dan would need to feed them, but at least he wouldn't have to cook. While waiting for the water to boil she ran to her bedroom and changed her clothes. She tossed her shoes and a towel into her bag and ran a brush through her hair.

By the time Dan retuned she was ready.

"The kids are free to watch television. They love to be read to. The rule with the toys is put them away when you are done and before playing with something else. And no Legos in the living room. Dinner is on the stove and you can warm up some green beans in the microwave. No milk to drink. Just water. Applesauce for dessert. That's in the fridge."

She pointed to a piece of paper taped to the fridge. "Here's my cell, although I turn my phone off while I teach. Here's the number for my mom, poison control, and their medical doctor. I'll be back in about ninety minutes. Any questions?"

Dan's eyes were wide and she feared he was going to retract his offer.

He shook his head. "I'm sure we'll get along fine. Try not to worry and enjoy your class."

Skye smiled. "I enjoy teaching. Thank you." She squeezed his arm gently before grabbing her keys and heading out the door.

The whole way to the YMCA she kept wondering why a single man as good looking as Dan would ever willingly take on her two monsters. Sure, she loved them, but he really had no idea what he had gotten himself into. She almost felt sorry for the man.

Almost.

She grinned. She was going to really enjoy her class.

~*~

Well, here was his chance. Didn't expect it to come this fast though, but it wasn't like he had anything else to do this evening. He checked the food on the stove. Kids probably didn't need to eat for a little while yet. He wandered into the living room and spied the desk in the corner. It was a taller one than usual with a slanted surface and several pieces of paper spread out. He picked one up. This must be her work. She was really good. He found some photos of paintings he supposed were hers. He sat back on the stool that was there.

Wow.

He stared at one painting and suspected that the real thing had been even more dramatic. This girl wasn't pretending. She was world-class. He forced himself to walk away. Looking at her paintings might be construed a violation of her privacy. Would he want someone looking through his journals? He wrote his heart out, but she put it in her colored brush-strokes. He sat down to keep an eye on the kids as they vegged in front of the television.

"Mr. Dan. You're b'aysitting us?" Meghan asked. She came to sit next to him with a book. Dr. Seuss. Couldn't go wrong with him. "Can you read this to me?"

"I might be able to manage that."

The television clicked off and Quinn came to sit on the other side of him. Dan shrugged, opened the book, and read it to them. Soon a stack of five books were on the coffee table.

"I'm hungry." Quinn announced. Dan followed them to the kitchen, heated up their dinner, and got it on the table for them. Quinn was going to dig in.

"Wait," Dan said. "Shouldn't we pray first?"

"Why? God doesn't need to save mac 'n cheese." Quinn lifted a fork to his mouth.

"No. He doesn't, but doesn't He deserve to be thanked for the fact that you have food to eat?"

Quinn frowned and dropped the fork. Both kids bowed their heads.

"Dear God. Thank You for this food and the hands that prepared it. Thank You for letting me spend time with Quinn and Meghan. Amen."

Meghan looked up to him. "I eat now?"

Dan smiled. "Yes, you can eat now." He sat down at the table as they ate and listened to their chatter. He was surprised when Quinn changed the subject and blurted out news.

"Mommy said we don't need to see Daddy anymore. She told her lawyer to make that happen."

"You don't like your father?" Dan asked.

"No," Quinn stated.

Meghan nodded. "Daddy mean."

Having met their father, he figured the kids weren't exaggerating. He found his admiration for Skye climbing.

When the kids were done, he cleared off the table, put food away, and loaded the dishwasher. He trailed them down the hall to their room. *Play?* The therapist wanted him to play?

Maybe these kids could show him how.

SIX

Find ecstasy in life; the mere sense of living is joy enough.
Emily Dickinson

"No, silly. Like this." Meghan giggled.

Skye had let herself in, closing the door quietly. Class went well and she longed for a hot shower. She peeked into the kitchen. It was spotless. She noted the stack of books on the living room table.

"I've never done this before," a deep voice spoke.

"You've never played with Legos?" the little boy asked, shock evident in his voice.

"Nope. So can I put this piece here?"

"You're not going to put a door on your house?"

"Is that what this is?"

Skye peered into the room. Dan sprawled out on his stomach on the floor surrounded by blocks and children. There was something sexy about a man playing on the floor with little kids. She shook herself for even going there in her thoughts.

Quinn and Meghan soaked up the attention. When did she last sit and play with them like this? She was always busy. She folded her arms and waited. It was several minutes before Meghan glanced up and noted her presence.

"Hi, Mom." She gave Skye a little wave, blew a kiss, and went right back to helping Dan with his project. He turned his head and flipped to his side.

"Ouch!" He moved a few blocks out of the way and looked back again. She failed to hide a grin. Her feet had met those plastic blocks one too many times. "You're home. How did class go?"

"It was good. Full gym but lots of fun. Do you mind staying until I've showered?"

Dan rose to a sitting position. "No. I really can't stay. It wouldn't be—"

"Proper?"

Dan frowned. "Thanks for teaching me how to play Legos."

Meghan threw her arms around Dan's neck and planted a wet kiss to his cheek. "You best ba'ysitter eber!"

"Yeah, you were fun." Quinn gave him a high five.

"Thanks, guys." He gave Meghan a hug in return and rose to his feet. "Guess I'll head out.

"You've been such a huge help today. I really appreciate it."

He grabbed his keys by the door and turned to face her as he held the knob. "It was...enlightening. Thanks for letting me help. You're a great mom, Skye." He turned and left, pulling the door shut behind him. She watched through the peephole as he entered his own apartment and closed the door.

Since the kids were playing well she took a quick shower and came out to fix some food for herself. She hated that it was dark so early. This year's winter was on track to break records for how cold it was, but she didn't think that was something to brag about. It wasn't a selling point for living here...but New York had far more snow and she didn't think she'd like to leave her mom.

She checked her e-mail and found a note from the art dealer. Her painting of Dan had sold for an exorbitant price and a publisher wanted to run a feature on her art in their magazine. A deep sense of loss rooted inside. That painting would never return to her. Sure, she owned the digital reproductions. One already hung in her bedroom. She never before attached herself so to a painting and didn't rejoice in its sale. The money would go a long way toward supporting her and the kids. She might even be able to get her car repair work done now.

She buried her head in her hands. Car repairs, kids, her ex, and an unexpected income. She hated bearing this burden alone. Sure, her mom would help when she could and Dan was a lifesaver tonight. That paycheck would help. Who knew how long before the money from New York would come and there were other paintings still for sale.

But the one of Dan—she wondered who bought it.

~*~

On Sunday morning, she struggled to get the kids ready on time for church. She wasn't even sure what she should wear. Did they expect her to come in a dress? She didn't own any. Jeans were her normal uniform when she wasn't teaching Zumba. She grabbed her nicest pair and soft fuzzy sweater that matched her boots for texture. She knew the boots were silly, but they were comfortable and kept her feet warm.

She managed to find the church, park, and soon the kids were settled into their classrooms. What they might teach a two and four-year-old was beyond her but it couldn't be worse than what they had been taught by Riley. She walked into the sanctuary and struggled to find a place to sit. She hung toward the back and slipped into a row. She moved to find a spot where there would be open chairs around her. She draped her coat on one, having forgotten to hang it up. She caught the notice on a screen to turn her cell phone off or to silent. No problem. Who would need her right now anyway?

The worship started, and she quickly got the melody of the song and tried to sing along. She wasn't much of a singer, but she did love music. She clapped when others clapped and managed to shake hands with a few people around her.

She settled down to hear Pastor Andrew speak. He was older than Dan. She got the drift from his stories that he was married and had children. He spoke today about the movie *Frozen*, the irony of how cold it was and the importance of allowing God to thaw our hearts...and how serving was out of love, not duty or to gain heaven. She had her phone out and a note pad application provided her with a spot to make some notes, since she'd failed to bring a pen and paper.

After the final song, she struggled through the crowds of people to wait her turn in line to pick up her kids. When she'd finally bundled them up and was ready to leave, she saw Dan speaking to someone. He glanced her way and his face lit up with a smile. Then he winked at her. He wasn't wearing his glasses today. Maybe he wore contacts sometimes? He was even cuter when he wasn't hiding his eyes. Heat rushed to her cheeks and she gave him a nod and ushered the kids out to the cold car.

The rest of the day she was haunted by the frosty windows and the pastor's words. Was her heart frozen and far away from God? Why would He want it anyway? She didn't understand any of it and resented that her focus was on these thoughts and not on her kids or her work.

Stop it. Just stop it. When she put her kids down for their nap, she picked up her sketch pad and colored pencils. And she drew.

She realized she'd been staring out at the icicle-laden sliding glass door. She never asked Dan about what really happened when his door was broken. She thought the reason was important.

Or maybe she wanted to see him wink at her again.

~*~

Dan trudged up the stairs. He missed being at church every day, and being there this morning was a mixed blessing. Welcomed warmly by many who didn't even realize he hadn't been around and those wanting to see how he was doing. The worship ministry was thriving under Nikolas's leadership.

And Skye.

She'd come. He didn't think she really would, but he was glad she did and eager to find out what she thought of the service and the message. Did the kids enjoy their classrooms? He itched to ask how the message impacted her. He entered his apartment slowly, hoping she would pop out her door to talk to him, fuzzy boots and all. She didn't, and he was strangely disappointed.

He made himself a simple lunch and settled into his favorite chair. He looked at his new sliding glass door, grateful that the warmth was reasonable now and the draft was gone. He sat and looked at his notes from the morning. He didn't like to think he'd walled off his heart in an igloo since Sharon's death. Grief seemed to be a burning-hot fever, not an icy-cold indifference, but the result was the same. He used his grief to hold everyone at bay.

Even God.

So what was he going to do about it? How did he begin to feel and open his heart to life and love and, yes, even play? He wasn't sure.

What did he always want to try but never had the courage to do?

Well, he was an athlete, but he'd never been skiing. Maybe he should try that. He really didn't want to do that alone, did he? He'd think about that. There was a place in Sussex. Anything else? Studying his Bible and writing notes about what he learned, but that only made him want to teach what he wrote. That wasn't recreation. He was learning new things, which was great. How often did he have time for that kind of in-depth study with his daily duties as pastor? Well, unless he was writing a sermon. In those instances, he would clear his calendar for prep time.

There must be other things he would enjoy. The fact that it was winter limited his options. Sailing could be fun. Or fishing. He doubted he would be able to relax and wait forever for a fish to bite, though. And sure there was ice fishing, but he couldn't imagine driving out on the ice with a vehicle. *Insane!* Pass on the fishing. They had a funny odor and he wasn't into cleaning freshly killed anything. That would mean deer hunting wasn't going to be on the docket come fall either.

Well, he could always explore the wonder of Legos some more. He smiled at the memory of the sweetness of Skye's children. He wondered at the neglect and abuse they might have suffered through the vile mouth of their father. Riley was lost. Skye was searching, and the kids were ripe for learning about Jesus and love.

Maybe it was no accident that he had moved into this apartment at this point in time.

~*~

The next morning at the YMCA, Dan saw Skye come in and warm up for her class. She really was somewhat cute when she dressed in normal clothes. Even with her hair in a ponytail she exuded positive energy. He lifted weights and surreptitiously watched her interact with people coming in for class. He was almost tempted to go in and try it.

Zumba? A pastor doing Zumba?

Well, why not? He wiped off his sweat. He was warmed up from the treadmill and lifting weights. Did he have it in him to dance for fifty minutes? How hard could it be?

He tossed the towel in the laundry bin, grabbed a fresh one, and walked to the studio. He entered the room and all conversation stopped. Skye turned to look at him with wide eyes.

"Dan? Can I help you?"

"Can anyone take this class?"

Skye nodded slowly. "Sure."

"Even guys?"

"There are many male Zumba instructors around the United States and the person who 'invented' it was a man."

"So I can give it a try?"

Skye grinned. "Sure."

"Where should I stand?"

"Stay right where you are. Since you are new to the class, being in the front makes it easier to follow me. If you can't figure out the move, bounce or jog in place. For every movement, there are different levels. To start, keep it low until you get the rhythm of the moves. If you come back for more in the future you can increase the intensity."

Adrenaline raced through his veins. He was going to watch Skye for fifty minutes as she jumped, bounced, and wiggled through this class? He swallowed hard. *You can do this.* He glanced around at the other women in the room, using the wall of mirrors to check them out. All kinds of women were present. Young and old. Fit and fat. He was probably going to be majorly humbled by them all.

The music started, and Skye addressed the class through a microphone worn on her head. "Let's go! I won't be giving many verbal instructions but I will point and you follow. Many of you know the routines pretty well. The rest, don't worry, you'll get there."

The bass vibrated under his feet and soon he was sweating and struggling to keep up with the shimmying and swaying. Women around him giggled, but he realized they weren't laughing at him, but at their own struggle to master the dance.

"It's OK to laugh. Have fun. Laughing burns more calories!" Skye called out to them as she clapped and stepped from the right to the left.

When the class finished, he grabbed his towel and wiped his face and head. Several women approached Skye, and he hung back. When they left, she approached him.

"You did pretty good for a first-timer. Did you

enjoy it?"

Dan couldn't stop grinning. "Yeah, I really did. Hey, I need to catch a shower, but I wanted to hear what you thought of things yesterday, and I never did tell you what happened with my sliding glass doors. Can I buy you a cup of coffee at the corner shop?"

Skye folded her arms and considered him. "As friends?"

"And neighbors."

She nodded. "OK. Give me twenty minutes to get cleaned up and I'll meet you there."

"Sounds great." He headed to the locker room and was out the door with his hair still wet, which he instantly regretted when he hit the frigid air. He dashed into the coffee shop and ordered his cuppa joe and settled into a comfortable chair to wait.

He was as eager as a teenager on a first date.

The very thought shocked him to the core.

~*~

Skye entered the coffee shop. Dan had already ordered and found a seat. She got her drink and went to join him.

"You and those fuzzy boots," Dan said as she settled into a chair adjacent to his.

"What do you have against my boots?"

"The first time I saw you, they were paired with short-shorts."

Her face grew warm and she was grateful some of her hair fell forward to hide her cheeks. "I like my boots. They keep my feet warm."

"They're growing on me."

"Like mold?" She raised an eyebrow, and he

laughed. His face changed today from her past interactions with him. There was a twinkle in his eyes and his smile was wider. Laughter. That was new coming from him. "How long has it been since you really laughed?"

He sobered up and shrugged. "It's been a long time."

"You enjoyed class."

"I did. It was a new experience to laugh at myself and enjoy not being perfect. It was OK because no one else was either, except perhaps you."

"You got a great workout as well."

"I already had a full workout before I came in. I suspect I'll be learning about muscles I didn't realize I had."

"You had 'em, they've been exercised in a new way and might complain a little."

"I'll survive."

"You'll come back?"

"I'd like to."

"You wanted to talk about what happened with your window?"

Dan nodded and proceeded to describe that day.

"Riley did that?"

"Yeah. He thought we were an item."

"He was jealous?"

"Yup. He wasn't too happy when I visited him in jail either."

"Why would you do something like that?"

"Because he's lost, Skye. He doesn't know Jesus and he's trying to fill up that hurt and emptiness with drugs, alcohol, and a vain attempt to control others."

"You went to tell him about God?"

"Yes. I forgave him for his actions. It doesn't mean

he'll escape the consequences, but at least I'm free from carrying any burden of resentment. He's God's responsibility now."

"Is it that easy to forgive?"

"Not usually. I don't have a relationship with Riley, so there's nothing really at stake. I can understand if he was deluded about us and really felt threatened. It doesn't make his actions right, but given how compromised his reasoning was, well, it kind of makes sense."

"How did he respond?"

"Rage."

Skye shrugged. "Sounds like typical Riley. I'm sorry you needed to deal with that though, and I'm glad you weren't hurt."

"I'm fine."

"You asked about yesterday."

"Yeah. What'dya think?" Dan sipped his coffee. She stared at his eyes, warm as a summer sky.

"I liked it. The kids had fun. The message got me thinking."

"Yeah, me too," Dan added.

"I haven't even seen the movie *Frozen* yet." She blew on her hot drink.

"Me either. Are you going to take them?"

"I hadn't even considered it. Money has been tight for so long. I sold some work, which will help, but might cause me to lose my food stamps and insurance. I've no idea how it's going to work out yet, so I need to be careful. It might be the only painting I sell this year."

"I saw some of the prints on your desk. You do beautiful work."

"Thank you." Did she dare tell him about the

painting that sold? It wasn't *really* him. He hadn't posed and she never intended to paint him. It just *looked* like him. He'd likely never see it since it had been sold in New York. He was a pastor in the northwest suburbs of Milwaukee.

"So, the message, aside from the movie. What'd you think?" Dan asked.

"You know how a sculptor will start with a block of granite, or wood, or even ice and envision what is inside and strive to bring it out?"

"I've heard of that." He leaned forward with his elbows on his knees as he nursed his drink.

"I envision God with His chisel and He's been placing it in tender spots and pounding."

"Sounds painful."

"Terrifying. None of that happened until you moved in. What is it about you, Pastor Dan? It's like you've cast some kind of spell and I'm trapped trying to figure a way out."

"Drop the pastor. I'm Dan. I'm rarely called pastor even at church. There is no spell. Would you be offended if I told you that I pray for you and your children?"

"Pray what, exactly? Isn't that almost the same as a spell?"

Dan shook his head. "Far from it. A spell asks for a specific outcome and expects it. A prayer is more a matter of the heart."

"So, you don't expect God to answer?"

"Oh, I expect God to answer, but not always in the manner or timing I prefer. He is in control over everything and He sees the bigger picture of what is going on in your life and heart. He knows your past, present, and future. Only He understands when and how to bring you to Him."

"You prayed I would accept Jesus. That I wouldn't only learn about God but, as Andrew said yesterday, I would have a relationship with Him?"

"Yeah. I did. I pray you would know the height, depth, breadth, and width of His love for you. Jesus is the bridge between you and an eternity with the God who created and gifted you."

Skye shook her head and sipped her coffee. The burn going down her gullet soothed her anger at the audacity of the man next to her. Praying for her? How dare he? "Why would you do something like that? Why would you even care?"

Dan bowed his head and sighed. "Because you matter to God, Skye. You know how you love your kids, even when they do wrong? Remember how Quinn ran away from you and hid in my closet? You were desperate to search for him so you could love him, care for him, and protect him. You are God's child, running and hiding, and He is seeking you because He loves you."

"What does that have to do with you? Why would *you* care or pray? That's what I don't understand. If I choose to remain hidden, I will."

Dan raised an eyebrow and grinned. "Did Quinn manage to keep you from finding him?"

Skye shook her head.

"Right. He could keep his eyes closed. He could have refused to respond to you, but you found him and dragged him out of the dark closet he chose to hide in. God can do no less for you. As for why I would pray? God dropped me into your apartment building and opened a door for you and I to become acquainted."

Susan M. Baganz

"I got the impression that you didn't approve of me when we first met." Skye wondered how forthcoming this man would be.

He frowned. "You were frazzled and your son hid in my apartment. You had those boots on and shorts and your hair looked like something from the 80s. I'll admit I looked down on you because of all that and your piercings. I'm sorry. I was wrong to judge you so harshly without even knowing you. I was frozen in my own block of ice and didn't appreciate the O'Connell *Titanic* bashing into me."

"Did I sink your ship?"

Dan leaned back and his eyes held hers. "I'm not sure yet."

Skye blinked.

"Have you ever skied?" Dan asked.

"Yeah. I used to do that when I was in high school. I wasn't great, but I managed getting down a hill without hitting a tree."

"I want to learn. Care to teach me?"

"I…"

"I'll foot the bill." Dan assured.

"That will only be if you don't break your foot in the process."

~*~

His accountability group noticed Dan's improved mood.

"What's your week been like?" Tony asked.

"Crazy and wonderful. I've been sharing the gospel. I played with Legos and took a Zumba class."

"You danced?" Simon asked and burst out laughing.

"I didn't say I was good at it, but I sure had fun," Dan said as he dug into his omelet. "And tomorrow I'm going to go skiing for the first time in my life."

"How are you doing with your grief?" Nick asked.

"Better. I was hiding behind that, and I can't believe how much life I allowed it to rob from me. Sharon is gone. I loved her and I miss her, but I'm learning better who I am now and what, outside of ministry work, I enjoy."

"You mean other than the Green Bay Packers?" Tony elbowed him.

"Well, they might have more draw right now if they'd made it to the Super Bowl, but man can't live for the Packers alone."

"Says you." Tony grinned. "Welcome back to the land of the living, Dan. We missed you."

SEVEN

Grief can take care of itself, but to get the full value of a joy
you must have somebody to divide it with.
Mark Twain

Skye agreed to meet him at a ski resort not far from Milwaukee. Old habits were sometimes good ones and for the sake of appearances, he would not ride in a car with a woman alone. Sure it might start out as nothing...but gossip and also opportunity for any kind of slip up were to be avoided. He rented boots, skis, and poles. The gal working the shop helped him get wax on the skis that was right for the snow they made. It had been a cold winter and while there was snow on the ground, fresh powder was nice, and this resort aimed to please.

Skye met him in her lavender ski outfit. "Looking good, Dan."

"You didn't need to go to any extra expense."

She shook her head. "No. I was pleasantly surprised that my gear still fit after all these years. Guess that Zumba helped. How do you feel?"

"I was sore the first day, but better now. Shall we hit the bunny trail?"

"Bunny trail? Is it Easter already?" She let out a full belly laugh. She wiped a tear and grinned. "How about a beginner trail. There's one over there with a tow lift to the top, but before I do that I should show you some basics, like how to stop, steer, and avoid getting your skis crossed."

"Can you help me avoid hitting a tree or careening off a cliff?"

"You really don't have to worry about cliffs on this section so we can skip that for now. As for trees? If you don't head in their direction they will generally leave you alone."

"Ha. Ha. Ha. Well, let's get this done. I'm eager to try these out."

Skye guided Dan through the basics and up the hill for the first run. "I'll go down and you follow."

"Are you sure I shouldn't go first so you can pick me up?"

"I've already shown you how to get up if you fall down. I think you'll be fine."

"You're mean."

Skye grinned. "Good. Maybe it will keep you from getting hurt."

"Why did you ever stop skiing?"

"I fell for a boy and got sucked into the wrong crowd. Doing anything healthy became a thing of my past. Recreation became about sex and drugs...not skiing, art, reading, or even Zumba."

"You consider Zumba recreation?"

"I get to go dancing a few days a week without someone trying to buy me a drink or proposition me, so, yeah, I do."

"And you get paid for it."

"Right, without it being a strip club." She winked at him. "Catch you at the bottom."

~*~

She took off down the easy slope, grateful that she had an opportunity to get used to the balance and movement on the skis. She missed this. Now she really couldn't afford a hobby. But for today she would enjoy herself. She slid to a stop at the bottom of the hill and turned to watch Dan. He was a strong man and she was confident that with a little practice he'd be mastering the most difficult hills.

She stood and held her hand up to keep the sun out of her eyes. Dan pushed off and slowly started his descent. He started out straight and slowly began to move to the right and left. He made it to the bottom and with a swish came up to her. "Shall we do it again?"

They went down that hill several times and moved to one slightly longer.

After their second time down that hill, Dan seemed to try to be a little fancier in his descent. She watched, giggling but pleased at how much he grasped in their short time there. As he came down the last half of the course, his ski broke and he somersaulted forward, the other ski bending his leg at an odd angle.

Skye unlatched her own skis and ran as fast as she could up the hill to the prone body lying in the snow. Ski patrol was on his way down. She dropped to her knees in the snow. Dan held his side and laughed.

"Pride goeth before a fall..." he gasped.

"Or a broken ski. That was not an issue of skill, Dan. Where are you hurt?" She leaned over to unhook what remained of both skis. He tried to straighten out his one leg. He groaned as he pushed himself to his elbows.

"My ego has a dent here..." Dan pointed to his ribs, "...and here." This time he pointed to his knee. "But I don't think I broke anything. I also don't ever remember doing a somersault in the snow before in my life. While I don't recommend it, or wish to do it again, it was quite fun."

The patrol arrived. Slowly, Dan rose to his feet, and they walked him down the hill. Once in the lodge and out of his ski clothes, the patrol looked at his side a little more closely.

"I think you should go to the doctor," she said.

"I will. Probably need an X-ray of my ribs, not that there is much they can do for that except it means no Zumba for a while."

"Would you stop smiling?" Skye couldn't believe how jovial he was in spite of his pain. "You might have been seriously hurt and you act like it's some joke."

"Oh, trust me, it hurts and it was definitely not a joke, but Skye, don't you see? I got out and played. I lived today. Not to serve anyone. Not to please anyone. Not to do any duty or job. I played and I had fun."

Skye shook her head. "I should never have agreed to this."

"I'm glad you did. I think part of the fun has been the company I've been with. You were a great teacher. Thank you, Skye, for making this such a memorable day."

"I'm totally lost here as to why you feel this way, but if you enjoyed yourself in spite of that tumble I'm happy for you. I, however, have responsibilities and need to get home to relieve my mom who is probably pulling her hair out with my kids."

"Your kids are great, Skye. Tell her to play Legos with them and she'll have fun."

Skye shook her head. This was a different man than the one she met only a few weeks ago. "Let me know what the doctor says?"

"Will do." He gave her a salute as he struggled to

his feet and zipped up his coat. Together they walked, well, Dan limped, to their respective cars.

The pastor was insane. Weren't they supposed to be serious? Staid? Boring?

This man really wasn't a pastor at all.

He was human.

~*~

Dan stretched out on his bed and reached for his bottle of water to take the pain pill the doctor prescribed. Every inch of him hurt, but he couldn't stop grinning. When had he ever had so much fun? Had he ever *really* played?

Memories of running around his neighborhood with his brothers and neighbors playing cops and robbers with sticks for guns. Racing bikes around empty parking lots. Kick the can. Soccer in high school and basketball. Yet with none of those did he remember feeling joy like he did today. His therapist was right. He hadn't been living. Hiding in his grief trapped him. He'd been entombed in ice and it took a spunky neighbor to help break him out of his shell.

He really should apologize to her. She'd been genuinely worried about him. Sure, he bruised some ribs and twisted his knee, but nothing was broken and he'd heal up soon enough. As he drifted off to sleep, he wondered what else he could discover to do that would be fun. He only hoped he didn't have to wait until he was healed up to find out.

~*~

On Sunday, he was back at Orchard Hill. He

didn't want to be anywhere else. He waited to see if Skye would show up and when she did, he approached her.

"Hey, kids all settled?"

"Yeah."

"Wanna sit together?"

"Aren't people going to talk?"

"It is what people do."

"No. I mean about us."

"There is no 'us' is there? We're neighbors."

She looked at him and shook her head. "Fine. Suit yourself." She walked away, and he stopped to pat someone on the back and grab a bulletin. He spied her toward the back on the right side.

He slid in next to her. "Why back in the shadows?"

She shrugged. "All the better to make out with you, I suppose." She covered her mouth quickly, and he spied her pink cheeks as she ducked her head and tried to hide behind her hair.

Dan wasn't quite sure how to respond to that. "Wow. Here I thought I was the one who got my brain rattled on that hill." He settled back to focus on the room. They had redecorated the stage. He liked it. He glanced through his bulletin. Skye settled back beside him but let her hair fall forward like a curtain shielding her face. Dan couldn't help but grin.

Sharon used to tease him like that early on, but not after he became a pastor. He hadn't even realized how much he missed that kind of repartee with a woman. Of course, Skye wasn't his wife so the comment was a tad on the inappropriate side, but it pleased him anyway. She must think he was attractive to make a comment like that, right? He'd forgotten what it was like to sit with a woman, as a man and not a pastor. Not that he would act any less honorably, but it was almost as if the role robbed him of the ability to…

Had Sharon been aware of that wall? They never touched, kissed, or in any way showed affection when in public. The thought grieved him. Another failure to chalk up to his frozen heart. The one that was cracked but now letting in the warmth of…what? Affection? Attraction certainly.

But she could never be a pastor's wife.

Why not?

She doesn't love Jesus.

Yet.

She's divorced.

So? She wasn't a Christian then and even if she had been, her divorce would have been permissible.

She doesn't look the part.

He paused at this. He looked around at the diversity in the congregation. So what? She didn't look like a cookie-cutter pastor's wife.

Wait a minute. Who started talking wife here? He wasn't in the market for a wife.

You're lonely.

True. But that didn't mean he had to pick up the first woman to cross his path.

She's about the eightieth if you had been counting. And the only one to shake you out of your comfort zone.

And he had definitely needed that.

He stood for worship but never forgot the woman next to him. When they sat for the offering, she leaned over. "You have a beautiful voice."

"Thank you." He pulled out his Bible and pencil to take notes. She took out her phone.

He scribbled his notes and she typed them on to a

blue note pad on her device. Interesting. He'd never thought of doing that before.

After they stood for the last song, he followed her out of the row of seats.

"See ya later, Dan."

"Yeah, later." She walked away and he quickly averted his eyes. Other bodies already interfered with the view. He moved out to the café to talk to people he knew before heading home.

Alone.

The emptiness of that word haunted him. Not so much now because of missing Sharon, but the fact that in a year since her death he'd done nothing to develop relationships where he might have company, to laugh, talk, or do something. He rubbed his wrapped rib. Not that he was even up for bowling right now. And laughter? Well, that rather hurt too. So perhaps home for a nap was a good call after all. He'd figure out the rest later.

~*~

The next day while painting, Skye found herself humming one of the worship songs from the day before. She did a quick search and found a radio station that played Christian music. The music moved her in new ways. There was more light in her painting than the previous ones. She finished one with a bird soaring. She chose watercolors today and the soft shades blended and created in her a sense of hope and freedom. Freedom. She leaned back in her chair to consider the work.

Would she ever feel that free inside? Would the darkness of her past always cast a shadow over her?

She never thought about that before. It took all she had to make it through each day caring for her kids and providing for them. But art was an introspective career and emotion was huge in her work. She looked at the bird and longed for it to be her. For her soul to be that free. To soar above the hardship and pain of life.

If God really cared for her like the songs she listened to and the pastor and even Dan had spoken about…why had she suffered as much as she had?

Because I made choices I knew weren't the best even at the time.

And why?

Because I was afraid of being alone—like my mom.

And where did that get you?

Divorced. Alone. With two beautiful children.

Tears ran down her cheeks. The thing she most feared had happened, but she survived. Didn't she? They were making it. The kids were doing better and she was starting to make some strides in her career.

I am so lonely.

She was also too busy to go out and make new friends who weren't doing drugs. Skye left not only their apartment, her husband, but also all their friends. She changed her phone number and moved outside of Milwaukee County to avoid any and all contact with people she used to hang out with. She didn't want to get sucked back into that lifestyle. She didn't want her children raised by a strung-out mom. Or killed in some drug bust gone bad.

This was all Dan's fault. She'd been content with mere survival until he showed up. Handsome. Caring. Asking questions that forced her to think, he changed everything.

Her kids were happy and wanted him to come

back to babysit.

Riley was in jail, this time for attacking Dan.

She'd attended church—twice. She'd gone skiing which she'd not done since high school, and up until Dan fell, she'd enjoyed it. She still couldn't believe how hard he laughed as he tried to get up from his strange and painful position in the snow. She almost wished she'd recorded a video of that run. It was funny, but at the time she was so concerned he was hurt.

He'd limped, and she noticed how carefully he sat yesterday.

She wondered how he was. She hadn't heard him leave his apartment. But where would he go? He couldn't work out at the Y and it was freezing outside. What did he do since he couldn't work?

She walked away from her painting. The music was still on and she flicked it off. The painting drew her eye again. Freedom. Was Jesus really the key to that? Her mom thought so. Dan did too.

But Dan's wife died. He'd been forced out of work he loved.

None of this made any sense, but logic didn't appear to be the qualifier for faith in Jesus. If she understood it correctly, faith was an act of believing without proof.

From where she stood, faith was equal to foolishness. Wasn't it?

But how many times had she believed in someone she could see and been disappointed, hurt, and betrayed?

Could an invisible God be better than the humans He supposedly created?

They aren't all horrible.

Yeah, but none are perfect.

I was.

"God?" she whispered.

Silence met her plea.

She shook her head and blew her nose. The man next door had some explaining to do.

She crossed the hallway and knocked on his door.

"Coming." The voice came faintly from inside and something crashed.

The door whisked open to reveal Dan in a T-shirt and jeans.

"Hey, Skye. Wasn't expecting you today."

"I need to talk."

"Like a sit-down kind of talk?"

She nodded.

"I could meet you for coffee in fifteen minutes. Would that be OK?"

"Do we really have to go out in the cold to do this?"

He frowned and nodded. "Listen. Don't take this personally. As a pastor, I need to protect my reputation, but it's more than that. You're an attractive woman. If I start spending time with you alone behind closed doors, it opens the door to intimacy and that might become physical. I would never want to dishonor you or any woman in that way, but I am a man and can be tempted. So, I play it safe."

He wasn't rejecting her, but protecting her. "OK. I'll meet you at the coffee shop."

He smiled. "Good."

The door closed and she went back to her apartment to grab her coat and purse. If it weren't for the fact that she had questions for him, she would almost anticipate this as a date.

Danger! No. He was right. There could be nothing

between them. He was a pastor. She was surprised lightning hadn't singed her fuzzy boots for daring to walk into the hallowed halls of a church.

Except Orchard Hill didn't look like any churches she'd seen before. It was filled with space and light outside of the sanctuary and no windows at all in the theater style auditorium. Not a stained glass window to be found. It was somewhat sad that the art that filled old church buildings was no longer a part of the current religious culture. Maybe God didn't need artists anymore like He did in centuries past.

She shivered at the cold in her little car. She didn't have a lot of time to meet before the kids would be home. As she walked into the restaurant, she got a text from the Y. An instructor was sick and they wanted to know if she could teach the class. Around dinner time again. She rolled her eyes.

Dan limped in and gave her a wave as he whipped off his stocking cap. His fingers raked through his blond hair making it spike on top. Soon he was sitting across from her at a tiny table, warming his hands on his cup of joe. His steamed frames were sitting on the table. She placed hers next to them.

"Coldest winter in forever around here."

"That's what the weathermen say." Skye drank him in. He was an attractive man, but up close he was overwhelmingly beautiful. No wonder her subconscious chose to paint him.

"Maybe I should find a church in the south or California?"

"Would you really move away?" Her hands shook as she blew on her hot tea.

He shrugged. "I've considered it as a possibility. Would I just be running away?"

"I tried running away. It helped a little, but the fact is I took my biggest problem along."

"And that was?"

"Me."

"I'm sorry," he said.

"It's not your fault."

"I realize—it's just, I understand all too well."

She nodded. "I have questions."

"About what?"

"God," Skye whispered.

"I'm not Him but I'll try to answer what I can."

"Why did God create man if he were to be so evil?"

"Initially man was good. It was all good. God made the world and everything in it and then made man. He realized man would be alone and created woman to be a helper. They were happy in paradise. I'm guessing Wisconsin is as far removed from that as possible, at least right now. They could go anywhere, talk with God. He only had one restriction on them. There was one tree in the garden that they were told not to eat from. That tree was called 'the tree of the knowledge of good and evil.'

"All they had ever experienced was good. Evil was a mystery to them. Satan masqueraded as a snake and teased and tempted Eve, the woman, and she ate of the fruit and gave it to Adam who also ate of the forbidden tree. They violated God's law and now full awareness of evil had been unleashed. They were banished from the garden and no longer would live eternally in paradise with God."

"So, they were given a choice?"

"God always gives us a choice. He doesn't want puppets to worship Him. He doesn't want adoration that is forced and false. He longs for us to come to Him with hearts filled with love and gratitude for the wonderful gifts He gives us. All of Scripture is filled with the history of man making choices and the consequences of those actions. Physical death is inevitable and didn't occur until after that first sin. That's what sin is at its most basic, a choice to disobey God."

"Physical death didn't exist?"

"Not until Adam and Eve ate that fruit. Spiritual death was also now part of our world. We are dead to God until we make a choice to follow Him. All lives are eternal. A small part is lived here on this earth, filled with sickness, sorrow, pain—but also God's beauty evident in His creation and expressed through gifts He gives us—like your art. But we all die. My wife, Sharon, is enjoying an eternity with no pain and only happiness and joy in God's presence because she made a choice to accept His free gift of salvation from eternal damnation."

"That's this 'accepting Jesus' thing I've heard about?"

"It's more than that. It's as simple as recognizing that He is God. That He died and rose again to save you and that, like a present given at Christmas, all you have to do is accept and unwrap that gift."

"I just say 'yes'?"

"It's not a flippant yes. It's a 'You are Lord of my life and I bend my need to follow You' kind of a yes."

"So, when a person does that, then what?"

"That person continues to live their life but now seeks to honor God with all their words, actions, and decisions."

"How would I learn any of that?"

"He gave us a book, the Bible. Here, do you have your phone?" He put his glasses back on as he reached toward her.

She handed it over to him. She grabbed her own frames and put her glasses on, grateful to see him more clearly. He punched some things and soon handed it back to her. "There. You now have a Bible app on your phone. I recommend you start in the book of John and learn who Jesus is. Because Jesus returned to heaven, He has not only left this book, but also His Holy Spirit to help us."

Skye looked at the phone and clicked open the app and found the book of John. "I'm not sure I completely understand."

"It's OK. I went to seminary to study this and I'm still learning and growing in my faith."

"Really? I thought pastors knew it all and had it all together."

Dan grinned. "Sorry to step off that pedestal, but I'm afraid of heights. I'm prone to temptation as any man or woman. I try, but sometimes I fail, more than I would like to admit, to think or do what would honor God most."

"Even thoughts?"

"He's God. He sees and knows everything about you."

"That's creepy."

"He's pursuing you, Skye. He's the best and most loving stalker you'll ever encounter. I'm not saying that choosing to follow God is easy or that your life will be better, but it is worthwhile and I believe many who choose that path are far happier than those who don't."

"I just don't want to be alone anymore."

"You never were. God's always been there, waiting for you to choose Him, even when you refused to acknowledge Him."

Taking a sip of her hot drink she let the warmth spread from her inside to chase the shivers of cold and fear away. "You've given me a lot to think about."

"I understand. I've been praying for you and will continue to do so."

"Thanks. I think. The first time you told me that I was furious at you for trying to interfere with my life. Things have been happening and it's been weird."

"What things?"

"My art has changed. I think it's for the better but I don't always understand the images I'm drawing and painting. Twice I could have sworn I've heard a voice, but no one was there. I was afraid I was losing my mind."

"You're not losing your mind."

"Can I change the subject?"

"Sure." Dan grinned.

"I got a chance to pick up another class tonight…"

"And you want me to hang with your kids?"

"If you would. Can you handle them with your ribs?"

"As long as Quinn doesn't want to wrestle I should be fine."

"How's the knee?"

"Tender but functional. I'm taking it easy so it can heal. It will be weeks before I can hit the treadmill and full press on the weights. When you came over I was doing some resistance band work and some hand weights to exercise what I can."

"So tonight?"

"Sure. I'll enjoy it. Your kids are great."

Skye looked at the time on her phone. "I'd better get home. Mom will be dropping them off soon. She's been sweet at bringing them home from their preschool program. She works there part-time but not in their classrooms."

"What time tonight?"

"Four-thirty?"

"I'll be there."

"Thanks, Dan. I really do appreciate it...and your willingness to answer my questions."

"I hope it helped."

Skye shrugged as she wrapped her scarf around her. "We'll find out, won't we?"

EIGHT

Friends are as companions on a journey,
who ought to aid each other to persevere
on the road to a happier life.
Pythagoras

Skye was out the door almost the instant he arrived.

"Gotta go. Thanks." Off she ran down the stairs to her car. Dan frowned but closed the door. Two pairs of eyes glanced his way before returning to the program on the television. He wandered over to Skye's art and examined some of her work. She mentioned her work had changed. He didn't know what it had been like, but what he saw was breathtakingly beautiful. These were all reproductions of the original but stunning in their detail.

He made his way to the couch and sat, watching the program with the kids. When it ended, they crawled up next to him with a stack of books. He read to them from a few of them before heading to the kitchen to prepare dinner. Skye left directions for making fish sticks and there were carrots and raspberry applesauce. He prepared and served the meal.

Quinn looked at him as they sat down. "Will you pray for us again?"

Meghan nodded and folded her hands in front of her.

"Sure." How could he resist such a request? "Dear

Jesus, thank You for this food and please be with Quinn and Meghan's mommy as she teaches her class and bring her home safe. Amen."

"Amen!" the kids chorused as they dug into their meal. When finished, he cleaned up and followed them to their room, like last time. He sat down and together they started to build with the Legos.

"Mommy says you're a pastor." Quinn looked at Dan. "What do pastors do?"

"Great question. We serve the members of the church, helping them use their gifts for God. We provide teaching, counseling, encouragement, and leadership."

Quinn scrunched his face and shook his head.

Dan tried again. "We try to help people know Jesus and grow in their understanding of Him."

Meghan stood up and spun around. "We go church, learn Jesus."

"What did you learn about Jesus?" Dan asked.

"Lub. Jesus lubs us," Meghan responded as she plopped back down and went back to work on her project.

"How about you, Quinn?"

"God is a father. I don't want another father."

"God is not a father like your dad was. He's a wonderful, loving father."

"He won't hit us?"

"Your father hit you?" Dan hadn't realized there'd been physical abuse in the marriage.

"Shhh. Mommy not know or he kill her."

"God will never hit you. You are wonderful and precious to Him."

"Really?"

"He created you. He gave you your dark hair." He

turned to Meghan. "And you got curls."

"Does He love daddy too?"

"He does, but He's not very happy at what your daddy did."

"He loves Mommy?" Meghan asked.

"Yes, God loves your mommy too."

"Will He help her to not cry so much?"

"Your mom cries?"

Quinn raised his shoulders. "I hear her at night. See tissue in the garbage when we get home from school."

"God cares about your mommy's tears. Even adults get sad sometimes."

"Did you ever cry?"

Dan nodded. "Yup. Lots."

"Why?"

"My wife died and I miss her."

Meghan rose and patted him on the back. "It be aw right."

Dan smiled and gave her a little side hug. "Yeah, you're right. It will. But sometimes crying is part of getting to 'aw right.' Do you guys like to sing?"

"I'z a girl." Meghan put her hands on her hips and scowled at him.

"But of course. My apologies."

She went back to playing. "I sing wheels on bus."

"That's a great song. Did you learn any at church?"

"Something about God's love..." Quinn's nose scrunched up.

"Did it have hand motions like this?" He raised his hands up and then down and out.

Quinn nodded.

Dan started to sing the song and the kids stopped

playing to watch him as he did the movements to it. Soon they were trying to imitate the moves but they didn't sing. He stopped and they smiled.

"Do you understand what that song means?"

"God lubs us." Meghan answered.

"Yes. More than you will ever know." Dan put a final piece on his creation and showed it to the kids.

"Good job, Mr. Dan," Quinn said.

The apartment door opened and Dan rose to his feet. "Guess that's my cue to leave. It's been fun."

Meghan came and hugged his leg. "Thank you."

Quinn came and hugged his other leg. "We like you taking care of us."

"That means a lot, but I do need to leave." He pried their arms off and dropped to his good knee. He pulled both kids in and hugged them close. He whispered, "Don't forget that God loves you and He hears you every time you talk to Him."

The two kids released him and he pulled himself up and turned, almost running into Skye.

"How'd it go?" she asked.

"Great. We had fun. How was class?"

"Surprisingly full given how cold it is outside. It was good."

"Wonderful. Have a good night, Skye. Kids." With a wave, he was out the door and back into his own apartment.

~*~

His phone rang and he looked at the number. Amy? "Hello?"

"Hey, Dan. I returned from Arizona for training and vacation with my family. I just discovered you're on a leave of absence, and wanted to check in and see how you are doing."

"Better than I was. It's nice to hear from you. How are you?" Amy had been Sharon's close friend and they used to meet as part of a small group. Amy was also one of the worship team leaders. She'd seriously dated a man, but broke it off shortly after Sharon's death. He often wondered why.

"I've waited a year to approach you, Dan. Figured you needed that long to grieve. Thought maybe we could do lunch one of these days."

"Sorry, Amy, but I don't do lunches or dinners with a woman alone. You know the policy."

"Dan, let's be honest. We like each other. We get along. We have many interests in common. We've hung out at the adult group a lot over the past year, and we've led worship together. I knew you needed time to grieve Sharon. I miss her too. But I thought, maybe now that you've had time to heal, we could…date."

Dan sat down and swallowed hard. If he'd been wearing a tie he'd be loosening it right about now. "Listen, I like you Amy, and I value your ministry and faithfulness at church. I enjoy your company when we are with others. You are a delightful woman, but I'm not interested in dating you."

"It's too soon? I totally understand. I figured that with you needing a wife, that maybe it was time to throw my hat in the ring."

"I don't *need* a wife. There is no ring to throw your hat into. This isn't some kind of sweepstakes drawing where I'm the prize. I'm not looking for a wife and even if I were, you would not be in the running. I don't think of you in that way."

"You can't deny we'd be great together. I'll give you more time, but you need to know I'm serious. I've been praying and I believe God has selected you as my life's mate. I intend to honor Him. If I need to wait, fine. I can do that. You'll see. You need me."

"Amy..."

"Bye, Daniel. Think of me."

The connection ended and Dan set the phone down while he shook his head. Sure, he'd been approached, but no one had ever called and asked him on a date before. He caught all the broad hints of interest at church in the groups he led, but he ignored them thinking they would die down in time. But Amy could cause problems for him with the worship team if he wasn't careful.

Amy was right about one thing though that he had been in denial about. He did need a wife. Just not for the reason she thought. He needed a wife to keep the Amys of the church away. They respected his boundaries better when he wore a ring on his left hand.

The memory of Skye's face as she leaned over him in the snow, so concerned and even ticked at him for laughing, made him smile. Now there was a woman who would keep him on his toes.

She doesn't know Jesus yet.

She's close.

She's not a typical pastor's wife. I haven't known her long enough. She came with two kids and an abusive ex-husband who wouldn't hesitate to make trouble for him, wedding ring or not.

All true. He sighed and rubbed his achy knee. Struggling to his feet he went to the kitchen to make his own dinner. It was about the only thing in his life he knew to fix right now.

~*~

He saw his therapist the next morning. Shirley sat across from him and waited.

"OK. I did what you suggested. I babysat the kids, twice. I played with Legos. I tried some new things. I took a Zumba class and went skiing for the first time ever."

"And?"

"I haven't been living. I've gone through the motions. Done what was expected. But now? I had fun. I laughed. I don't know when I ever laughed last. Even when I bruised some ribs and twisted my knee—I laughed."

Dan spent the rest of the hour recounting his adventures.

"You've made great progress. What are you going to do about Amy?"

"I don't know."

"It is interesting that you've done coffee with Skye twice, but won't do lunch with Amy. And you sat with Skye at church."

"How did you know that?"

Shirley grinned. "I was there on Sunday and saw you. I suspect Amy and others did as well."

"We're neighbors. She's been asking a lot of spiritual questions. That's all there is."

"That's fine, Dan. But think about how it looks to others. I'm not saying you need to change anything. Your behavior is above reproach, but that doesn't mean your choices, as noble as they are, won't have consequences."

"What's that supposed to mean?"

Shirley gave him a smile and instead of answering bowed her head and prayed for him. When she finished, she said, "Think about it and I'll see you next week."

Dan's hands were fisted as he strode out of the office. Right now he wished he could run on the treadmill, but the doctor suggested a few weeks off to heal his knee. It still ached but that pain didn't ease his anger. "Choices have consequences." He wasn't two years old anymore, he didn't need a reminder that everything he did and everywhere he went he was under a microscope.

No. He wasn't a movie star stalked by paparazzi, easily detected by their cameras. He was a pastor, and people from church could be anywhere watching him. Judging him. Trying to decide if the Jesus he proclaimed was really all he claimed.

As if *he* were God. They expected him to be perfect. Flawless. Superhuman.

But he wasn't.

He was a man. A lonely man. A widower.

He sat in his car and wept. Then he drove home.

~*~

That evening the buzzer for outside the building rang.

He wasn't expecting a visitor. He pushed the intercom. "Who's there?"

"It's Amy. I brought you dinner."

Dan rolled his eyes. Now what was he to do?

The buzzer rang again. He opened his door and ran across the hall to Skye's door.

She opened it. "Dan?"

"You gotta help me, Skye. There's a woman downstairs who brought me dinner. I don't want to let her in. How do I deal with her?"

The buzzer rang again.

Skye grinned. "Hold on a sec. Quinn, Meghan!" She thrust them at him. "Kids, I want you to go in to Dan's apartment. Turn up the music loud and dance and sing." She turned to him. "Return them when you're done." The kids ran in and cranked the volume on the stereo.

"What?" Dan yelled at the door closing behind Skye's grinning face. Dan could hardly hear himself but went to the intercom, and pushed it, opening the door to the downstairs and waited for Amy. He stepped out into the hallway and hoped the kids weren't destroying anything.

Amy came up the stairs. She worked as a realtor and was dressed in black boots, a skirt, and a long red coat. Her head was covered by one of those silly little black beret type hats that did absolutely nothing to keep anyone warm. At least in his opinion. She carried a paper bag.

"I wasn't expecting anything or anyone."

"Well, I thought that since you didn't want a public lunch or dinner, that a private one would be better. No one would need to know until we were ready to be public with our affection."

"Amy, there is no affection on my side. I'm sorry."

A crash and a cry came from inside the apartment.

"Hold on." He went in and closed the door, putting his foot by it in case she tried to force her way in. "Are you OK?" Both kids gave him a thumbs-up and big smiles. He slipped back out to the hallway.

"Aren't you going to let me in?"

"I'm sorry. I can't. I have company right now and they're a little wild at the moment."

"Company?"

"Yeah. You picked a bad time. But I really don't want you coming back here. My address is not in the church directory, so I'm only assuming you snooped to get it. This is an invasion of my privacy."

"But Dan…"

A scream erupted from the apartment. "I'm sorry, Amy. Gotta go before they kill each other." He slipped back into the apartment and locked the door behind him.

She banged on the door, yelling his name, but he remained firm. He egged the kids on to be louder and silently laughed at their antics. He wasn't feeling too bad about turning Amy away. It was inappropriate for her to come.

Dan looked out the peephole as the outside door slammed shut. He went to turn the music down and gave the kids a hug. A soft rap on the door told him Skye had returned to them.

He answered the door and almost tripped over the bag of food. "I can't believe she left it."

"You might as well enjoy it."

"Thanks for your help. I really do appreciate it."

"It's the least I can do for the man who has twice helped me out of a bind. The kids have done this routine for me when I've had unwanted suitors. Nothing deters a man and dampens his hormones more than screaming children."

"I bet."

"Wasn't she the one leading the singing on Sunday?" Skye asked.

"Yeah. She has 'thrown her hat in the ring' to be

the next Mrs. Daniel Wink."

"There's a ring?" Skye winked at him as she escorted her kids across the hall.

"No. No ring. No open positions either. She doesn't seem to understand my English."

"She understands, Dan. She just thinks she can change your mind. But take it from me. If she controls your courtship, she'll micromanage your marriage."

"I am not marrying her—or anyone!" He slammed the door and heard her laughter as she shut her own.

The apartment was suddenly quiet as a tomb. He picked up the bag and found that Amy hadn't cooked anything. She purchased take out from the local restaurant, DeLuca's. He pulled the food out and enjoyed the healthy helping of lasagna and garlic bread.

Rejecting a woman never tasted so good.

NINE

*People grow through experience
if they meet life honestly and courageously.
This is how character is built.*
Eleanor Roosevelt

Skye wasn't sure what to think after meeting with Dan to talk about God. Listening to her kids talk about how wonderful he was, and now his little run in with that woman, left her confused about the man.

He was an attractive guy, but she didn't think women, Christian women, chased men. Even she never chased boys, although once she had one she'd done everything to keep him. That didn't work out too well for her. She didn't want a man who didn't respect her, want her, or care about what she liked or didn't like.

Well, now she had kids and the label of "divorcee." While that wasn't a negative from where she came from, it was a failure she carried with her. A failure to make a better choice. A failure that she wasn't worth a man loving and caring for her and their children.

She spent time reading in the book of John from the Bible like Dan recommended. Jesus was wonderful. She didn't understand how someone like Him could ever love someone like her. No man ever really had, so why would Jesus be different? She was carrying her past with her. Her sins and failures surely prevented a God from ever loving her.

Didn't it?

She thought about Amy. How had the woman ever deduced Dan was looking for a wife? Skye hadn't known him long, but when she met him only a few weeks ago, he was deep in grief. While he seemed better now, she had no doubt it was going to take time for him to heal. He repeatedly said he wasn't interested in marriage. She suspected it was because his had been so wonderful he feared no other woman could compare.

Sharon probably had no idea how treasured she'd been.

Who would mourn Skye when she died? Her mother and children. That would be it. Well, her Zumba class would miss her until they found a replacement. OK, and maybe that dealer out in New York who loved her work. Maybe after she died she would become a world-famous artist. Isn't that what happened to most of the great talent in the world? Their true value was recognized only after they passed away in poverty.

She put the kids to bed after listening to them pray. It was something they insisted on, having learned it at church and from Dan. She stepped into the dim living room, picked up her paints, and pulled out a new canvas.

Her palette was shades of gray and black. The shadows that haunted her emerged on the page. Splotches of red represented the death of dreams and tears shed over them. The painting was dark and moody.

Dan deserved someone like Amy. *If* Dan were ever to remarry.

What must it be like for his wife to have been loved so well? She would do almost anything for a man who would love her like that.

But Dan wouldn't be the one. Not some agnostic, single mother with a history of drug abuse and a jealous and abusive ex-husband. She moved her finger to the piercing on her lip. Why'd she do that anyway? She reached up, gently released the ring, and set it up high on a shelf. She went to the bathroom and looked in the mirror. Her second piercing was in her eyebrow. She removed that one too. There would be scars if she let them heal up, but she would look more normal, whatever that was.

Who was she kidding? Even without the piercings, men of Dan's caliber would never look twice at her.

Her future stretched out before her long and lonely. She put her paints away and went to bed. Alone.

Always alone.

I am with you.

I'm beginning to understand, but God, are You enough?

~*~

Skye had just checked the kids into their rooms at church. She was eager to learn more about God. Amy intercepted her.

"You sat with Pastor Dan last week. I'm warning you to stay away from him. He's mine." The woman hissed at her.

"Is this how Jesus behaved? I haven't read that far so I'm curious." Skye's heart thumped, but she was determined to stand her ground. She didn't have any claim on Dan, but neither had this woman. Her respect for the worship leader plummeted, and it hadn't been too high after her attempt to impose on Dan the other night.

"Excuse me?" Amy placed a hand on her chest and her chin went up a notch.

Skye decided to press the issue. "My understanding is that Christians are to model their lives after Jesus. Is there an example in the Bible that shows Him acting like this?"

"Like what?"

"Rude. Petty. Jealous and possessive of a man who has no desire to claim you."

"You little interloper. You've crossed the wrong woman." Amy's voice had raised at this point.

"Excuse me." Pastor Andrew had been close by during this exchange. "We haven't met, I'm Andrew."

"Skye."

"It's a pleasure to have you here, Skye, and your question was insightful. Jesus doesn't ask us to threaten others. It is not a way to show the love of God to those who don't know Him." Pastor Andrew motioned to Amy. "You're coming with me."

"But I'm singing back-up on the team this morning. We start in a few minutes."

"They'll need to do without you this morning. Head to my office and I'll be there shortly."

Amy sputtered but obeyed. She strode away, bumping into people as she went.

Andrew turned to Skye. "I'm terribly sorry that happened. You're new to visiting Orchard Hill?"

"Yes. Dan is my neighbor, and he's asked me difficult questions and I came because I want to learn more."

Andrew grinned. "I'm glad you've come. As you can tell, our faith doesn't change us all at once and even believers fall into behaviors God doesn't consider pleasing."

"Passion is a powerful emotion."

"So is jealousy. I hope you won't hold Amy's inappropriate behavior against us as a church or the God we proclaim."

Skye frowned. "It's sad that He uses such imperfect people to be His ambassadors."

"That's a good word for it, but it is also a way for Him to show His power as He changes and grows us. Listen close this morning. I'll be talking about some of my past mistakes and how God changed me."

Skye nodded as he glanced at his watch. "I need to go. It was nice meeting you."

"Thank you, pastor."

"Andrew."

"Thank you, Andrew."

He bustled away and she stood there for a few moments, wondering how he would deal with Amy. She'd been inappropriate and beyond rude. Skye was used to that kind of behavior in high school, but they were all adults now. The one thing it did prove to her was that she was not good enough. Not to be forgiven by God. Why would He forgive her? Even here it was like the filth of her past hung as a cloud over her head. A neon sign flashing "sinner" to everyone she met.

She ducked her head, accepted the bulletin, and found a corner on a different side of the sanctuary to sit. She didn't see Dan anywhere.

~*~

Dan walked in a few minutes before the service started and saw Amy stalk toward the offices. Andrew strode purposefully down the hallway on the phone. When Andrew spied Dan, he motioned for him to follow.

"I understand it's a change of plans and I'm sorry. Trust me on this. Go ahead and I'll be in there soon. Tom is doing the announcements. I will be there before the message." Andrew clicked the phone off and pulled Dan into the conference room and shut the door.

"What's going on?"

"Amy laid into a young woman outside of children's ministry a few minutes ago. Name of Skye? Gal had pluck and nailed Amy to the wall on her inappropriate remarks. I pulled Amy off the team and she's waiting for me in my office. What's going on?"

Dan let out a deep breath of air. "Amy believes she is God's answer to my unacknowledged need of a wife. She tried to get into my apartment a few nights ago. She's called wanting a date. I've told her I'm not interested in dating right now and she is not someone I would consider for a wife. I don't like her that way. She doesn't want to take no for an answer."

"And Skye?"

"She's my neighbor. I've been sharing with her about God and she's been asking lots of questions."

"She's cute."

Dan shrugged. He agreed, but he wasn't going to admit it to his boss.

"What do you propose I do about Amy?"

"I wish I could tell you. I'm not sure why she's latched herself on to me. I've never shown her any preference over any other woman."

"You're single, attractive, love God. It's a potent combination." Andrew ran his hand through his hair.

Susan M. Baganz

"I'm pulling Amy off the team until she can meet with Mary Beth and if Mary Beth can clear her to serve I'll accept her back on. I don't want her there causing trouble for you when you return."

"Thanks."

"Skye seems sweet, Dan. She's seeking and my prayer is that Amy didn't derail her."

"I'll try to talk to her soon."

"You're being careful?"

"All the rules I followed on staff, I still hold to now."

Andy nodded. "Good. Call me. I want an update on how things are going. I'm hoping you'll be back soon?"

Dan smiled. "I'd like that. The time away though has been revealing to say the least."

Andy squared his shoulders and headed to his office.

Dan slipped into the back of church, near where he'd sat the week before with Skye. He didn't see her.

When Andrew came to preach, he talked about how God saves everyone, and forgives even the worst of sins. He even talked about his B.C. days (before-Christ). Dan worked with Andrew for years but didn't know about his previous descent into drug use while younger. No wonder he was such a stickler for boundaries in ministry, but also had such grace for those who fell and repented. Dan was once again grateful to be under his leadership.

After church, he slipped out a side door. He wasn't sure how many people had witnessed or were aware of Amy's folly that morning, or a few days prior, but he wanted to avoid the questions. Cowardly, maybe. He called it self-preservation. He didn't know how many others would think they needed to 'throw their hats in the ring' as it were.

Once home, he picked up his guitar. He tried to play but gave up. How could Amy look at him that way? He was all too aware, far too late, of how he'd failed as a husband. Why would anyone want him? Sharon was a saint to put up with him for as long as she had.

Lord, am I destined to always be alone?

~*~

Dan sat with his accountability group on Wednesday. Tony already had his turn and put the focus on Dan.

"How's it going, Dan?"

"Crazy. I got hurt having fun, and for some reason single women at church decided I'm back on the market."

"That's rough. What do you do about that?" Simon asked.

"I don't know."

Tony shook his head. "I remember those days before and after Stacy…until I met Renata. By then, I think everyone realized I was off-limits, and that if I were interested I would approach them. Any overtures by them would not be reciprocated."

"And Renata was not an easy catch for you. I think you enjoyed the challenge. The first woman not to fall down at your feet desperate for your company," Simon said.

"You're right. We spent time together, but while we weren't alone a lot, we became friends. I didn't learn until later on why she was so cautious about men. I'm glad I respected her boundaries, but I think the fact that she respected mine was one of the things that made her more attractive to me." Tony sipped his coffee. "Sure glad she decided to trust me enough to actually marry me."

"Sharon never chased me down either. We met, hung out at school in groups where we met other people and gravitated toward each other. We became comfortable together, and it was certainly easier than trying to date around while attending seminary. We became best friends and fell in love." Dan frowned. "Now I look back and wonder if I found her too convenient and took her too much for granted. I put everything into ministry and she always supported that, but I wasn't ever really there for her. I think that's why losing all those babies was so hard for her. She longed to have someone around, to love and care for. All those years I thought we had a great marriage and now all I can see is how I shortchanged her."

"Ouch," Simon said. "You can't keep beating yourself up for that. Sharon loved you and she accepted you for who you were. You need to forgive yourself and move on."

"My fear is that I would forget my mistakes and make them all over again with another woman. Andrew was right to force me into time off, although initially I resented him for that. I didn't understand who I was apart from Sharon and ministry. I didn't know how to have fun. I had no hobbies."

"So you finally get to grow up and discover who you are," Nick said.

"I'm still not there yet, but I've had some fun and laughed…even when I cracked my rib and twisted my knee skiing."

"And you did Zumba?" Tony elbowed him. "That I would have liked to see."

"Hey, don't knock it till you try it. It was a great workout and a lot of fun. Pastors don't get much chance to dance, you know."

Simon grinned. "And Legos? How deprived was your childhood?"

"Sorry. We had Lincoln logs and other toys. Lots of books."

"When are you going back to work?" Tony asked.

"Might be soon. I meet with Andrew tomorrow. Pray that I'm ready when the time comes."

The men nodded and moved on to Nick.

Dan was grateful. Sometimes the spotlight shone a little too close for comfort. And while he shared...he still held some of his closest fears to his heart.

There were some things his accountability group didn't need to know.

~*~

It was weird walking into church and not going to his desk. He walked into Andrew's office and sat on the couch.

Andy rose and closed the door. "So tell me how it's been going."

Dan gave him a brief overview of some of the things he'd done and been learning during his time off. It had only been a few weeks.

"So how close do you think you are to being able to come back and work in a more balanced manner?"

"I'm getting closer. Still not sure how I would handle the situation with Amy though."

"I've decided that for now I'm continuing to have

Niko oversee that ministry for a few months. He's a strong leader and Specific Gravity is working on their next album. This gives you time to adjust your schedule with other things and not have to be overloaded when you come back."

"Will I be able to lead worship?"

Andy frowned. "I suppose periodically that could be good, but I would suggest it not be on a team with Amy."

"How did she respond to your 'talk?'"

"She cried. She'll be following up with Mary Beth."

"OK. It hurts to think that I'm losing the worship ministry..."

"You're not losing it. You'll still be the pastoral oversight for the ministry, but Niko will have the major responsibilities for now. He's a little spooked about taking your baby from you so you might want to connect with him."

Losing leadership of the worship ministry was both a relief and a curse. "I'll reassure Niko."

"Good. Listen, you've taken a lot of hits and I'm sorry I didn't push you to take this time away earlier..."

"You couldn't. Budget time, Easter, staff vacations, and fall were all busy and everything got into full swing with Christmas. You couldn't have spared me."

"We would have survived for you to take time off. You make me sound like I used you. It wasn't like that, Dan. I was praying and waiting and to be honest, I was afraid." Andrew leaned forward. "You're my friend, Dan, but you had even shut me out. There isn't hard and fast protocol in any 'ministry handbook of standard operating procedures' that I could go to. I knew what God wanted me to do, but I was a coward and I didn't obey as soon as I should have."

"What were you afraid of?"

"That you'd quit. That you'd toss it all away. Ministry, music…and maybe even your life."

"I'm surprised you didn't ask me to sign a suicide contract."

"I thought about it."

"So did I." Silence hung between them. Dan swallowed hard. "Listen. I'm sorry for causing so much concern. I was angry and resentful. I did consider whether it was time to move on, and not necessarily in ministry. I've learned a lot in the few weeks you've given me. It forced me to face myself and come to grips with some hard truths."

"Hard? Like how?"

"I thought my marriage to Sharon was good. I've realized I wasn't as great a husband as I thought I was. She never complained, but I shortchanged her in so many ways. And I shortchanged myself. I never got to tell her I'm sorry."

"You weren't aware. Maybe the gift now is learning this so you'll be a better husband next time around."

"*If* there's a next time."

"You liked being married."

"I did, but I never gave myself permission to play. That's where I hurt myself."

"Play is hard, isn't it?"

"Yeah. I think if I had kids it would be easier. It's not like Sharon and I didn't do things together, but it was mostly work around the house…I'm trying some new things though and when my ribs are healed up, wanna try some racquetball at the YMCA?"

"You know how to play?"

"Nope, but I'm willing to learn and look like a fool while I try."

"I'll teach you. I'd enjoy that."

"Andrew, we're cool. I'm grateful now that you forced this time away. Thanks for caring enough to push me even when I resisted."

"Anytime, Dan. I'm glad you're still around to serve with. So, another two weeks?"

"Yeah. Sounds reasonable."

"And remember, coming back doesn't mean you have to put in sixty-hour weeks. Take what you've learned, scale back, and do what's reasonable."

"Got it. Easier said than done, but I think I understand this all a whole lot better for having had this time."

"Good." They both rose and shook hands.

Two weeks. Pretty tall order to be all healed up in two weeks. Almost as tall an order to be over your wife after a year. Was he ready to come back?

He'd find out soon enough.

TEN

Paintings have a life of their own that derives
from the painter's soul.
Vincent Van Gogh

Skye hung up the phone in a daze. New York? She really needed to go to New York. But how? She snagged the interest of an agent who wanted her out there to do a showing and sign a contract for larger retailing of some of her work in the Christian market? That was never on her radar. She needed to be gone for two nights and three days.

She heard the key in the door across the hall and ran to open hers. "Dan."

He turned and gave her a smile. "Hey, how are you, Skye? I haven't seen you in a while."

"Doing OK. How are the ribs?"

"Tender. No Zumba or heavy weights for a while yet and the most I can manage for cardio is the bike."

"Well, at least it's something."

"Yeah."

"Can I ask a favor?"

"Sure. I can't guarantee I'll grant it."

"Fair enough. Would you pray for me?"

"Sure. Anything specific?"

"My agent wants me in New York for an art show. Next week. I can't take the kids. I need to figure out what to do."

"Your mom will help, right?"

"Mom can pick them up and take them to their

Susan M. Baganz

morning programming but beyond that, she has her own work. Her own life."

"So you need someone who will be with the kids when they come home and during the night."

Skye bit her lip. "Yeah. For two nights. But I don't know anyone and I don't want to hire someone I've never met. I've hardly ever used a sitter. Well, except for you."

"When's the trip?"

"I'm supposed to fly out next Thursday morning and get back Saturday night."

"Flying out of Milwaukee?"

"Yeah. I'm a little nervous about that. I've never flown before."

"I like it. Exhausting, but it can be fun."

Skye smiled. "Thanks for praying."

"I'll do more than that, Skye. I'll take care of the kids."

Her mouth dropped open. She shook her head. "I couldn't ask that of you."

"Do you trust me with your kids?" Dan asked, leaning against the door.

"Well, yes."

"I can't exercise much and I'm still off work."

"You really don't have much experience."

"Well. The offer is on the table. I'll pray, but if you are willing to trust me I'd be glad to help. You've got great kids."

"For two hours they can be angels. Three days might be enough for you to swear off ever having any of your own someday."

Dan's eyes sank to the floor as he shook his head.

Skye covered her mouth. "I'm so sorry. Dan. I didn't mean..."

"No. I get it. Being a parent is hard and I've not experienced that pleasure, or pain. Just don't count me out because of it." He closed the door to his apartment and she heard the latch click.

Skye slid back into hers as well. She loved her kids. She really did. There were just days when being a single mom was too much to bear. Quinn was better since they'd not seen their father, but he was still a precocious four-year-old, up to mischief. She couldn't believe she would have been so insensitive to Dan's pain to say something like that to him knowing that he wanted kids but he and his wife had lost several to miscarriage. Skye had never been down that road and couldn't imagine the heartache. Even when things were bad in her marriage, she eagerly anticipated becoming a mom. To have been robbed of those dreams time after time…

It didn't make sense how someone could go through all that and still trust God. How did a loving God do that? Take babies from their mother's and father's eager arms? Deny those children a chance at a loving family? Sure he was single now, but didn't that just prove God's negligence? He not only took Dan's kids, but his wife as well. She didn't understand how Dan could still believe.

He offered to babysit so she could pursue her art dreams in New York. Tears sprang to her eyes at his kind gesture. But surely that's all it was.

~*~

Her mom dropped off the kids.

"Mom, I asked my neighbor to pray about this trip next week."

"And?" Her mom walked over to her drawing table and fingered through some of the portfolio she had started to put together for her trip.

"He offered to watch the kids for me."

"Well, guess you got your answer to prayer, then."

"No. Mom. I can't expect him to watch my kids."

"Why not?"

"Well...I..."

"Listen. He's watched them before. He's a pastor and from what I understand, a good one. I've heard him preach and he's solid. He's also pretty talented with the guitar and can sing. If he's offered, you should take him up on that."

"I can't afford to pay him."

"Did he ask for money?"

"No. We didn't talk about it."

"Maybe you should. From the looks of these pictures he's had some influence over your work."

"Why do you say that?" Skye walked over to the table. Her mom pointed to the print of the painting that had been her one big sale.

"That is Pastor Dan Wink."

"It could be anyone."

"Nope. It's him. And you know how I know?"

"How?"

"His eyes. It is the way you painted his eyes." Her mom pointed at the print. "Painting an anonymous person, you would never have put a gray star in his blue eyes like that—almost white to the outer edge and rimmed in a dark gray. Not many people have eyes like that."

"How did you know?"

"I met him at a wedding and noticed his eyes. They are stunning, even when he hides them behind those geeky glasses. I'm not surprised that you noticed those details even if you weren't aware of it at the time. This is not an 'anonymous' man. Does Dan know you painted him?"

"I wasn't even intending to paint him. It just...happened, and I was as surprised as you at the similarities."

"He didn't sit for this portrait?"

"No. Sure he's handsome, but I haven't used live models since high school. Well, except for my children."

"Well, you might want to tell him since you're selling his image for big bucks."

"Do you really think I need to?"

Her mom nodded. "It would be a kindness."

"He might get the wrong idea."

"About what? That you like him? That you find him attractive? That he's handsome?"

Skye shook her head. "I couldn't."

"Well, you better hope that you don't sell too many of that print. It is stunning and probably your best work, although some of these others are special too. Listen, sweetheart, you do what you think you need to do. But let that boy take care of the kids. Go and follow your dream in New York and see where it leads you."

"Riley would have never let me go, much less taken care of the kids while I was gone."

"And Riley is currently in jail and not around to interfere or sabotage your dream. And even if he were, I suspect your neighbor next door is man enough to handle him."

"Mom..."

"Well, 'nough said. I'm off. Tell me what you

decide."

Skye walked her to the door. "Thanks, Mom."

The door closed and Skye leaned her forehead against it. Tell Dan that he had inspired some of her best work? Some of those paintings came out of the turmoil his questions caused her. Sleepless nights and moody days as she struggled. It wasn't fair that the first man she was attracted to after her disaster of a marriage happened to be the man least likely to ever even look at her with romantic interest. And she had no interest in God...well, not enough to consider ever being a pastor's wife. Didn't they need to know how to play the organ or something?

She never saw an organ at Orchard Hill. Hmm. The last keyboard player she saw there was a man. Interesting. She wondered what pastors' wives at this church did? Work in the nursery? She'd shave her head before saddling herself with a ton of kids for over an hour. It was one thing to take care of her own, but others? Even as a teenager she hated babysitting. It was one of those things about herself that made her wonder if she would ever be an adequate mother for her own kids. Well, so far they appeared happy, healthy, and she had managed to keep them alive. Maybe she wasn't doing too badly.

~*~

She almost ran over Dan the next day at the YMCA. He caught her in his arms and she jumped back as if shocked. Her heart rate quickened faster than if she had taken a high intensity aerobics class.

"Hey, you OK?" Dan frowned.

"Yeah, I'm fine." *Only you've stolen my ability to*

breathe. Why did he need to be so good looking in that T-shirt and work out shorts?

"You looked like you were escaping a fire," Dan joked.

She smiled. "No. Just spastic today. Don't want to miss the yoga class I sometimes take. You coming to Zumba?"

Dan shook his head. "Got a few more weeks, unfortunately, and by then I'll be back at work when your class is being held."

"Everyone has their excuses not to work out, don't they?" she quipped.

"That and it seems some single women at church think hunting season is open on the widowed pastor. If they found out I was doing Zumba I'd have them all here and probably sticking their number in my pockets. I'd feel like I was at a strip club."

"And how do you know what a strip club is like?" Skye was curious.

"I've seen bits in movies. Never could understand the appeal or why women would want to do that."

"Some don't think they have a choice. Make money or starve. Some are forced."

"Sounds like first-hand experience."

"Friends from my former life..."

"Sorry. I didn't mean to imply."

"No, Dan. It's me that needs to apologize. I was unpardonably rude yesterday, and I'm so sorry I hurt you with my thoughtless words."

"You didn't say anything that wasn't true."

"Maybe so, but I didn't need to rub your nose in your losses."

"They are invisible, gaping wounds I carry with me. I can't expect everyone to recognize and remember that every time they are around me. I don't want to spend the rest of my life wearing a black band on my sleeve to remind people of all I lost."

"How do you continue to believe God, given your history?"

"How could I not?"

"I don't understand."

"I still had my best friend. The One who created me. The One who called me. The One who died for me, walking by my side through the power of His Holy Spirit to lead and guide me in my deepest, darkest hours. Honestly, He is the only reason I'm still alive today."

"You thought of...?"

Dan nodded. "The last year was rough."

"Are you doing better?"

"Yes. By the grace and mercy of God, yes. And you've been a part of that."

"Me? What did I do? I'm nothing. I'm a nobody."

"No. You're an extraordinary woman, a great mom, and a phenomenal artist. You are honest about your questions and struggles. I admire you for that. You're not a victim. You've worked hard and risen above your past."

"Maybe outwardly. Inside I'm still a loser."

"Hey, God calls you His child. His heir. That would make you a princess. I don't think princesses are allowed to call themselves losers."

"A princess?"

"Yup."

She wiped away a tear. "How am I supposed to make it through a yoga class now?"

He bent over and whispered in her ear sending off a chain reaction of goose bumps. "You could always skip. The world won't fall apart."

"You are a temptation, Mr. Dan Wink."

He wiggled his eyebrows. "Really?"

"Yeah. And I'm going to take you up on your offer."

"My offer?"

"To watch my kids next week."

A smile spread wide across his face. "Really?"

She nodded. "Yes."

"Thank you for trusting me. I'm so glad you're going to go. You deserve a little time away and the opportunity to see where your dreams and your art takes you."

"Thanks for believing in me."

"I'd be a fool not to. You have talent."

"I appreciate that." She glanced at the clock. "I have one minute. Later, Dan. Gotta go." She took off for her class at an easy lope. It was a challenge to get her heart to slow down though at the thought of Dan, snug T-shirt and all, along with his sweet comments. He really did seem too good to be true. And then she remembered the old saying.

If it's too good to be true, it probably is.

~*~

Skye managed to stay away from Dan until the day before she was to leave. She knocked on his door.

She was stunned again at how attractive he was.

"Hey, Skye. What time do you need me tomorrow?"

Thrusting a piece of paper his way, he took it and glanced it over. "I have another request."

An eyebrow shot up on his handsome face, and

she looked into those eyes—for the first time really registering the stars. Her mother was right. Fascinating. She shook herself. "I'm not feeling safe leaving my car down at long-term parking at the airport. Plus, it would cost a fortune. I could reimburse you gas if you would be willing to—"

"Give you a ride?"

She nodded.

He frowned. "Your car would be safe enough down there. It's not that I don't want to take you, it's just a policy I have…"

"A policy?"

"Well, boundary is probably a better word. Guideline. I don't allow myself to be alone with a woman for any period of time that would be conducive to intimacy."

"In a car? You're afraid I'm going to debauch you in a car? On the highway to the airport? I think I can restrain myself."

To her astonishment, he blushed. She didn't realize men could do that. "Listen. I'll give you the money for the parking or cab fare both ways. And it's not because I'm afraid you'll do something to me. It's because, well, I'm a single man. Lonely and over time it could lead to temptations I'm not sure I'm strong enough to withstand. So I err on the side of caution…"

"And there's that whole 'appearances' thing too, right?"

He nodded. "It's part of the burden of being a pastor. People are watching all the time. Even something innocent can become fodder for gossip or for hindering someone in their faith."

"Apparently, not everyone holds to your values."

"Amy. Listen. I'm sorry that happened. She was

wrong. Sitting next to you in church seemed to throw the gauntlet down amongst the single ladies looking for me to 'put a ring on it.'" His left hand flung forward and he did a little wiggle with his hips as he sang the last words.

"Didn't know you listened to that singer." Skye was impressed.

"I'm a musician as well as a pastor and I try to stay abreast of the trends in the culture. The song's actually not that bad. The video? Well, I wish she would have put more clothes on."

"She was covered."

"Leaving nothing to the imagination."

"So did your wife wear denim jumpers that go practically to the ankles, have long hair, and refuse makeup?"

"No. She wore jeans and T-shirts and dresses on occasion. Her hair was short because that's the way she liked it. She wore a little makeup most of the time. But she was modest. She was heavier set than some women, didn't like working out at all, but she dressed attractively. We didn't always have a ton of money so she liked hitting the thrift shops."

"Interesting."

"So...cab fare? Or I could try to call someone at church and see if they could give you a lift?"

"You would do that?"

"Sure. Why not?"

"The question is, why?"

"Skye, you've been coming to our church. I like you. God adores you to pieces and He has some wonderful things in store for you. Why would I want to stand in the way of all that when I possess the means to help?"

"But you won't drive me yourself."

"If you were dying and the only way I could get you to the hospital was to drive you, we'd be on our way right now. But this isn't an emergency and there are other options."

"You confuse me."

"I do?"

"Yeah. If you can find someone willing to help me both ways, that would be great. The times are on the sheet there as is my cell phone number."

"I'll get back to you. Anything else I might need for my stay at your place?"

"Your pillow and clothes?"

He smiled. He had beautiful teeth. "I think I can manage that. Since you won't be taking your car will you leave the keys in case I want to take the kids anywhere? Probably easier to use your car with the car seats than to transfer them to mine in this frigid weather."

"Sure. I'll leave them hanging on the hook by the door." She cleared her throat. "Listen, I didn't even offer to pay you...and I'm not sure—"

"—you don't have to pay me anything. I offered and don't want the money. You, however, need this opportunity. So go, take it, and have fun in New York."

"Oh, OK I guess."

"Are we done?"

"Yeah. Thanks again, Dan. The kids are really excited to be able to spend time with you."

He grinned. "I am too."

She turned away, and he closed the door with a soft click. Skye wandered back to her own apartment and thought about the enigmatic pastor who lived across the hall. Would she ever understand men? Or was this one an alien? He was so far removed from her ex-husband that it was a startling comparison between the two.

~*~

The next morning, an older woman from Orchard Hill Church came to pick her up for a ride to the airport. Skye already kissed the kids goodbye when they left that morning with her mom. She dropped off the key to the apartment with Dan who wished her a great trip. He'd also slipped her an envelope she'd been afraid to open. She'd do that later while waiting for her plane.

"Cora, thank you for being willing to take me to the airport."

The older woman grinned. "Gives me something to do. I'm retired and my husband is too. This gets me out of the house. I love being able to help others."

"Well, I'm grateful."

"Pastor Dan tells me you're an artist."

"Yeah. This could be my 'big break' as they say."

"Would you move to New York City if it is?"

"No. I wouldn't want to live that far from my mom, and while my ex is currently not a suitable person for my children to visit, our divorce agreement restricts how far away I can live with them."

"Well, Wisconsin is a nice place to raise a family. I've lived here all my life."

"Me too. This is my first time going further than Chicago."

"Well, you are on quite an adventure then, aren't you?"

"Yeah."

"I will pray for your safe travels, dear. I'll return to pick you up on Saturday afternoon. You have my phone number so you can call if there are any delays. I'll bring a book though so I can always catch a cup of coffee here and read while waiting for you. Lots warmer inside than waiting in the car."

"Thank you. That's sweet of you."

"Don't worry about it. So many people helped me out when I was younger and now it's my turn to, what do they call it now? Oh, 'pay it forward.'"

"Yup. I think you're right. How did someone help you?"

"When my first husband died, neighbors helped with the kids while I worked and one even mowed my lawn and shoveled my walk."

"That's sweet."

"Yes it was. He was single. I ended up marrying him and we had two more kids together."

"So he was your happily-ever-after?"

"Well, don't get me wrong. I love my husband, but men are a different animal and sometimes they can get on a woman's nerves. My first marriage wasn't as good as my second. This man treats me well and I do adore him even with his quirks."

Skye laughed. "I agree they can be perplexing."

"Yes," Cora grinned, "but the perplexing ones are the ones that make life more interesting, don't you think?"

"Maybe so." Skye thought of Dan and how different her life had become since meeting him.

Cora pulled up to the terminal. "Here you are. I'll see you in a few days, and have a marvelous time."

Skye removed her bags and thanked the woman again before heading into the ticketing concourse.

Once she checked in and made it through security, she opened the envelope Dan thrust at her that morning. It contained a letter and a VISA gift card.

Skye,

I'm thrilled you get this opportunity to travel and see new places and meet new people. You really are a fabulous artist from the little I've seen and I am praying God richly blesses your work on this trip and that you get the affirmation you are looking for as you try to provide for your family.

Thank you for trusting me with your children. That wasn't an easy thing to do, and you really are a great mother and take such good care of them. So relax and enjoy your time away knowing they are safe and that we will have some fun together (as much as my ribs will allow).

I hope the card will help with any unexpected traveling expenses.

I am praying for you.

Dan

Too good to be true...but maybe that's because the men she had previously known didn't know Jesus. Maybe Jesus wasn't too good to be true if he could make a man this nice.

Definitely something to think about.

ELEVEN

I'm going on an adventure!
J.R.R. Tolkien

Dan wondered if he was ready for this challenge. He'd never had any kids and now he was going to spend three days with these two?

When they arrived at lunchtime, he welcomed them with hugs. Quinn and Meghan headed straight to the kitchen table where he had set out some grilled cheese sandwiches and tomato soup in mugs.

"Thanks for dropping them off, Sandi." Skye's mom was heavier set and her once red hair was a soft auburn mixed with gray.

"I appreciate you making it possible for Skye to chase her dream."

"My pleasure."

"Enjoy yourself and I'll see you in the morning." She gave a wave to the kids and was gone.

Dan turned to the kitchen and sat down to eat his own sandwich. "So kids, after your naps, what do you think about a trip to the Children's Museum in downtown Milwaukee?"

Meghan squealed for joy, jumped off her chair, and danced around.

Quinn grinned as he shoved his sandwich in his mouth. He nodded vigorously.

Once the kids settled down for their naps, he cleaned up the kitchen. He settled down on the sofa with a book. He couldn't focus on the text before him.

Leadership. Only a few days left of his leave of absence and he was reading a book on leadership? He dug into the bag he brought with him and dug out a novel. Mystery. Hmm. Now that would be relaxing.

~*~

He almost jumped out of his skin when Quinn vaulted over the back of the couch a little over a half an hour later. Dan closed the book and looked at the four-year-old.

"I thought you were taking a nap?"

Quinn shook his head. "Couldn't sleep." He yawned.

"Right. Let's give this another try." He picked up the wiggly little boy and hauled him back to the bedroom and half-lay, half-dropped him on the mattress. Dan resisted the urge to tickle him. He put his index finger to his lips and backed out of the room.

He walked past Skye's bedroom and the door was open. He took a step in and saw a canvas leaning against the wall. He tipped it back to look at a painting that took his breath away with its beauty. Skye painted in such vivid colors and all he could think of was the artist had opened herself up to the truth of the gospel.

It was the woman at the well but not like any other painting he'd ever seen. It was contemporary. It wasn't a woman from biblical times but from 2014, the United States of America. Broken and lost. Worshipping Jesus.

Dan stared at it for a long time. Why had Skye been drawn to that story? Did she understand the depth of love God showed that woman? Did she realize that He saw everything in her past and still offered her Himself?

He slowly set it back against the wall. If this was what she left behind, what had the work been like that she already sent for the show? He walked back to the living room. Skye had told him he could sleep in her bed, but he wouldn't. He'd sleep on the couch.

Before long the kids were up, and he bundled them up for the trip to the Children's museum. They were excited and so was Dan. This was someplace he'd always heard about and never had a chance or reason to explore. Hands-on learning for kids? They'd only have about ninety minutes, but that was more than enough time to help wear them out.

They arrived, and the kids took off running in an enclosed space for younger children. Several moms were there with their little ones, but Dan was the only man. He sighed. He took off after Meghan and started to play with her before taking some time with Quinn. Soon he was sitting on the sidelines, exhausted, as he watched them run around and explore.

At five o'clock they traipsed out to the frigid car and headed for home in the middle of rush hour traffic. About twenty minutes out from the apartment, a little voice yelled from the back seat.

"I need to go potty."

"Meghan, you'll have to wait. There's no place to get off here. I told you to try at the museum before we left."

"Mr. Dan, I'm hungry," Quinn whined.

Dan shook his head. Oh, yeah, he'd bitten off more than he could chew big time. How did moms do this every day?

He finally got home and managed to get Meghan into the bathroom in the nick of time. He started water boiling on the stove to make spaghetti noodles while he hung up coats. He threw a glass bowl filled with frozen peas into the microwave to heat them up. He set the table when Quinn chased Meghan around the apartment yelling at her.

"That's mine!"

Meghan half-squealed, half-laughed and then she tripped over the coffee table.

Dan rushed over. She was bleeding from her mouth. He checked her little teeth, went to grab a washcloth and run cold water over it, and had Meghan hold it against her gums. He held her in his one arm as he stared at Quinn.

"Quinn. You need to apologize to your sister."

"I sorry," Quinn said. "But it was my toy and she took it."

Dan looked at Meghan. "Did you take Quinn's toy?"

She nodded her head.

"You need to apologize to Quinn."

"I thorry" came out from the washcloth. Dan heard a sizzle from the kitchen. He ran into the kitchen to find the water boiling over. He turned the burner down, dumped the noodles, and set a timer. Pulling out the peas from the microwave, he set those on the table. Once the noodles were strained, he added the bottled sauce. After everything was ready, he put it all on the table and got the kids to sit down.

He paused and took a deep breath. "Let's hold hands and pray."

"I wanna pray," Quinn said.

Dan nodded. "Go ahead." He bowed his head and Quinn began.

"God, thank You for Mr. Dan and the fun we had today. I like skettie but hate peas so please don't make me eat them. Amen."

Dan fought back a chuckle. "You need to eat a few anyway."

"No."

"No peas mean you don't get dessert."

Quinn's eyes grew big, but it was Meghan who asked, "What's dessert?"

"Ice cream." Dan wiggled his eyebrows.

Meghan squealed with joy and dug into her peas. Failing to nab them on her fork she started to pick them up with her fingers and pop them in her mouth.

Before long, peas were on the floor, tomato sauce stained their faces and ice cream encircled their mouths. Dan struggled to clean up the kids and then the kitchen. He put the food away and sat with the kids on the sofa. They read a few books.

With one kid tucked under each arm, Dan knew a satisfaction he'd never experienced before. He got them off to change for bed and sat with them in their room.

"I miss Mommy," Meghan said.

"Me too," Quinn responded.

"Why don't we give her a call?" Dan pulled out his phone and dialed the number. There was no answer so he texted her a message.

Kids miss you and wanted to tell you they love you.

A text returned quickly

In a meeting, can't talk. Tell them I love them too.

Dan read the text to the kids. He listened to their prayers, tucked them in, and turned off the lights. "I'm sleeping on the couch if you need me."

Dan headed to the bathroom and changed into his favorite T-shirt and sweats for sleeping in the living room. He grabbed his pillow and blanket and tried to stretch out. Another text came in just as he got comfortable. He reached for the phone and almost fell off the sofa.

Did you have a good day?

Took the kids to the museum. They had fun. Got them to eat peas.

Lol. How did you do that?

Threatened to hold ice cream hostage.

Good threat.

How is it going?

So far so good. My agent is OK and should be meeting a publisher or two in the morning. The exhibit is tomorrow evening.

That's wonderful!

It's late. Need to sleep.

Me too. Have a good night.

You too.

Dan set the phone down and reclined back on the sofa. *Lord, please guide Skye and protect her in New York. More than that, open her eyes to who You are.* He closed his eyes and drifted to sleep.

~*~

Someone is watching me. Dan cracked open an eyelid to see Meghan standing in front of him.

"Did you need something?"

"You don't smell stinky."

"I think that's good? Thank you." Dan propped himself up on one arm.

"Daddy always smelled stinky. He was mean in the morning."

Dan reached for his phone, it was fifteen minutes before his alarm had been set. Well, so much for that.

He turned it off. "I'm not too grumpy first thing in the morning. But I do get better with some coffee." He pulled back his blanket and Meghan's eyes grew wide. "What?"

"You wear clothes to bed?"

"Yeah." Dan was afraid of what was coming next.

"Not Daddy or his girlfriends."

Oh, boy. "Well, I like to wear clothes most of the time." He leaned in to whisper to her. "They keep me warm."

Meghan smiled. "I'm glad." She rubbed her tummy. "I sick."

"What's wrong?" Dan sat up straight.

Her answer was to throw up on him. Dan jumped to his feet. The odor of vomit almost made him want to run to the bathroom and do that himself. He ran to grab a dishtowel to wipe some off. He dug out a plastic bowl and brought it back to Meghan. "Next time, use this."

She dropped to the middle of the floor, picked up a doll that had been left there, and started to play. Dan folded his blanket and put the pillow on top. He grabbed his bag and headed to the bathroom to shave and change. He'd planned to catch a shower later at the gym while the kids were at their program. With a sick kid, all bets were off.

When he came out of the bathroom, Meghan had thrown up on her bed and Quinn was moaning. As he rolled over, Dan tried to get the wastebasket to him before the little boy lost it, but it was too late.

Dan picked up the phone to call Sandi.

"How'd it go last night?" she asked. "I'll be there in thirty minutes."

"Don't bother coming. I've got two kids with the

flu. Throwing up."

"Ouch. Anything I can do?"

"No. You need to get to work. Can you call them in sick?"

"Sure. I'll take care of it."

Dan hung up, ran to get some towels, and stretched them over Skye's bed. He changed the kids' clothing and had them rest there with their empty ice cream buckets he'd found under the sink. He ran the dirty bedding down to the washing machine. Once he got the load going, he ran back upstairs to check on the kids.

They'd fallen back asleep without any further vomiting. He did a quick search on his smartphone. Toast. He'd try to feed them toast when they woke up.

It was going to be a long day.

~*~

Skye stretched in her soft bed as she awoke. No kids calling for her. Only her phone beeping to tell her it was time to meet the day. She loved her kids, but it was a refreshing change to not deal with their demands.

After her shower, she dressed in the new, more professional and conservative outfit she had managed to find at a thrift shop. She looked at herself in the mirror. She didn't recognize herself. She wore a dress that ended above her knees and heels. She was a sneakers, flip flops, or fuzzy boots kind of gal. Dresses? The last time she wore one was her wedding day. She left her red hair down, and her black glasses helped her feel more professional, although she wondered again whether contacts would be a better choice...if she could ever have afforded them. *Ah, vanity. You are an artist, Skye, and you look like a business woman today. It's not right.*

Skye pulled out leggings and a purple tunic-type dress that went to mid-thigh. She grabbed her pink fuzzy boots that Dan thought were silly. It didn't matter. She loved them and they were comfortable. New York was colder than she expected. She put on some large hoop earrings and her favorite necklace, which she rarely wore anymore since babies grabbed everything.

She looked in the mirror now. Much better. She added some lip gloss, grabbed her purse and jacket and headed down for breakfast before her new agent would pick her up to meet some art publishing people in town. Her big show was tonight. At least now, she looked more like herself.

"Skye, I hope you slept well." The tall, reed-thin woman reached out a hand and shook Skye's firmly. Dressed in a conservative blue suit with three-inch heels, Skye wondered that the woman could stay upright.

"I appreciate you helping me, Sally Ann."

They caught a cab and Skye held tight as her agent kept up a running monologue of all the places they passed. Arriving at the address, they exited and Sally Ann paid the driver.

"Well, once you signed that contract, it was the least I could do. There was no time to waste in this competitive world." They walked into an office building that was all marble, glass, and gold trim. Stark. Art was important to this company?

Skye followed the woman to the elevator and up to the fifth floor where they got off at a Christian publishing house that specialized in mass marketing Christian art. Sally Ann Rogers led her to a large desk.

"We're here to see Ronald. Could you let him know?"

"Yes, Ms. Rogers."

"You'll like Mr. Weston. He's one of the good guys." The door opened, revealing a polished man whose dark hair was edged with gray.

"Sally Ann, how wonderful to see you. And this must be our new artist." He thrust a hand to Skye. "Ms. O'Connell, it is a pleasure."

Skye allowed his large hand to envelope hers and draw her into the lavish office decorated in rich woods and carpet, a large mirror on the wall, and no artwork anywhere. Skye sat across from a large mahogany desk, suddenly self-conscious, and terribly out of place in this fancy room with these posh people. She suspected that to them she smelled like the dairy State, and they probably expected her to chant "Go! Pack! Go!" at any moment. Midwest was her roots but trailer-trash was her heart.

"Let's talk business. We loved these pieces you've done and would like more of them." He laid out several prints she had forwarded. "This doesn't mean you still can't sell these images in larger formats, but like Thomas Kincaide, you can do both. Cards, calendars, journals, and possibly other things. Thomas is no longer alive and we've been looking for someone to fill that space in our market." He shoved a piece of paper toward Sally Ann. "This would be your contract."

Sally Ann picked up the paper and scanned it over. "This is standard. Go ahead and sign it, Skye." He slid the paper to her side of the desk and slapped an expensive pen down on top of it. Both people looked at her expectantly.

She picked up the paper and started to scan it. She couldn't make much sense of it.

"Skye, the point of having an agent is that I vet the contracts for you. This is a good one and, for a first time out, it's fair. Once they see how your work sells, they might offer you more."

Skye sighed. She signed the paper and pushed it back to her agent who signed as well.

"Wonderful. Keep sending stuff to your agent and keep painting such inspired pieces." The man stood. Skye did as well and followed Sally Ann out of the office.

"That was wonderful. One more publishing house to visit today and then I'm taking you shopping to find the perfect outfit for your show." The woman looked at Skye, scanning her from head to toe. "And maybe have something done with that hair."

Skye frowned but followed her agent. The same scene played out at the next publishing house and after a fancy lunch and an exhausting trip, Skye was back in her room to prepare for the evening. What she really wanted was to take a nap. She picked up her phone to call Dan.

"Hello?"

"Dan, it's Skye. How are things going?"

"Well, we're all still alive and no one has visited the emergency room—yet."

There was a teasing tone to his voice, as well as exhaustion. "Is this too hard for you?"

"How do you do this day in and day out? The kids are great but they missed school today because they both got sick. Between washing all the bedding, scrubbing carpets, and empting their slop buckets I've not had a moment to breathe."

"They're sick?"

"A touch of the flu. They haven't tossed their cookies for a few hours, so I'm hoping the worst is over. How is New York?"

"Loud. Busy. Cold. Exhausting. I don't fit in here."

"Not the adventure you hoped it would be?"

"No. I'm signing contracts right and left and something feels wrong about it all. Most of the people I've met are nice but my agent...she's a bit pushy. She insisted I wouldn't fit in to the crowd with the outfit I brought for this evening...without even seeing it."

"Regrets?"

"Maybe. My art is as close to me as my children. They are pieces of my heart and it seems callous to be selling them."

"You need to live. You don't paint with your kind of talent only to hide it away. God's given you a gift."

"Maybe so...still, it's been weird. Listen, I'm sorry the kids got sick. I'll be home tomorrow afternoon and you can rest, and I hope you don't catch what they have."

"You were with them before they got ill as well. If a bug is going around you might have been exposed. I hope you don't get sick while you're out there."

"Thanks for taking good care of them."

"Don't worry. Your mom's been checking in with us too. We're going to survive this."

"I really do appreciate it."

"Glad to help. I'll continue to pray for your show tonight."

"Thanks."

Skye hung up and looked at the slinky black dress.

She at least managed to talk her agent out of four-inch heels. Sure, she was on the short side but she was comfortable with her height and didn't want to risk a twisted ankle. There were classes to teach when she got back. She sighed and got dressed for the show.

She surveyed herself in the mirror. Her hair had been braided and twisted into an intricate updo at the salon. Skye frowned. Her agent wanted her to forgo her glasses, not believing that she really did need them. The image looking back at her in the mirror with the heavy makeup and fancy hair wasn't her.

Skye went to wash off her face and applied her own minimal makeup. She looked at the mirror. Her head ached from how tight the braids pulled at her scalp and the bobby pins stuck in everywhere. She glanced at her watch. There was time.

~*~

Skye walked into the art gallery and was pleased her work was displayed so beautifully. Wait staff dressed in tuxedos served wine and hors d'oeuvres. Skye saw Sally Ann before she was spied. The agent gasped when she caught a glimpse of her protégé.

"What have you done?"

"It is the dress and boots you purchased."

"But your hair. Your face. It's all wrong."

Skye folded her arms. "For who? It's right for me." Her hair wasn't stick straight after those braids, but she suspected by the end of the evening the waves would work their way out.

Sally Ann shook her head. "It's all wrong. You are presenting the wrong image."

"And what image is that? I'm the artist. I'm

representing myself and no one else here."

"You represent my agency."

"Would you rather I leave?"

Someone cleared their throat from behind Skye and came alongside her. "Sally Ann."

"Chet, this is Skye O'Connell, the artist you are displaying."

Chet turned a stunning smile to Skye. "Here I thought you were a patron, and instead I behold an artist as compelling as her work. Enchanté." He lifted her hand and kissed the back.

"Thank you for showing my paintings."

"How could I not after you'd been so gracious to let me sell a few of your previous pieces. You made me decent income and if we are lucky, tonight will be a huge success."

"You sold with Chet before?" Sally Ann frowned at Skye.

"Well, yes. Before I signed with you Chet sold a few pieces."

"I was thrilled to get a full collection to showcase. I've had people asking after you especially after a photo of your fabulous painting appeared in that national magazine this past week."

"Which one?"

"That wonderful one of the man…"

Oh, no! But Dan wasn't a magazine reader from what she could tell. "Excuse me." Skye strode down the room to the restroom and leaned against the sink. What were the chances that Dan would ever see that magazine? Especially if the painting was buried inside? She shook her hands at her side. *Calm down. It's going to be fine. Who doesn't want a painting to be noticed? Am I nuts?*

She went back to the room as more people in fancy dress came to peruse her paintings. Most did not recognize her as the artist so she would hang around to look at a painting and listen to what people said.

"Oh, darling. I love the colors in this one. It would look lovely in the back hallway," an older matron said to her husband. Skye didn't know whether to take it as an insult or compliment.

At another painting, "Pietar, you're the expert. What do you think of this one?"

"Interesting composition and the brush strokes are flowing, which show a serenity of spirit as she painted this. I think this would be lovely in your studio."

Serenity? She painted that one when in dark despair, worried, and wondering about what the future held. She shook her head. That was the beauty of art. Every person looking at a piece could draw something different from it based on what his or her experiences were. She should be happy that at least the comments were positive.

Well, at least until she got to the next one. The man's nose was in the air and his glasses clouded any clear view of his eyes. He shook his head and whispered to her,

"Who could this artist be? A nobody, I bet. Trying to fly in the big leagues. Well, she isn't any Rembrandt or Monet that's for sure."

Skye looked at the painting in front of them. "Who do you like in the art world?"

"Moi." He placed his hand on his chest with dramatic flair.

"What do you paint?"

"Everything. Landscapes, people, kittens."

"Kittens?"

"They don't sit still very well, I must admit. I take their picture and paint from that."

"Interesting method."

"Someday the world will notice my genius. This artist?" He motioned to her painting. "A blip on the scene. Here today and gone tomorrow."

"Skye?" Chet came up to her. "You've met Mr. Ambrose? He's here to give a review of your art."

Skye cringed inside. Obviously, it wasn't going to be a good one. "We've not been introduced. He was telling me how much he hated my style of painting and predicting the demise of my career."

Mr. Ambrose turned to look at her. His jaw dropped. A hand came to cover his mouth and he turned and took off helter skelter out of the room, nearly hitting people.

"Did he really trash your work in front of you?"

Skye frowned and swallowed hard. "I don't think I'm cut out for this."

Chet put a hand on her arm. "Don't worry about him. He's all hot air and puffed up consequence, but he generally gives artists a good review. I've heard him raving over some of the paintings."

"He's not going to hold it against me that I didn't introduce myself?"

"There's a photo of you in the brochure. He should have been able to recognize you."

"You printed my photo?"

"Well, considering we were advertising that the artist would be present at the show, yes."

Now Skye wanted to run back to the bathroom and throw up. Maybe she had the flu like her kids did? Wouldn't that be inconvenient…and messy?

He wrapped an arm around her shoulder with

creepy familiarity. "Come, darling, let us meet societies' elite."

The night flew by in a blur, but her paintings had sold and her agent was thrilled. She didn't run into Mr. Ambrose again.

Back at the hotel, she sat by the window taking in the view of the lights from the city that never sleeps. This whole trip felt like one big mistake. Did God even care? Sure she had contracts, but too much legalese and her street smarts started to make her second guess her every decision. Every signature seemed like a mistake. Had she signed all her dreams away?

So, God? What is it You want for me? Am I another mistake? One after another? Am I ever going to feel like I fit in? That I'm worth even having a chance at something worthwhile? Even some security would be appreciated. She rose to change and paused as it hit her. The only person who ever made her feel OK with being her—was a certain pastor who was sleeping on her sofa and had spent a day cleaning up after her kids. The one person who she used, unintentionally, to get where she was. Not with the babysitting...but by being an inspiration for her very best piece of art.

She fell into bed. Her feet hurt from wearing heels and standing the entire time. Snow was falling in the Big Apple and she longed to be home. Sick kids and all.

And she wanted to see Dan. She had some explaining to do.

TWELVE

*Every moment and every event of every man's life on earth
plants something in his soul.*
Thomas Merton

Dan stretched out on the couch. Skye would be home today. He made all the beds, including Skye's after the kids had thrown up there as well. They finally settled down in the afternoon and even after their naps, they were lethargic and wanted to watch television. He let them. He was beyond exhausted. Every cough during the night had him jumping up to make sure someone hadn't vomited somewhere. He feared walking down the hall in his bare feet and finding something he didn't want to step in, but thankfully, it never happened.

The kids ate toast for breakfast and a banana each. Everything had stayed down so he was hoping macaroni and cheese for lunch would be a hit. The phone rang.

"Hey."

"Hi, Dan. How are the kids?"

"Much better today but still tired. Low energy but other than that, good."

"I'm glad."

"How did the show go last night?"

"Everything sold and some collector expressed a desire to purchase more."

"That's amazing. Congratulations. I'm happy for you."

"Thanks. But I have bad news."

"Yes?"

"There's a blizzard in New York. The airport shut down. I can't get a flight out until tomorrow."

"We'll survive. Maybe you can catch a Broadway show while you're there?"

"I doubt it. Those sell out way in advance and nothing right now interests me."

"You are going to come back from New York without doing anything touristy?"

"I don't have the money and I don't want to be out in this city alone. And, in case you forgot, there is a blizzard going on. Not the day to visit Central Park."

"Good point."

"I'm exhausted after yesterday and how often does a single mom get an entire day to herself? I have my sketchpad so I might go people watch in the lobby, read a book, or take a nap."

"As wonderful as those all are and you definitely deserve them, I'm sad that you can't pamper yourself more on this trip. Does the hotel even offer massages? That would be a wonderful treat."

"The price of that would be worth six months or more of macaroni and cheese for my kids. I can't waste that kind of money."

"OK. Well, try to enjoy your day."

"I will. When I get home though, I do have something I need to share with you."

"I look forward to that conversation."

"You might not when I'm done."

"Did I do something wrong?"

"No...but I have. Thanks, Dan. See ya tomorrow."

"See ya."

Dan hung up the phone and stared at it for a

minute. What had she done wrong and why did she need to tell him? He wasn't a priest.

When the kids were down for their nap, Dan ran next door to get a change of clothes for the next day. Church. He rolled his eyes. He'd be taking two kids, who were not his, to church. Wouldn't that get the tongues wagging? Maybe he should skip? After all the kids had been sick. He shook his head. What kind of coward had he become? He was helping a friend. If that friend had been Tony, he wouldn't be worried. But it was an attractive woman who happened to be his neighbor.

You can't control other people's actions.

True, but I can keep from feeding fires.

Fire? There's no fire and maybe he was shortchanging his congregation.

And maybe it will be a non-issue. He'd never done anything to put his reputation at risk before. His integrity went before him. He needed to not worry about this. The kids needed Jesus just as much as their mom did.

They'd go.

~*~

The sofa three nights in a row for a man of his height, could definitely rate as cruel and unusual punishment when coupled with nightmares and a little girl missing her mommy. Dan didn't even bother sleeping until his alarm, but did get a much-needed shower in before the kids found him for whatever it was that they needed next. Moms deserved sainthood.

The weather was frigid, but at least they didn't have a blizzard. He got the kids bundled up and into the car, but the car wouldn't start. He hauled them back inside the hallway to wait where it was warmer. He practically froze his gloved fingers off transferring the car seats to his sedan. He finally got the kids in and buckled up, and they barely made it to church in time. He checked them into their classrooms, grateful that at least the lateness meant not as many people saw him with the children. Not that he was ashamed, but it meant fewer people to question him. He would not be so lucky after the service when he needed to go pick them up—along with every other parent there.

He sat in the back of church. He'd spied Amy down toward the front in the audience. He didn't hate her for her presumptions, but he wondered what made a woman so desperate, pathetic even...to pursue a man so aggressively. He didn't mind strong women. There were many he worked with over the years in ministry, who were respectful of his position and authority, but also unafraid to express their opinions and not play games with him over anything.

Not all of these women were the older ones either. Some were younger and could teach ones older in years some lessons. He longed for a mentoring program in the women's ministry that wouldn't place "older" women over younger necessarily. Kind of a default in the Mother of Preschoolers program because the older women were the ones who had gone through having young children. But even then, they had to be careful of the mentors in charge. Character. Integrity. The refusal to engage in gossip or lewd behavior.

And a respect for men.

He worked hard with the men's ministry to see that the men who were growing in their faith...were worthy of that respect.

He tried hard to focus on the message. A guest speaker was there today. Dan forgot his Bible with his pencil and notebook but remembered Skye using an app on her phone. He quickly found the app, downloaded it, and started to take his notes there. He really hated virtual keyboards. He missed his previous phone with a real keyboard that slid out.

Faith. Faith in action. Faith that waits. *My soul longs for your salvation; I hope in Your word. My eyes long for Your promise; I ask, "When will You comfort me?"* Something about Psalm 199:81-82 resonated within him.

Several weeks away from the office. A new wind blew through his soul since he moved and was forced to look inside. Forced to try to figure out who he was beyond being a pastor. To learn that he hadn't been the wonderful husband he once thought he was. To discover that he hadn't really been living. Salvation had been his all along, but he, a pastor who knew better, violated his own values...of resting and trusting in God for his comfort. Instead he tried to handle it on his own by burying himself in his work. And failed miserably.

He stood with the people around him as the final song was sung. Switching his phone off, he bowed his head for Andrew's prayer and send-off. He moved out into the aisle and made his way through the crowd. He had kids to pick up today. He stood in the line for Meghan's room first.

"Why are you here in line?" Stephanie asked. She was married to Roberto, an attorney who also attended the church. Now there was a relationship that had endured challenges.

"I'm helping a friend with her kids this weekend."

He flashed his two tags.

"You? Babysitting?" The blonde winked at him. "Good for her...and you. Learn anything?"

"Yeah. Mothers are saints and single mothers deserve to be honored."

"Have your friend check out our Mother of Preschoolers group. Sounds like she could use it."

"After only a few days I feel like I could use it." He gave a short laugh. "Seriously. I had no idea what it all entailed and these aren't babies. At least I was spared the diaper changing."

"Diapers aren't as bad as—

"Vomit" they both said and chuckled.

"So you had some of that too?" The line moved forward.

Dan nodded. "Yup."

"Good for you. Give this mom my number and we'll get her into MOPS and connected with other moms who can encourage her on her journey."

"I will. Thanks, Steph."

"Anytime, Dan."

He handed his card in and Meghan ran to him. He lifted her up in his arms and planted a kiss on her cheek. The little girl giggled and wrapped her arms tight around him. With a nod to Stephanie he wandered to Quinn's room and a shorter line that existed there. Tony stepped up behind him with his two daughters in his arms. "Skye's not back yet?"

"Blizzard hit New York City."

Tony grinned. "So how do you like single parenting?"

Dan tried to cover up a yawn and Tony laughed. Meghan giggled.

"Guess I have my answer. I look forward to

hearing about it on Wednesday. Have a great day back tomorrow."

"Thanks." Dan watched his friend walk away with his delightful twins on either side of him. Tony was a lucky man. He was also due to become a father again any moment.

As the chatter of people surrounded him and bodies bumped against him, he clung to Meghan. Her hair carried the scent of baby shampoo and tickled his nose. Her two little hands cupped each cheek and she pressed them together giving him fish lips. She giggled. Dan grinned as she dropped them to wrap her arms around his neck. Soon Quinn walked alongside. He noticed the strange looks as he walked to the coatroom.

Cora stopped him.

"Are these Skye's children?"

"Yes. She didn't make it back last night."

"Oh, I know. I was supposed to pick her up at the airport but will do that this afternoon instead. I must say though, Dan, those children look very good on you." She gave a nod and slight grin as she walked away to greet someone else.

He spied a friend in the lobby. "Come on kids...one last conversation before we head home." He walked up to a man in a leather jacket. "Titus, I've got a single mom's dead car in my parking lot. Could you take a look at it?"

"Sure, I'll come over now. I'll follow you home."

"Wonderful." Dan turned to walk out and Titus followed. "Come on, kids. Let's get home and prepare for your mother's return."

~*~

Skye settled into her cramped seat on the plane. Her agent had called that morning, wanting her to produce more art immediately. Didn't Sally Ann realize it didn't work that way? An artist couldn't force their work to happen. She wasn't even home yet.

And what if she couldn't paint? What then? Her biggest fear as an artist was coming to a point in time when the creativity dried up and there was nothing new to paint. Nothing breathtaking to share with the world. When all colors appeared gray and flat. What then? How would she support her family then?

She'd spent time reading in the Bible the previous evening and even that morning before going to the airport. This Jesus was called the Light of the World. Was it a coincidence that light was a new feature in her paintings? And the way he treated the Samaritan woman was respectful. And the woman caught in adultery? Jesus never condemned her.

Light.

Love.

Respect.

Truth.

Was Jesus the truth? Dan thought so. He believed it. He had staked his future, his life, and his career on it. He was the one to ask about her faith, or lack thereof. And other than making fun of her fuzzy pink boots, he had always treated her with respect. Even when he took her Zumba class, a class that some men thought of as an opportunity to flirt.

He never flirted with her. She understood that he was grieving his wife, but even married men often plied their flirting trade with her when the opportunity arose. Some of that happened at the art show. Whether they realized she was the artist or not didn't matter. She was female and, therefore, an object of lust.

She might have walked away feeling flattered by the men's attention, but instead it disgusted her. Those men wore high-end suits, but they were as slimy as some she met in the inner city of Milwaukee.

But not at church.

A man sat next to her on the plane. She was on the side with only two seats, so that meant no sandwich between strangers. The man was older, with white hair.

"Well, little lady. Leaving New York for Wisconsin?"

"You would be as well." Skye hid a smile as she looked straight ahead at the stewardesses checking the overhead bins.

"I'm going for a visit."

"Then it's good you're on this plane," Skye responded.

"What brought you to New York?"

"Art."

"Ahh, a connoisseur?"

"An artist."

"A little thing like you?"

"Yeah."

"What is your inspiration? Your muse? Don't artists have those?"

Skye didn't respond right away. She shook her head. "I don't know. My art comes from deep within. Emotion expressed in images, color, shading, and brush strokes. Where that comes from? I have no clue."

"God was the ultimate Artist. He paints the sky every morning and gives each human a unique fingerprint, personality, family, and history. Scripture talks about every good gift coming from Him."

"Art has been a gift, a curse, a healing, and a question."

"A question?" The old man turned to face her, his bushy brows drawn together.

"Yeah. Sometimes I paint and I look at the image and wonder what I'm trying to tell myself through that painting. The depths of the images perplex me at times."

"Has it always been that way?"

"Not initially…only recently."

"What changed?"

Skye whispered, "I'm not sure." But it was a lie. What changed? A certain grieving pastor offering her the hope of the world in Jesus. That's when it all changed for her. Her paintings were good and she had some sales, but it wasn't until that one, that things changed. The one where she was asking the most questions about faith. Attraction. Love.

"Get some rest young lady. I'm sure you'll figure it out."

"What about you?" Skye asked.

"What about me? I'm an old man on my way to see my daughter. We've been estranged since she was a teenager. Recently she's come to know God and has forgiven her old man. I hope that maybe I'll even meet my granddaughter. I hear she has some kids too. Hard to believe that after all these years of living alone and having to deal with the fall out of my sins, that I'll finally have a family."

"What sins kept you from them?"

"Drugs. Alcohol mostly. Caused my wife to leave. She remarried, gave my daughter a different name. I didn't fight it. I knew they could provide a more stable life. It wasn't until a few years ago though that I heard the truth. Got myself to church. Found God. Joined Alcoholics Anonymous and reached out to beg her forgiveness. For years she ignored me, but she kept my information. I may be old, but I wasn't very wise. It was only recently that she reached out to me and accepted my olive branch."

"I'm happy for you. It's nice for someone to get a happy ending."

"You don't have a happy ending?"

"I didn't have a happy beginning. I don't hold out high hopes for the end."

"Listen to an old man, for whatever it's worth. God's got His hand in your life, even when you can't recognize it. He loves you more than you'll ever understand and wants good things for you."

"I've had so little evidence of that." Skye avoided looking at him.

"You probably have more proof than you realize."

Skye leaned back and closed her eyes. She didn't want to talk anymore. Cinderella stories were not for girls like her.

~*~

The plane landed and Cora was there waiting for her at the baggage claim.

"Come along, dearie. We'll get you home to those adorable children of yours."

"You've met my children?"

"Dan brought them to church this morning."

"Oh, well, that's good I guess."

"You've been bringing them."

"Yes...but, well, they'd been sick and it's really

cold out. I'm surprised he bothered."

"I don't think it was a bother." The woman winked at her.

She was dropped off at the apartment complex and noticed a man by her sedan. "Hey, that's my car."

"Are you Skye?"

"Yes."

"Just replacing your battery. The other one was beyond resuscitating."

"Oh, well, thank you. What do I owe you for that?" Her nose was freezing.

"Nothing. It's all taken care of. Get inside before you freeze to death." He let the hood slam shut and handed her the car keys. He gave her a nod and jumped into his truck that was parked next to her car and had been running.

Skye obeyed and went inside and dragged her stuff up the stairs. *Thud. Thud. Thud. Thud.*

Her apartment door flung open and two little people ran out. She plopped her bags at the top of the stairs and dropped to one knee to hug them.

"Mommy, I missed you," Megan said as she clung tight.

"Mr. Dan was nice. Is he our new daddy?" Quinn asked.

"Oh, no, sweetheart. Mr. Dan is our friend and neighbor. Did he take good care of you?"

The kids nodded and pulled her into the apartment. The place smelled like savory roast beef and her bags had been brought in. The table was set for three.

Dan leaned against the wall with his arms folded. "Ready to take charge?" He gave her a wink.

"I think I can handle it from here. Thank you."

Dan started to move to the door and Skye stopped him. "My car?"

"Didn't start this morning. It should now."

"Who do I pay?"

"No one. Some of the guys from our church like to help out single moms in need at no cost to the owner of the vehicle."

"Oh."

"Dinner is in the slow cooker. Enjoy."

With a quick grin, he was gone. The door closed softly behind him. She heard the click of the one across the hall and her kids once again demanded her attention.

Skye put the food on the table and sat with her kids.

"Mommy, we pray now." Both children bowed their heads and folded their hands. Quinn spoke, "Jesus, thanks for Mommy being home and for Mr. Dan taking good care of us and making us yummy food. Amen."

Meghan gave an enthusiastic "amen" herself and they looked expectantly at their mother.

"Amen?" Skye responded and was rewarded with big grins. She served up the meat, potatoes, and carrots and her stomach rumbled. It seemed wrong they were enjoying this feast, and Dan was alone next door probably eating soup from a can or a frozen dinner.

She was amazed at bedtime. Both kids knelt by their beds and prayed. Skye tucked them in and planted kisses on their cheeks. She walked out of the room, entered her own, and stopped. Her suitcase sat on a bed made with care. She unpacked, readied herself for bed, and climbed in.

The old man on the plane had been right after all.

She'd been blessed more than she realized.

THIRTEEN

There is nothing on this earth more to be prized than true friendship.
Thomas Aquinas

Dan spent the night in the bathroom. *Great. Catch the flu bug just as I'm about to go back to work.* Every time he threw up, his ribs hurt all over. By morning he was blurry-eyed and exhausted, but at least his insides had quieted down. He showered, dressed, and headed out into the frigid cold Wisconsin Monday.

He arrived at church before other staff and started the coffee pot...even though the thought of a cup didn't appeal to him at the moment. At least the aroma of the coffee beans didn't make him sick. He poured a cup for himself anyway, more to hold and warm up his hands rather than drink. It would make for a nice prop.

He flipped open his work laptop and logged in. His email was overloaded with thousands of messages. He started with the oldest first and began to work his way through, making a note of who he needed to contact and about what. He returned a few brief ones, apologizing to those who didn't realize he'd been out on leave. Many were notes of encouragement. There had been several from Amy. The early ones started out flirtatious and later ones, apologetic. Her last one indicated she wanted help to connect with Skye—to apologize to her face to face with Mary Beth as a safety for them both.

He wondered how Skye would react to that. She

hadn't filled out a contact card yet, so he didn't feel right giving out that information without her permission. He picked up the phone to give her a call.

"Hello?"

"Hey, it's Dan."

"Oh, thank you for everything, the car, the roast, taking such great care of my kids. They couldn't say enough good things about you."

"It was an enlightening experience. And my pleasure. Listen, I need to ask you a question."

"Shoot."

"Remember that woman who confronted you?"

"Yeah, I get it, you are an attractive single man, you probably need to carry a baseball bat with you to get to your office."

"Nothing of the sort. But thanks for the compliment. Amy wants to meet with you to apologize. She would do it here at the church with our Women's Ministry Director, Mary Beth. Could I give her your phone number to set it up?"

"Mary Beth or Amy?"

"Well, Amy asked, but if you're more comfortable with me giving it to Mary Beth instead, I'm fine with that."

"I'd feel safer with Mary Beth. I'm willing to meet. Should be interesting."

"This would probably need to be in an evening due to Amy's work schedule."

"I'd need to find a sitter."

"Let me know and I'll watch the kids for you."

"Why? Why should you give up your free time so Amy can unburden herself? That seems wrong."

"Maybe because I'm your neighbor, skiing partner, and erstwhile Zumba student, and I love your kids and want to help?"

"I must be crazy to always question you on your motives. I'm sorry about that, it's just—"

"It's OK, Skye. I have a hard time asking for help too, and it takes time to learn to trust people. From what little you've told me, you've had that trust betrayed one too many times."

"Yeah. Thanks for understanding. Go ahead and have Mary Beth set it up. How's the first day back?"

"Brutal. I caught your kid's bug and was sick last night. Better now but beyond exhausted. I don't think I'm going to want to eat for a week after that."

"I'm sorry you got sick."

"It's not your fault. It happens."

"I realize that, but, if you hadn't…"

"I could have still caught it from someone on a Sunday morning, or at the grocery store, or even here in the office."

"Well, thanks again. Try to have a good day. I need to get to class here in a little bit."

"Let me know if you have any trouble with the car."

"Thanks. I will."

Dan hung up and couldn't help but smile remembering her as she crested the stairs yesterday and sank to her knees to hug her kids. She wore her pink fuzzy boots and even though she had to be exhausted, she glowed when she looked into their eyes and listened to their chatter.

That was a gift he would never experience. The pain of every child they lost ached anew, compounded by such a beautiful example of love he saw. Being with those kids, even while they were sick, reawakened a longing inside. For a wife. For a family. Maybe it was time to start thinking of moving on and finding one.

But how did a single pastor do that? Everyone would watch. Judge. And how did he even begin to find a woman who would have the courage and stamina to take on the position and weight of a pastor's wife? It could be isolating to be in that role. Pastors' wives knew too much, and the expectations of them were high. He wasn't interested as much in a partner in ministry at church...but a partner in the ministry of raising a family.

He leaned his head back and sighed. It had been easier in high school. Find a girl, ask her out, and if it didn't work, move on to another. But here? In the church? In a venue where so many people watched? Why would any woman willingly step into that?

A rap on the door startled him and he snapped forward.

"Andrew."

"Welcome back, Dan." Pastor Andrew stood in the doorway with his own steaming cup of joe lifted in a toast.

"Thanks. It's good to be back."

Andrew frowned. "You don't look so hot."

"Tired. Caught the flu from the kids I took care of. Better now, just wiped out."

"If you need to leave early, go ahead. No rush. No appointments today. I realize you'd need to catch up with your e-mails and the stack of memos on your desk."

"Thanks. I might take you up on that. Or take my laptop home and work from there."

"Either way, let Joanie know so she can forward or redirect your calls."

Dan groaned.

"What?"

"I totally forgot the voice mail. There's probably a million of those too."

"Sorry, could be possible. I'll let you get to it."

"Thanks."

The door closed and he grabbed a fresh piece of paper to start jotting notes from his voice mail. It was going to be a long morning.

~*~

By 11:30, Dan was barely awake, so he packed up his laptop and drove home. Skye's car wasn't in the parking lot, which concerned him because she was normally home at that time to meet the kids. He went inside, placed his stuff in his apartment, and went across the hall to knock on her door. No answer.

The outer door downstairs opened, and the kids came running up followed by their grandmother.

"Dan? I thought you started work today."

"Yeah, home for lunch. Where's Skye?"

"She's not here?" Sandi Richards went to knock on the door while the kids wrapped their arms around each of his legs.

Dan shrugged and dropped down to give the kids hugs.

"There's no answer. I have a key but I can't leave the kids alone and I need to get to my next job." Sandi looked at him with pleading eyes and pursed lips. "Dan, I'd hate to ask…"

"Why don't the kids hang out at my place till Skye gets back?"

Quinn and Meghan cheered and ran into his apartment.

"Are you sure about this?" she asked. Dan watched through the open door. The kids scattered their boots and coats all over.

"No, but they need to be somewhere safe, and I'm home."

"You got the flu, didn't you?"

Dan nodded and frowned. "Last night. Didn't get much sleep."

"And you left work to come home to rest."

Dan nodded. "Guess I better go make more coffee."

"I'll text Skye to tell her. Hopefully she's on her way and you'll be relieved soon."

"Thanks, Sandi. Skye is lucky to have you."

"I'd like to think so…but she's also blessed to have you in her life."

Sandi took off down the stairs and out the door. Dan sighed and went to his apartment and turned on the television. While the kids settled down he tried to figure out what, in his meager store of food, he could feed them.

~*~

Really God? This is how You show Your love? Skye huddled in the back of the squad car. The officer had been nice enough to give her a blanket to help her warm up and the heat was on. Her head throbbed, but at least the seatbelt kept her from hitting the steering wheel when she'd been rear-ended at the stop light. As luck would have it, the driver who hit her drove away. Although his green car with a smashed front end should be easy enough for the police to locate in time. A song had been playing on the radio when she got hit, and the lyrics were about God making everything work together for her good. *I think they've got it wrong*.

And her phone? Batteries were dead. She'd totally forgotten to hook it up to the charger last night.

Her car was old and from what she could tell, undrivable. A tow truck was called to take it away. Oh, and lucky for her, car seats were not to be used after being involved in an accident. She was grateful at least her kids hadn't been with her, given how the back end had scrunched the rear seat forward.

Now she needed a new car and new car seats. She hardly had any money. She borrowed a phone to try to call her mom, but there'd been no answer. Her mother wouldn't answer her cell while working. So where were her kids?

The officer returned to the car. "Your tow-truck is here. You sure you don't want a trip to the hospital?"

"No. I need to get home to my kids." She got out of the squad car and handed the blanket he had given her to the officer. "Thank you for letting me warm up."

The officer pointed her to the man hooking up her car.

"Miss O'Connell, I thought this was your car. Are you OK?" Titus, the mechanic from yesterday, was her tow truck driver.

"A little shook up, but also in need of a ride home."

"I can do that. Hop into the cab, the heater's on. I'll only be a minute." He turned to finish securing her beat up car. Where would they even take it? What was the point?

"Can I borrow your cell? I need to call my insurance."

"Sure." He handed it over and she headed to the

cab. She inhaled the warm air and shivered deep inside. She dialed the number, gave the information, and got a location as to where to drop off the car. Titus jumped back in and she handed him the address and filled out her insurance information for the towing.

"Well, Miss O'Connell, why don't we get you home first?"

She nodded. "That would be great. I've been really worried about my kids. My cell phone battery was dead…"

"Don't sweat it. God's got this covered."

"How can you say that? My car was just totaled."

"And you survived. Sure, your neck is going to be sore—I know a great chiropractor by the way—but it will heal. Your kids still have their mother. That's cause to be grateful. Trust me, not every car I tow has a driver who walks away on her own two fuzzy, pink feet."

"Are you making fun of my boots?"

Titus chuckled. "They suit you."

"Oh."

He dropped her off in the parking lot. Dan's car was already there.

"Looks like Dan came home early. You need anything you let him know…including a used car. Part of his job is connecting people together to see that needs are met. Not sure how he does it, as I swear most of that information is in his pretty, blond head." He waved a hand at her. "I'm not putting him down. He can bench press with the best of them. He's a great guy and I like to josh him a bit about the attention he gets. Leaves us more rugged characters in the dust."

"Well, um. Thanks again, Titus. I'm sorry that battery was a wasted deal."

The mechanic shook his head. "Don't worry about it."

Skye stepped down out of the truck and hauled her purse and gym bag after her. She gave a final wave, shut the door, and headed to the apartment building.

A note hung on her door. *Kids are at Dan's.* It was signed, *Mom.* Skye let out a sigh of relief and opened the apartment, dropping her stuff inside and plugging in her phone right away. She headed next door. She knocked and heard a muffled, "Give me a sec," from inside.

The door cracked open and Dan stood there with his finger pressed to his lips. "Shhh."

She walked inside. Pillows and blankets were strewn all over the middle of the living room.

Dan whispered, "They're napping in a tent fort."

"How...?"

"Are you OK? Your mom was really worried, and I tried calling."

Skye shook her head. "My car was totaled in a hit and run. He hit me from behind at a stop sign."

"I'm so sorry."

"Titus, the guy who fixed my car yesterday, was the tow truck driver. He brought me home. My phone battery was dead and I borrowed a phone to call my mom, but it went to voice mail. She must have been at work by the time I was able to try." She looked at Dan. "Are you OK? I thought you were back at work today."

He pursed his lips and pointed to the laptop on the kitchen table. "I was sick during the night and came home to take a nap. I was here when Sandi arrived with the kids."

"Thank you, again. I don't know how I could ever repay you for all you've done for me."

"I don't help you so that I can get anything in return." His arms folded across his well-defined chest, and his voice was a little louder now.

"Shhh! I don't understand why you would help me."

"And why not?" Dan motioned for the door and they went to stand out in the hallway. "Listen, I know you've got some baggage from your past, but not everyone is a dirty lowlife wanting to take advantage of you. Sure, it's wise to be careful who you trust. By now you should realize that I don't do things to get something in return."

"Then why?"

"Because you are an image-bearer of God. He created you. Special, talented, and unique. And you, like me, carry wounds from our past. Not to rip open by nasty behavior, but to be healed by your Creator. God loves you, Skye. How could I treat you in any other way than to help when I am able and to care about you as a person, because you are my neighbor? You know, you've helped me too."

"I have?"

"Zumba, skiing, you let me play with your kids. Skye, the heartache I've carried for years of longing for kids? You can't imagine. Every baby we lost was a knife stabbing in my heart. Sharon hurt even worse but she's free of that now. Me? I still don't have what you do in those precious children. I don't begrudge you them. You have a difficult life as a single mom. But you've shared them and some of that has helped me in my own healing."

"You'll marry again someday and have a family."

"Maybe. But you can't promise me that. One of the hard things I learned was that I wasn't as good a husband as I thought I was."

"Did your wife ever complain?"

"No. That wasn't her style. But that doesn't mean I didn't hurt her anyway." Dan shook his head. "I'm not the prize women think I am, Skye. And I don't know if I ever could be."

"Aren't you the one who says God loves me?"

"Yeah."

"Then He loves you too, doesn't He?"

Dan nodded.

"How come His love is good enough for me to have faith in but not yourself?" She held a hand up. "I'm sorry. That was uncalled for. Give me a call when the kids are up and I'll come take them off your hands. And again, thank you." Skye turned and escaped into her own apartment.

She went to make a cup of tea to warm herself up and took out some of the meat from last night to make a sandwich. She couldn't believe she challenged Dan like that. He was a pastor. He knew this stuff better than her and she was lecturing him? She noticed how he treated people. She knew how he treated her. She'd seen the way he mourned his wife. Whatever his perceived sins were, they weren't as bad as he thought they were. She was jealous of Sharon. His dead wife. A woman who held the steadfast love of a man.

Something she'd never know.

Susan M. Baganz

FOURTEEN

We are either in the process of resisting God's truth or in the process of being shaped and molded by His truth.
Charles Stanley

Once the kids were gone, Dan surveyed the damage. He managed to sleep for a short time on the sofa while the kids rested under their fort. Without a pillow though, it wasn't the deep rest he needed. He dragged himself to the computer to keep hacking away at the e-mail, deleting some, making notes on others, and responding to many.

He finally pushed away from the kitchen table, made a baked potato in the microwave, slathered on some butter and ate it for dinner. His first real meal of the day and even then he couldn't keep it down.

Skye's words irritated him. She couldn't see God's love even though he and others had been showering her with it for weeks. Then, she turned the tables on him.

She was right.

She unflinchingly challenged him. Who had ever done that to him unless they had an agenda? At least that was sometimes his experience in ministry. Everyone thought their favorite ministry was the most important and would fight tooth and nail for every dollar of the budget they could get not realizing that the bigger picture of the church meant that they were all important.

But even relationally, very few were willing to

challenge his faith and his walk with God. Andrew had, and sometimes his accountability group were willing to wade into those waters. It wasn't that he was hard-headed, but most people thought he should have it all together. They thought that he never struggled through times when prayer was difficult and God's word seemed dry to his soul. They didn't know he sometimes questioned the goodness of God even as he tried to remind others of how much God loved them.

Few understood that loneliness ate at him and the silence of his apartment taunted him with all he had lost.

And Skye called him on it. She'd been in a car accident, shaken up and frantic over her kids, and still, she looked past that and pierced the core of his issue. She wasn't just an artist. She was a gift, a curse, and a beautiful temptation all wrapped up in one package. And she hadn't accepted Christ yet. At least he didn't think she had. He wanted to smack himself in the head. He hadn't ever followed up with her. He'd never asked her about her reading in John and what she thought.

And he realized why.

Those conversations could lead to intimacy. Intimacy that was tempting and dangerous. He really needed to get her connected to some other, more mature women, to disciple her and answer her questions. He wanted to watch her grow in her faith, but he was too close and it could only lead to danger.

Not that she was a threat to him.

He was worried he would be a threat—or even a stumbling block to her.

Obviously he hadn't been doing as well as he thought anyway.

He finished cleaning up from the meal and turned off the lights. It was early, but he didn't care. He was depressing himself and he was bone weary. He collapsed into bed like a limp noodle.

~*~

Dreams were supposed to be revelations, weren't they? So why was he dreaming of her? Holding hands, taking a walk, and occasionally bumping into each other. The look of concern on her face as her petite figure towered over him in the snow. He believed she wanted to slap him when he started laughing. Her passion as she taught her fitness class. The love that shone through her eyes as she spoke to her children.

He wanted passion, love, touch...and he wasn't afraid of a woman who poked the bear now and again without flinching.

He wasn't on a pedestal to her, but he didn't understand why. How could he get others to take him off without him crashing and burning in the process?

~*~

The next morning, he dragged himself to church, made the coffee, and prepared for the staff meeting.

"Welcome back!" was the common refrain but his head pounded. He forced the smile and took his notes and listened to all that was going on in the church. Mary Beth came to visit him in his office when it was done.

"Dan, you don't look so hot." She sat across from him in blue jeans, blouse, and cardigan sweater. Her office was always pretty cold.

"I was sick over the weekend, and I still haven't recovered."

"I heard you have a neighbor."

"Yeah, single mom of two little kids."

"You had those kids with you on Sunday. How'd that go?"

"The kids were great. It was eye-opening."

"Re-open wounds?"

Dan shrugged. "I grieve what Sharon and I lost. Being a single dad would have been a really difficult path to travel on top of the grief that almost buried me."

"It's hard to look at loss like that in light of future blessings, but it doesn't minimize the weight of that pain and the dreams that shattered with each death. Not only of those babies but also your wife."

"Yeah. It's a difficult thing—being grateful and sad at the same time."

"Job must have struggled too. Losing all his children, his business, all his worldly possessions, his health...and then after struggling with his faith, God gave him all that and more."

Dan rubbed his forehead. "But that's no guarantee...no promise..."

"God didn't ask Job to worship to get a reward. Ultimately, our greatest promise is heaven. No pain, no loss, no sorrow or people betraying us."

"A place with no sin. I can't imagine." Dan fought with the desire to hasten his journey there and victory didn't mean the thoughts still didn't intrude.

"I understand. Hang in there. Wait on him. Keep healing and who knows? Maybe God will drop a wonderful surprise in your lap."

"Maybe. Before you go...here's Skye O'Connell's

phone number. She said I could give it to you, but not Amy."

"This is the young woman Amy threatened?"

"Yeah, from what I was told by Andrew."

"Great, I'll get something set up."

"She's seeking, Mary Beth."

"Good. We'll pray that she opens her eyes to a Savior who is drawing her to Himself."

"The ultimate love story."

"Yeah, definitely. Try to have a good day, Dan. I'm glad you're back."

"Thanks."

The soft click of the door echoed in his head. He'd never had migraines before but now? He folded up his laptop and put it in his bag. He told the secretary he was leaving and went home.

He heard the thump, thump, thump of music coming from Skye's apartment. She was probably painting. He paused though. It wasn't standard rock 'n roll, but the local Christian station. As bad as his head hurt, he wasn't about to tell her to turn it off or down. He went into his apartment, dropped his stuff on the sofa, and made a beeline for the bedroom. He closed the door behind him and shut the shades. He crawled under the covers and drifted to sleep.

He slept through till morning.

FIFTEEN

Only people who are capable of loving strongly
can also suffer great sorrow, but this same necessity of
loving serves to counteract their grief and heals them.
Leo Tolstoy

Wednesday morning was accountability group. Dan arrived before everyone. His headache was gone, but he still wasn't feeling one hundred percent well. His ribs still throbbed from his night of running to the toilet. The doctor said those injuries took a long time to heal. He motioned for Clarisse, their usual waitress, to come and fill his coffee mug.

"Heya, handsome. Flying solo today?"

Always. "The guys will be here soon."

"Great. See ya in a few." She carried her coffee pot away.

Dan stared into the dark drink. Dark. Winter. Why was Valentine's Day in winter? He thought back to all the effort he'd put into doing something special for Sharon. This year it fell on a Friday. This year, he'd be working and going home—alone. For the second time since Sharon left him.

Left him? Yeah. *Abandoned. Not good enough. She went to a better lover.* And in some ways he resented both Sharon and God for that. A widower he was acquainted with online often said his wife "ran away with Jesus." How could a man not be jealous that God took his wife? And maybe even angry that his wife so willingly went.

Sharon didn't have a choice. The aneurism that took her life was like a stealth bomber. She never knew what hit her when it exploded in her brain.

Tony arrived and soon Simon and Nick. Coffee mugs filled as greetings were exchanged and Clarisse took their orders. She probably had them memorized since they'd been meeting for years in this spot.

Simon talked about some health concerns and the men prayed over him. Nick's wife was struggling with the cold and isolation her illness caused, and he was too. Tony was excited about a new baby on the way and struggling with what to do for Valentine's Day since it was the busiest day for his restaurant and the anniversary of when he proposed. Way too soon the focus turned to Dan.

"How's it been being back to work?" Simon asked. "Inquiring minds want to know."

Dan grinned. "I got sick...I haven't been in the office much, and so far I'm buried under a sea of e-mails and voice messages. Staff meeting yesterday. My days were short with recovering from the flu. Today's the first day I've felt relatively normal." He pointed his fork at his plate. "And hungry."

"Does talk of Valentine's Day bother you?"

Dan sat back to think on it. "Honestly? Yes. I don't begrudge any of you—your love, your families, your struggles. This will be my second one without Sharon. We really never did much to celebrate, but in hindsight, even though she said she didn't need that...I was wrong to believe her."

"So self-flagellation is on your calendar for Friday?" Simon asked.

"Maybe..."

"Have you thought about dating?" Nick tilted his

head as he asked the question.

Dan sighed. "No. Yes. It's just the who and how. I was married before I became a pastor, but to navigate this under the microscope of the church is terrifying. Why would any woman even want to do that?"

"Flying under the radar isn't possible, is it?" Simon sipped his coffee.

Dan shrugged. "There are people everywhere who know who I am. I'm not some kind of covert operative with a disguise I can don. Who would want that anyway?"

"Obviously some of our single ladies would," Nick joked.

"I know most of those women. Many sat in my office over the years to pour out their struggles and sorrows. It doesn't feel right to even consider them as a dating pool. It's like it crosses a line and the risks are high. I need to be careful with any woman I meet with. Too many sex scandals have rocked the church over the years, and I don't even want a whiff of that to come from my office, by accident or suspicion."

"So the church is your bride?" Tony asked.

"The church is the Bride of Christ and I adore her. I wouldn't do anything intentionally to tarnish her image."

"Do you wait for God to drop someone in your lap?" Nick's eyebrows wiggled.

"I don't know. I'm not even sure if I'm ready." He sipped his coffee. "But I am lonely. Not missing Sharon so much as missing having someone in my corner, who understands me, and doesn't look at me through rose-colored glasses."

"We'll pray God will answer that prayer." Tony placed a hand on Dan's shoulder. "Let's pray for you now..."

~*~

Dan headed back to church. He grabbed his mail and took it to his office and started to leaf through the pile. An envelope with a sticky note on it came from Andrew. *You need to see this.*

Tossing the rest on the desk he plopped into his chair and opened the envelope. It was a magazine and the front cover was a painting that looked very much like—him. He stared at the work. It was beautiful. Surely, that wasn't him though? He looked inside to see the artist.

It was Skye.

Skye painted him this way?

When? He never sat for this but...the eyes. He used to be made fun of in school for the stars on his pupils. It was a rare thing. Of course, Skye, being an artist would notice that detail. Not many people looked him straight in the eye, they were too busy trying to hide their shame from God to face him when they sat across from him for counseling. Well, except for some of the women.

He tossed the magazine on the desk. He didn't know whether to be angry or honored. Why hadn't she told him? He groaned. Great. Now people would think he was only a handsome guy and not someone who could preach, counsel, and lead. Maybe he should stop working out. Put on a few pounds. Grow a shaggy beard. Try to look less like that image staring back at him from the cover of that rag.

No. He liked working out. It relieved stress and he needed the stamina to do his job. His body was a resource to be stewarded as much as the church budget, and the people who served. Not neglected or abused.

The phone rang.

"Yeah?"

"Thought you'd like to be aware that Amy and Skye will be here tomorrow night at six," Mary Beth reported.

"I'll make myself scarce."

"Might be wise. I don't want to break up a catfight."

"Seriously? You think they'll go tooth and nail over *me*?"

"Probably not, but women...well, there's a reason you hired me, right? Because neither you nor Andrew wanted the sole burden of dealing with this messy stuff."

Dan laughed. "Mary Beth, you are a jewel. Thanks for wading into this."

"Anytime, Dan. That's what we do here as staff. Look out for each other. Have each other's backs when the slings and arrows come. Never anticipated having to fight off Cupid's arrows aimed for you."

"Just in time for Valentine's Day."

"Yeah. Praying for you as you head into year number two with that. Remember that anniversaries of special occasions can be hard."

"I'm aware. I do counseling as well."

"Yeah, but sometimes we neglect to give ourselves the same compassion we extend to others."

"Touché."

He hung up the phone. There was work to be done and the church budget process headed the list. Still, he'd rather deal with that as opposed to being in the midst of the issues that emerged at times between women. He never did quite get it. They were all on the same team after all.

~*~

Titus stopped by and Sandi agreed to come watch the kids while he took Skye out to get new car seats.

"Hey. You ready?" Titus held the door open for her as she pulled herself up into the cab of his truck.

They stopped at department store and Titus grabbed the cart. "Where to?"

"This way. I really appreciate your help with this."

"I felt bad for what happened to you. How is your insurance working out?"

"They totaled the car, and I should have the check tomorrow. Friday might be the earliest I can consider purchasing anything."

"Craigslist is a good place to look unless you want to go to a dealership. What are you looking for? Do you have a price range?"

She gave him the amount of her check and he frowned. "It's not much, Titus, but it's all I have. Hopefully my art will start making me money but being self-employed, I can't get a loan for a car. I don't have steady enough income for that. I wouldn't want the debt when I'm not sure I could make the payments."

"You want a small car like you had or a mini-van?"

"I'm fine with a sedan. It's just me and the two kids, and the gas mileage is better."

"Sometimes we have cars donated to our Garage Ministry, but we don't have anything right now. Let me take a look and I'll let you know if I find anything in your price range. Maybe Friday we could go take a look at one or two."

"Not Friday. It's Valentine's Day," Skye protested.

"I'm not dating anyone right now, so Friday is just another day for me...unless you have plans?" He swung the cart down the aisle to the baby department.

"No plans but also no sitter. My mom has plans."

"Saturday I'm working the wrecker. Got anyone else who could help if I fed you the info?"

"I don't know. I'll see." She sighed.

He walked beside her as they strode down to the car seats and cribs. She quickly selected her items. The tall man next to her was ruggedly handsome, but he reminded her too much of her ex. Titus was all that was courtesy, and she had great admiration for those who could handle the mechanics of a car, even with dirt under their fingernails. He cleaned up nice. She just couldn't envision him in her life or as a father to her kids.

What am I thinking? I'm not on the prowl for a man. Still, the fact that he had come to help her out showed either a kind heart, like Dan's, or an ulterior motive, like her ex.

"Can I ask you a question?"

"Sure."

"Why are you helping me?"

Titus stopped and looked at her. "The truth?"

"Yes. Please."

"My dad abandoned my mom when I was just a kid. She worked hard and struggled to make ends meet and keep me out of trouble. Trust me when I tell you that was a full-time job in and of itself." Titus shrugged and they started walking again. "Since I've grown up and have skills with cars, I took over the ministry at church to help single moms when they had auto needs. I understand how important it is to own a reliable vehicle, get food, transport the kids, get to work, and get help when you need it. Dan oversees the ministry.

He, along with others from church, have taught me that being a man is about helping others, and that a man of God treats women with respect. Single moms aren't often given respect, as my own mother found out. Dan pointed me your way because you needed help. I felt bad when I realized what had happened to your car and promised myself I would do what I could to give you a hand."

"That's it?"

"Pretty much. You're important to God...He gave me the opportunity to help with the gifts He's given me. Accept the blessing, Skye. I'm not hitting on you."

Warmth flooded her cheeks. "I wasn't..."

"Yes, you were. Someone hurt you, and now you're cautious. As you should be. But you're also an attractive woman. I respect the fact that you aren't trying to jump into a relationship and even put me off with the car thing. Trust me. I'm not after you. But—" He held up a hand, "—I would like to be your friend if you'll let me."

All she could manage was a nod. What kind of faith was it that made men act like this? Then she recalled Amy...and sighed. Obviously, some people weren't changed all at once. She wondered what that meeting was going to be like.

Titus dropped her off and helped her lug the car seats to her apartment.

"Thanks again, Titus. I appreciate all you've done to help."

He looked at her with chocolate-truffle eyes. "You don't get it, do you?"

"Get what?"

"God loves you, Skye." He winked at her and took off down the stairs.

Skye stood there for a moment. *God loves me?* Dan said that too. But that didn't make her worth all this effort. She was nothing special compared to other single moms out here. So why her?

She turned to walk into the house and her kids greeted her with hugs.

Because you are mine.

SIXTEEN

Friends...they cherish one another's hopes.
They are kind to one another's dreams.
Henry David Thoreau

Skye was up late searching for a car and thought she finally found one. She e-mailed Titus about it to ask if it looked good. He said he would go check it out for her on Saturday in between towing calls. It was Thursday and she survived the long walk to the YMCA, but was so cold. She really needed a car. She changed and made her way to her Zumba class. Dan was just getting off the treadmill.

"Hey, Skye. Did you get a car?"

She shook her head. "Not yet. Titus's going to check up on one for me."

"You could've called. I'd have...given...you..."

"And compromise?"

"It is deadly cold out there. That constitutes an emergency. I'll give you a lift home when you're done. I need to talk to you about something anyway. Got time for a coffee?"

She looked at those spectacular eyes. How had she painted them without realizing how unusual they were? He wasn't smiling. Something was off with him today. "Sure. Thanks. That would be great." She gave him a wave and headed to her classroom.

~*~

186

After class, she headed to the shower, but kept her hair from getting wet. At least she wouldn't stink when she met with Dan.

And why would I care about that?

She told herself that it was only because it was cold outside and she didn't have time to dry her hair and didn't want to go out with a wet head.

And she didn't want to make Dan wait for her. Surely, he needed to get back to work. He was supposed to be at the church, wasn't he?

He waited for her in the lobby and gave her a nod as she came up beside him. "Ready to brave the elements?"

"Much easier to face when it's not the entire walk home."

They hit the frigid air and soon were sitting in his car. It barely warmed before they got to the coffee shop. They ran inside and Dan went to get them both a drink while she sat at a small table, shivering. Soon a hot mug was in her hands and she savored the warmth. She hadn't even taken off her coat.

"What did you want to talk about?"

"This." He placed a large manila envelope on the table. He pulled out a magazine cover and slid it her way.

Her eyes grew big. "Oh! I didn't realize they were going to put that on the front cover. It was supposed to be an inside story." She looked at up at his frown. One eyebrow arched upward. Her shoulders slumped. "I didn't know how to tell you. I didn't even realize that it was you until my mother pointed it out to me."

"What gave it away?"

"Your eyes."

He shook his head. "You're an artist. You're aware

of details like that. You really didn't know you were painting a portrait of me?" Anger laced his voice.

Skye looked into those eyes shooting darts more than stars. "My painting is different now and I don't understand some of the images that emerge on the canvas. This was one of them. The first. I used to have a firm vision of what I was going to paint, but now it's as if someone else holds the brush and it's not me. I won't deny I painted it. I did. I remember every brush stroke. I didn't realize what the finished product was going to be until it was you staring me in the face, and even then I denied it to myself. 'It's a man that looks like my neighbor.' Or I'd say, 'he inspired it but it's not really him.' Dan, I'm sorry. I deceived myself. The painting sold and I didn't know how to tell you. I didn't understand what it meant."

"What do you mean, you 'didn't know what it meant?'" His eyes softened and the scowl was gone.

"Painting has been therapy. Release. But lately, it's been spiritual. I don't know how to describe it other than that. You told me to read John. Light. Love. It's all there in my work." She chanced a glance at him. "But it never was before."

He looked down at his mug and back up at her. "I'm sorry I got angry. It's just…I'm tired of people looking at me as the pretty boy." His voice went high, 'You should be a model not a pastor.'"

She giggled. "Your good looks are a curse?"

"Maybe. Listen, I married before I became a pastor and it kept the women from pursuing me. Well, most of the time. But now with Sharon gone, and this image out there? I don't want to be loved because of my looks. Or that I'm a pastor. I want a woman who will see me for who I am inside." He leaned back in his chair. "You were right, you know."

"About what?"

"You said something about telling you that God loved you but not accepting it as true for myself. Do you realize how rare that is?"

"What? That God loves you?"

"No. That anyone would dare call me on the carpet for my own internal hypocrisy."

"I'm sorry. I didn't realize..."

"No. Don't be sorry. You spoke truth and you did it in a way I could hear and, well, thank you for that. Listen. I don't hate you for painting the picture. It's a beautiful piece of work and the imagery is powerful. I'm honored that I get to be part of your journey and that it was received well."

"Well? Do you want to know what that sold for?"

"No. I don't. I only hope you get a large chunk of whatever number that is."

"We'll see. I'm not sure I trust my agent, but thankfully that sale was made prior to her."

"Why don't you trust her? And if you don't, why did you sign with her?"

"I was desperate so I signed. As for trusting her? She wouldn't let me read the contracts and still hasn't sent me copies."

"You should have had those before you left New York."

"Yeah. I tried but well, the blizzard provided a convenient excuse for them not being delivered."

"I'm sorry."

"It's not your fault. It's my own. I chased fame and yet I'm not in control of what even happens on the canvas. This," she pointed to the magazine, "was the first of many that emerged and confused me."

"Maybe God's trying to talk to you through your work?"

"Can He do that?"

"He's God, isn't He? You've read about the Holy Spirit?"

She nodded.

"God gives grace so that you can discern his message. The Holy Spirit is who brings you to Jesus and to saving faith."

"I thought that was what you and Titus and others at your church were trying to do."

Dan shook his head and one corner of his lips rose. "The individual is a messenger, a vehicle for God to use to open your heart to Him but we can't save you. The church is a place for those who believe to grow in their faith. It can be a messy process but life is hard and none of us are perfect like Jesus was."

"Hence the stuff with Amy."

"Yeah. Sorry about that."

"Wasn't your fault, Dan. You've done everything you can to be pure, and I happened to be your friend, sitting with you in a service one week."

"Are we friends, Skye?"

"I'd like to think so."

"Thanks."

"Listen, Dan, maybe the Holy Spirit is trying to sway me. I still have so many questions."

"That's why it's called faith."

"I just leap and trust that God will catch me? After everything I've done and been through?"

"Yes. Especially then. I've been through tough stuff too. We all go through hard times. Life is hard. I can't imagine walking through that without God. The Holy Spirit is our Comforter. Granted, we can shut

Him out as much as we want, but He waits for us. In the book of James it says, 'draw near to God and He will draw near to you.' He's waiting Skye—with open arms."

"I read about the crucifixion and resurrection. It was a steep price to pay for my salvation."

"For anyone's, but it was necessary. Man disobeyed and death was the consequence. Only the perfect sacrifice could remove that stain, and Jesus was perfect. He was man and God. He faced all the fears and temptations we do but He never sinned...all we have to do is own our sin, accept the gift, and live our life in gratitude for what Jesus has done. Thankfully, we don't do that alone. He gives us the Holy Spirit...and church. A bunch of people struggling just like you to understand it all and live as He would want us to."

"Why did you decide to become a pastor?"

"I was going to be a musician." He laughed. "I really wasn't good enough. Oh, I have skills, but I don't possess the innate talent of Nikolas Acton or Johnny Marshall from Specific Gravity. I'd been praying about it and it hit me. Music was wonderful, and it ministered to many people at one time, but what I did best was face-to-face, one-on-one interactions. Sure, some of that can happen after a concert, but it was where I found the most joy. Seeing someone grow in their faith. Or accept Christ. Knowing I get to be part of that journey is fuel for me. Ministry is hard. People are messy and sometimes there are days when I wonder why God called me to do this. Especially when He took our babies and then took Sharon. I didn't know if I could go on."

"You wanted to die?"

Dan nodded. "Not many people realize that was how dark it got. I'm glad I didn't give into that temptation to escape my pain that way. Some days it still hurts. But while I'll always love my wife, I'm ready to go on living again."

"Will you remarry?"

He shrugged. "Maybe. I won't rule it out. But being a pastor's wife is a hard life for a woman. I failed far too much in my marriage. I worry that I would again."

"I thought God was in the business of changing people."

"Yes. He is. When I moved next door and heard all the music and chaos and Quinn hid in my apartment, I wasn't very happy with that news. But God has used you as part of my healing, and I'm grateful." He pointed down to her fuzzy pink boots. "I've even become fond of those."

Tears pooled in Skye's eyes. "And you've been pushing me to God and it wasn't until then that I was forced to look more closely at Him. My mom had been urging me for a long time…but it was you…"

"Guess He knew what He was doing." Dan's phone rang and he answered it. "Yeah? Oh, OK. I'll be there soon." He hung up and put it in his pocket. "I'd better take you home. I need to get to the office. Something came up and I need to deal with it right away."

"You're kind of like an emergency room doctor, only for souls instead of bodies." Skye zipped up her coat and finished her coffee as she rose.

"Yeah."

Skye looked at the magazine on the table. "Did you want this or can I take it? They never sent me a copy."

"Take it, Skye. Congratulations again. I'm honored."

"Better than angry."

"Well it might still cause me some embarrassment when some see that, but I'll survive. I've survived worse."

"We both have." Skye settled into the car for the short ride to the apartment. "Thanks for the ride, Dan."

He gave her a grin and a wave and was gone.

Now if only she could find a man like that to marry.

~*~

Sandi came to hang with the kids and loaned her car. Skye braved the cold to go to church for this meeting. She'd seen Dan's car at home when she left. She walked to the reception desk but no one was there. Office hours were over. But people were around. How odd. She rang the bell.

A woman called out. "Coming!" and soon emerged from the hallway. "Are you Skye?"

Skye nodded.

"I'm Mary Beth. Come with me." She escorted Skye down the hallway to a small but cozy office. "Amy will be here soon. Dan told me you're his neighbor and have been coming here for a few weeks."

"Yeah."

"What do you think?"

"Of what? Church? God?"

Mary Beth smiled. "Why don't we start with church?"

"I like this place and my kids love coming. The

music is good and the messages make me think, but in a different way from what Dan does."

"What Dan does?"

"He asks questions that make me think. The talks on stage are different. The questions come in my own mind, not aimed directly at me." Skye looked around the room before settling directly on Mary Beth. "What I don't understand is your purpose. Dan tried to explain it to me, but I'm still not clear. You're not a social services, goodwill organization but you've all helped me even when I didn't ask. Don't get me wrong. I'm not complaining. I just don't understand."

The older woman nodded. "The church is more like a family. This one is big, but the fact is, we all try to help each other when we are able. Dan is in a unique position of knowing many people, their gifts, passions, and ministry involvement. So when someone with a need crosses his path, if he can find someone who loves meeting those kinds of needs, he connects them. That's why we gather to worship. Yes, we are taught from God's word, and that can be challenging, but praying together, singing together, even having a cup of coffee, is a way to connect with each other and with God. He uses each of us as His representatives here on earth to reach others with the love of Christ. Sometimes his people, individually and corporately, don't get that right. But we try."

"Family? All I know of family is brokenness and pain."

"That can happen here too. We all still struggle at times with sin and we will until we get to heaven. If we are really following God, we will let our failures be a springboard to repentance, forgiveness, and relationship. All of which change us, mature us, to be more like Jesus."

"I didn't realize I was coming here for more teaching." Skye held up her hand. "I'm not upset about that. Just surprised. And, I was the one who asked the questions."

"Well, to be honest, I was the one who started us down that path."

A knock came at the door. Mary Beth brought Amy in and closed the door behind her.

Well, this should be interesting.

"Hi Skye, I'm Amy."

"Sit down, Amy." Mary Beth motioned to a seat across from Skye and sat down in her own chair. "Amy?"

The worship leader leaned forward. "I wanted to meet to apologize for my behavior a few weeks ago on Sunday. I've always had a crush on Dan, but he was married, and when his wife died I started to dream that maybe...," she waved her hand in front of her face. "Anyway. I was wrong and out-of-line in coming to you like that and no matter what I believed or thought, it was inappropriate and you were right to challenge me. I'm sorry. It's none of my business what friends you or Dan choose."

Skye wasn't sure what to make of this. "I'm not sure how I'm supposed to respond."

"I wanted to meet to ask you to forgive me."

"Me? What do I need to forgive? It seems to me it's Dan you've harassed and embarrassed by your actions." Skye pursed her lips. *Did she really say that out loud?*

Amy's eyes grew wide. "Yes. Of course, I need to apologize to him too...but I don't want my bad behavior to do anything to get in the way of your relationship with God. You pointed out to me that Jesus wouldn't have acted that way, and you were right. My behavior not only could have hurt your faith, but the faith of those around me. I can't apologize to them, but I can to you. Will you forgive me?"

Skye nodded. "Sure. Dan's a good-looking man and he's sweet. I can understand why you would find him attractive as a potential husband. He's a friend and neighbor. I'm sure I would be the furthest possible candidate to take his wife's place. He loved her very much."

"Sharon was my friend," Amy said. "Well, as much as she felt she could be in her position. She adored Dan too. They had a good marriage."

Mary Beth held up her hand. "This is going to stop. We are not going to spend our time talking about Dan and his merits as a husband or the quality of his marriage. That borders on gossip, ladies."

Skye nodded. "You're right."

Amy frowned. "You said Dan is your neighbor?"

"Yeah."

"So…you're aware that I tried to stop by?"

"It was somewhat hard not to notice. You spoke loudly in the hallway."

"I dug myself in deep with this one. Mary Beth, can you help me apologize to Dan? I don't think that's a conversation that should be done alone."

"I'll help. Are we done here now?"

Skye shrugged.

"Yeah, I think we're done," Amy answered. "Skye, I don't suspect you would ever want to be friends but I do want you to know that you are more than welcome to our Thursday night gathering for young adults. We're not meeting tonight though. Dates are posted online and in the bulletin."

"I appreciate that, but childcare can be a challenge." Skye rose. "Speaking of, I need to get home so my mother has her car back."

"Thanks for coming in. Can I pray for us all before you leave?"

"I suppose." Skye settled back into her seat. What was with all this praying anyway? What was the point?

Mary Beth bowed her head. "Jesus, thank You for showing us forgiveness. Thank You for a peaceful resolution here, and I pray that You would heal any wounds we are unaware of so that You can be fully at work in the lives of Amy and Skye. You are worthy of our love, adoration, and our obedience. We praise Your name. Amen."

Skye looked up and gave Amy and Mary Beth a smile.

Mary Beth rose. "Thank you for taking time to come, Skye. Have a safe trip home."

"Thank you." Skye bustled out into the brisk air. Her nostrils almost froze together before she could reach the car.

~*~

Later that night when the kids were in bed she snuggled into her own pillow and let her mind wander. Forgiveness. Who did she need to forgive? Riley of course. Her father. The idiot who totaled her car. Her pushy agent.

Herself.

She flipped the question. Who did she need to ask forgiveness from? She hadn't been an angel. Riley? Maybe. Her mom? Certainly. Her kids...she'd be asking them to forgive her for the rest of her life.

As for herself? She had no clue how she could ever do that.

~*~

Dan rolled over and his hand landed on the pillow next to him. Valentine 's Day. He saw the photo of Sharon and him from their wedding day on that side of the bed. Loss sucker-punched him and he struggled to breathe. Panic attacks didn't happen too often, but when they did...He closed his eyes and forced his muscles to contract and relax. He took a deep breath, held it, and slowly released it. He did that several more times. The tension oozed away leaving him a basket case.

It's OK. It was a panic attack. It happens, and I'm going to be all right. Jesus, when will this end?

He lay there praying for peace, but it wouldn't come. He dragged himself to the shower and dressed for the day. The offices were closed but he would go in. There was plenty to do and he was scheduled to preach next week. He had some serious message prep. And Niko was coming in to talk.

SEVENTEEN

Color in painting is like enthusiasm in life.
Vincent Van Gogh

The office had been unnaturally quiet. Even though the church was closed, it was common for several staff to take advantage of the quiet and work. A rap on the door startled Dan. He looked up to see Nikolas Acton, the interim Worship Director. Dan motioned for him to enter.

"Hey, Niko." He rose and patted his friend's shoulder while motioning to a chair at the desk. He sat down at the matching one, turning it to face Niko.

"Nice to have you back, Dan."

"You've done a great job keeping things going on Sundays."

"Thanks. Your shoes are not easy ones to fill. Tia's been great about the time I've needed away to handle rehearsals."

"It's not easy, but I couldn't think of a better man to have handed the baton to. You've got more experience dealing with the whims of singers and musicians and communicating with tech people than I do."

"I'm not so sure about that. Specific Gravity was always the same people, so we grew close. This? Every week this is a different group. A unique combination on stage and in the tech booth. That can make for some interesting conflicts."

"Yeah. Hard to make things happen while

tiptoeing around egos, huh?"

"Most of the team is great. They have a heart to serve and ego has nothing to do with it. Those who are teachable are wonderful to work with, even if they don't have the level of skill I'm used to on the road. It's the knuckleheads who think they know everything and don't like me telling them to do it differently that get my goat."

"Anyone in particular?"

"Yeah…"

The rest of the time they discussed preparations for Easter and finally Niko left. No one else was due to come in, so Dan locked up the church building, returned to his office, and shut the door.

He could die here and no one would miss him or even notice until Sunday…if even then.

Well, isn't that a cheerful thought?

He jumped to his feet and paced. He needed to shake this depression. The heaviness of the day. The loneliness ate at him, gnawed at his bones.

His stomach growled. Great. He'd forgotten to pack a lunch, so either he braved the cold to go through a drive-thru or he lived on coffee for the day.

He left his office and strode into the darkened sanctuary. He strolled halfway down an aisle and plopped into a seat, propping one foot up on the back of the seat in front.

*What do you want God? Really. I don't know that I can do this alone. You are with me, but it's too heavy…*He tilted his head back and allowed his eyes to close. *Help.*

The weight of the seat pressing down next to him was his first clue someone else was there.

"Rough day?" Andrew said.

"Yeah."

"I suspected that."

"I'm not going to kill myself."

"You thought about it?"

Dan nodded even though he knew Andrew couldn't see it. "I don't have the guts, but that doesn't mean I don't wish for it to just be over."

"What's the hardest part?"

"No hand to hold. No one there at the end of the day. No one to look forward to seeing. An empty apartment. An empty bed. I miss Sharon, but it's more than that. I miss being married. I regret not doing more for her."

"The whole reason God made woman was because He knew we shouldn't be alone."

"Are you sure it wasn't because most men are morons and women tend to keep us from doing stupid things?"

Andrew chuckled. "Speak for yourself."

"Touché."

Silence hung between them for several minutes.

"How can I help, Dan?"

"I wish I knew. Pray for me. I need to get through this. Tomorrow will be better."

"That's it?"

"You helped a lot coming here. How'd you guess?"

"Just a hunch."

"Could you have Jennifer call my neighbor and invite her to MOPS?"

"The artist?"

"Yeah."

"I liked her painting of you on that magazine cover."

"Is there anyone who hasn't seen it?"

"It was really good. Maybe we can buy one of her pieces to hang in the office. If they are as good as that one...well, I wouldn't mind owning something like that."

"I'll ask her. She has an agent now. I'm not sure she can sell direct."

"Check it out. It would be nice to support someone like that."

"She asks a lot of questions. She's the only woman I know who's been willing to challenge me."

"You like her?"

"Yeah. She's cute and smart. A great mom."

"Why do you think God made you her neighbor?"

"So I could share Christ with her."

"Is that it?"

"No. She's been an important part of my healing the past few weeks. I think I scared several years off her life when I somersaulted down that bunny hill after breaking my ski. I injured some ribs and couldn't stop laughing. I swear she wanted to break more of them for me." Dan couldn't help but smile at the memory.

"Maybe God has more planned?"

"I don't see how. You understand how brutal ministry can be to pastors' wives, and even if she came to Christ—and I think she's close—she'd need time to grow in her faith before she latched on to a has-been like me."

"You're not a has-been."

"Tell my spirit that."

"I think I just did. Have your ribs healed enough for you to play racquetball yet?"

"Maybe."

"Wanna go give it a try?"

Dan thought about it. He let out a deep sigh. "Tempting offer but I'm going to pass today. I need to get started on that message."

"You sure?"

"Yeah. Go home to your wife. Kids will be out of school before long...enjoy some alone time with her."

"You'll call me if you need me?"

"I won't."

"Just know I'm here. No matter the time of day."

"Thanks. I appreciate that."

"Get that message written. I want to see at least an outline on Monday."

"Yes, sir." Dan gave a small salute to the dark as Andrew left the dark room.

OK, God. You sent help. Thanks. Now, how about an assist on that message? Dan dragged himself out of the room and back to his office.

Before he dug in, he made a decision. Maybe even if he didn't have a wife, it didn't mean he couldn't do something nice for someone. He called up a local flower shop and had a small bouquet of flowers, not roses, delivered with no note. Maybe he didn't have the right to tell someone they were loved, but God could.

~*~

Class that morning had been a pain. She walked again. Too proud to ask Dan for help. That was going to get her frostbite. Hopefully, Titus would approve of one of the cars she'd found and she'd have a vehicle soon. She hated borrowing her mom's car. Her mom had her own life. She got home and tried to warm up in the shower. When her mom arrived at lunchtime, she was ready for the kids.

Sandi stepped inside. "Honey, remember how I told you I found my dad?"

"Yeah. How did that go?"

"Really well. He'd like to meet you and the kids."

"Why?"

"Because he missed out on knowing all of us as we grew up, and you are his family too."

Skye shrugged. "You'd need to bring him here."

"I can do that. Tomorrow?"

"Sure. Why the rush?"

"He needs to get back home. He flies out on Sunday evening."

"Tomorrow is fine. Do I need to fix a meal?"

"No. That's too much pressure on all of us. How about just coffee?"

"Sure. What time?" Skye asked.

"Ten?"

"OK."

"Any Valentine's Day plans?"

"Nope."

Sandi's face fell. "I'm sorry, honey. I hoped, maybe…"

"Maybe what?"

"Well, your neighbor is cute and then there's that mechanic, what's his name?" She snapped her finger. "Titus."

"All just friends. No cupid shooting arrows around here."

"Someday, sweetheart, a good man is going to recognize the treasure you are and snap you up."

"That would not be today."

Sandi leaned over and gave Skye a kiss on the cheek. "Well, I love you."

"Thanks, Mom. I love you too."

Her mom left and Skye got lunch for the kids. The dubious chicken nuggets. Well, it was protein, right?

Once the kids were down for their naps she started to paint.

~*~

A buzz at the outer door shook her from her trance. Well, at least that's what the experience resembled as time flew away when she was lost in her art. She pressed the intercom. "Who's there?"

"Delivery for Skye O'Connell."

Delivery? Curiosity compelled her to buzz him in but caution kept the door locked until she could see exactly what the man carried as he came up the stairs. She let him knock on the door and then opened it.

"Miss O'Connell?"

"Yes."

"These are for you. Happy Valentine's Day." The courier left and she brought the package inside. She opened up the cellophane wrapper and exposed a beautiful bouquet of flowers. Carnations and daisies, baby's breath and fern-like leaves. She inhaled. These flowers actually had a scent. She looked for a card but found none. Who sent them?

And why?

Did she have a secret admirer? Was she being stalked? Riley never bothered to buy her flowers or gifts, much less a card. This was unusual. She placed the vase at the middle of the kitchen table and shot up a quick prayer that her rambunctious kids wouldn't tip it over and break it.

She wandered back to her painting filled with

pastel flowers and a sweet little girl playing in the midst of them. Where had that come from? Was Dan right that the Holy Spirit was speaking to her through her art? Was He using that to draw her to Himself?

Dan hadn't sugar-coated faith. If anything, the hurts he suffered made his talk of faith more credible. He was right. Life was hard. But what would it be like to walk through it with God by her side?

She agreed she was a sinner. She understood about Jesus' death and resurrection and that it was a real historical event. She needed what He offered. But was she ready to bend her knee, her will, to God? She understood that some paid lip service to faith but she couldn't make that leap without being all in.

She walked back to the flowers on the table. *Wait. Those flowers. Those colors.* She brought the vase over to the painting. How would anyone have known that she was painting similar flowers and colors? It was Valentine's Day and the standard gift was roses...but there were none in this arrangement and none her painting. The rest? All there.

She put the vase back on the table and sat down. Had God sent her flowers? How else would these blooms come to her?

God? Why? Why would You even care about me? I don't understand.

~*~

She heard Dan come in late, his tread heavy on the stairs. She watched him unlock his door and close it quietly behind him. She went across the hall and knocked on his door.

He opened it and dark shadows hinted at his

weariness.

"Hey, Skye."

"Long day?"

"Hard day."

"I can imagine. I'm sorry. I wanted to offer you a piece of homemade banana cream pie." She thrust the plate forward. "Oh, and the kids made you cards."

Dan grinned and reached for the plate and cards. "Feeling sorry for the lonely bachelor?"

"Maybe it's just that I understand a little how hard a day like today can be. And I'm grateful for all you've done for me and my children and wanted to do something nice in return."

"I appreciate it. Bananas? So if this is my dinner it's actually health food, right?"

Skye grinned. "Sure. Have a good night."

"Thanks, Skye. I appreciate it."

She gave a little wave and went back to her apartment where the kids watched a movie.

~*~

At bedtime, the kids knelt for prayer again. Quinn prayed, "Jesus, thank You for loving us, and take care of Mommy and Mr. Dan. We love them. Amen."

Skye fought the tears. It was beginning to dawn one her that maybe she loved Dan too.

~*~

The next morning, she put the coffee on and the kids happily played when her mom arrived with Sandi's long lost father.

Skye opened the door and her jaw dropped. "It's

you?"

The older man grinned. "I have been praying for you since I met you on that plane. Now I find you're my granddaughter? I am a blessed man indeed."

"Come in, Mom and..."

"Rick Neill at your service. And you must be Skye."

"Yes. And these are my children, Quinn and Meghan." The kids came up to stand by their mother.

"You have a beautiful family."

Skye closed the door and motioned to the table. "Won't you have a seat?"

Sandi pulled out a chair and noticed the flowers. With raised eyebrows she looked at Skye. "Who are those from?"

"There was no card. But they came after I painted this." Skye went to grab the canvas and brought it to show them.

"You did that?" Rick asked.

"It's beautiful," Sandi commented. "But you got the flowers after it was painted?"

"Yeah. Does God send flowers?"

"He might use someone else to send them, but with no note?" Rick asked.

"I don't know."

"Any new men in your life?" Rick inquired.

"There's Dan across the hall. He's a widower and has been super-nice and there's a mechanic, Titus, who is helping me find a new car. Neither has expressed any romantic interest in me."

"Guess it will remain a mystery, but my bets would be on Dan." Sandi winked at her.

"Why?"

"He seems to be that kind of guy. He was so

worried about you when you had your accident and we couldn't find you. He didn't hesitate to offer to help with the kids." Sandi sipped the coffee Skye placed in front of her.

"He's a nice guy. That's all."

"A man who takes care of your kids? He must be in love to do that. Mark my words. And you, my dear granddaughter, are worthy of a man who will treat you well," Rick said.

"Thanks, um, Rick. Or should I call you Grandpa?"

"I'll answer to Rick…after not being in your life all this time, 'Grandpa' probably should be earned."

The next hour was spent in getting acquainted, and soon Sandi and Rick were gone. All those years with few men in her life, and now she had a grandfather who seemed like a great guy. He credited it all to God saving him.

The phone rang.

"Hey, Skye?"

"Yeah, Titus, did any of those pan out?"

"Yeah, the second one did. You want me to get it for you?"

"Sure, I guess. I can write a check out, the money has cleared the bank."

"I'll stop by for the check and then return with the car and install the seats for you. You'll have to do the registration on Monday."

"That's fine. And thank you."

"Not a problem. I'll be there soon."

Within fifteen minutes, Titus was at her door. Dan came out of his apartment. Titus looked at him. "Ready?"

"Wait. Dan what are you doing?"

"Well, someone has to drive the car back. It's a two-person job." Dan headed down the stairs after Titus and they were gone. Forty-five minutes later, Titus came to give her the keys and the title.

"There you go, little lady. It's purring like a kitten and has a full tank of gas. I've checked the battery and it's good. Tires are relatively new as well. She's all yours."

"Wow. Thank you. Where's Dan?"

"He stepped into his apartment. Glad we could help you though. Stay safe and warm out there, OK?"

"Yeah, you too, Titus. Thanks."

The mechanic gave a quick wave to the kids and headed down the stairs.

Skye looked across at the closed door. Dan. He'd helped her, again. She looked at the keys in her hand and went downstairs to the front of the building where the parking lot was. She looked outside at her new car. A car she'd never driven. Was she insane to trust these two men with her money and in making that choice for her?

She'd chosen the last car though, and it had been a lemon from the get-go. Riley was useless in knowing anything about cars other than what hubcaps might be worth more. She frowned. The guy wasn't stupid. She'd seen such potential in him when they first hooked up. Now she was embarrassed to admit that she'd had such low morals. How would she ever talk to her daughter and keep her from making her own mistakes? Or talk to her son and keep him from following his father's example?

She returned to the apartment and tossed the keys in her bag before putting the kids down for their nap. Too many questions with no easy answers.

~*~

It was his first Sunday back on staff. He was up for announcements, but other than that his job was to connect with people and handle any issues congregants had. Mary Beth came up to him during a quiet moment.

"Dan, wanted to let you know that things went well between Amy and Skye."

"No catfight?"

Mary Beth grinned. "No. Skye was perceptive though. She challenged Amy that the person Amy really needs to apologize to is you."

Dan frowned. "Really?"

"Yup. We'll get something set up soon. OK? I'll be in on the meeting to protect your virtue."

Dan chuckled. "Good. Can you come with me Thursday night? It will be my first time back at the adult ministries group."

"Safety in numbers, Dan. You'll be fine." She took off to go meet someone who was walking in the door.

He spied Skye coming in with the kids and Quinn and Meghan escaped her grasp and ran to give him hugs.

"Hey, kiddos. How are you today?"

"Great!" Meghan answered as he picked her up.

Skye walked toward him and he had a momentary wish that she was doing so as his wife. The smile she gave him wrinkled the corners of her eyes behind her black glasses. "Hi, Dan. I see you found my kids."

"Or they found me." He tried to hand off Meghan who was now in his arms, but she refused to budge. "How's the car?"

"It's great. So much better than my old one. Thanks for helping with that."

"Not a problem." Meghan was tickling his neck. "Should I help you get them to their classroom?"

"Sure, if you don't have other work to do."

"I'm good. I have a few minutes until the service starts. I need to be in there by then." They walked side by side down the hallway to the children's ministry and in spite of her reluctance, Meghan finally agreed to go into her room. Quinn gave him a high five before he sauntered into his class.

"Thanks for the help. They can be a bit squirrelly." Skye looked at him and stepped a few inches further away. "I'd better go find a seat."

"Yeah. Me too." He watched her walk away. With a sigh, he headed off to his own seat close to the front of the stage so he'd be ready to do his part.

~*~

After the service, he bounced from person to person who wanted his attention. He spied Skye leaving with the kids, but they hadn't seen him this time so he avoided having to explain why those two little people latched on to him.

Not that he minded though. He loved those kids.

He hung around through second service, but spent it in his office working on next week's message. He finally had an outline fleshed out and e-mailed to Andrew. They'd talk more about it tomorrow. He put two commentaries in a briefcase to take home to look at...after he took a nap.

EIGHTEEN

This love is silent.
T. S. Eliot

Thursday morning found Dan at the gym in the racquetball court with Andrew.

"You're going down!" Andrew whacked the ball and it bounced off two walls and headed straight for Dan.

Whack. The racquet met the ball. "You keep saying that but you'd be so wrong."

The ball bounced off the racket as Andrew returned it. The game went on for another thirty minutes until both men were sweaty and tired. They finally packed up their stuff and headed out of the court.

"That was a great game. Thanks for coming with me to play." Dan wiped the sweat off his forehead as Andrew zipped up his equipment bag.

"It was fun. We should do this more often."

"I agree. All work and no play was making Dan a very dull man." Dan opened his water bottle to down the contents. "Ahh. That hit the spot."

"How's it been being back at work?"

"Good. It's going home that gets hard."

"I know we discussed it, but your message outline for Sunday is solid. Feeling ready to deliver it?"

"Thanks. It feels like forever since I've preached. I'm a little more nervous this time around."

"Why?" Andrew asked

Dan plopped on the bench. "I keep seeing my neighbor in my mind and wondering, will she understand this? Will this make sense? Will it compel her to come to Jesus?"

"You do realize that's God's job, right? Not yours?"

"Yeah, I do, but I don't want to be a stumbling block either."

"Preach the truth and let the Holy Spirit do the rest." Andrew threw on his coat. "I'm heading home for my shower and to have lunch with Jennifer and the kids before heading back to the office."

Dan gave him a wave. "I'm going to hit the shower here and head in to work."

"Lunch?"

"Probably stop somewhere and pick something up."

"See ya later. Tonight's your late night, right?"

"Yeah, first time back since the beginning of the year."

"Try to enjoy it." Andrew grabbed his keys and headed for the lobby.

Dan picked up his stuff and headed for the showers. When he was done, he stalled for a few minutes in the lobby pretending to check his phone. He really did check his e-mail until he spied Skye coming toward him.

Her eyes grew wide as she saw him standing there. "Dan?"

"I had a racquetball game this morning with Andrew."

"Pastor Andrew?"

"Yeah."

"How'd it go?"

"He beat the pants off me but since it was my first time, I didn't do too badly. I'm sure I'll be sore tomorrow."

"If not later today after sitting at your desk." She headed out to the freezing cold.

"You got time for a cup of joe?"

She stopped, and looked at him. A shiver shook her. She nodded. "I'll see you there."

~*~

Skye pulled into the coffee shop parking lot and found Dan's car pulling up next to her. She really wished she'd showered at the gym. *This is not a date, so don't worry about it.* She got out and he held open the door to the restaurant for her. The scent of coffee beans made her smile. Soon she'd feel warm. At least for a few minutes until she needed to brave the cold again.

She found a place to sit, and Dan brought a hot drink and placed it in front of her. She sniffed it and looked up at him, puzzled. "This isn't coffee."

"No, a chai latte. I remembered you had some in your cupboard at home and not much in the way of coffee. You keep your coffee maker on top of the fridge, indicating you only use it on rare occasions."

She took a sip and warmth spread through her. Not just from the drink but also from the man who noticed that coffee was not her preference. "Thanks. That was sweet of you."

"Nah, just observant. How's the new car working out?"

"I like it. It's much nicer than the one I had."

"How are you recovering physically from the accident?"

"My neck is still a little sore. I can't fully turn it to the right so I need to turn my body to look over my shoulder when backing up. Makes some of my Zumba moves more difficult, but I manage. I can live with that. Hopefully, with stretching, it will get better."

"No chiropractor?"

"Considering it, although I suspect it would have been better to go right after the accident."

"Maybe, but it might still help." Dan slid a card across the small table. "This guy goes to our church. He's helped me in the past and he's good. Takes State insurance too. I asked but didn't mention your name. Since it was an accident, I suspect it will have to go through that insurance. Did they ever catch the guy?"

"Yeah, they did. I'm not the only one he hit. He was on some prescription that had 'do not drive' listed as a caution he failed to heed."

"I'm glad they got him."

"And he had insurance. The company has already called me to make things right. They did say that seeking medical help was covered. They were surprisingly nice about it."

"Good. I'm glad. How's the painting coming?"

"My art is going surprisingly well and I can't help but think you are right about your talk about the Holy Spirit. I went back to read John, chapter seventeen, where Jesus talks about going away. He asked God to bless those who didn't even know Him yet. The request was to keep us from the evil one."

"Right," Dan whispered as he leaned forward and she was drawn to the stars in his eyes.

She swallowed. "I started to think of all the ways God had already done that. I don't know how I got out of that marriage alive. God put Riley in jail and doors opened for me to walk through. It wasn't easy, but it could've been much harder. That brick he threw through your window was intended for me. It might've harmed one of the children, or myself. I walked away from the car accident, the children were not hurt, and you took care of them when I couldn't even call anyone.

"And then, Friday—Friday was the weirdest one of them all."

"What happened Friday?"

"It's almost too weird to share."

"Try me."

"Fine. I was painting and in my zone. When I stepped back, the picture on the page was nothing like I ever imagined. It was beautiful. I couldn't believe I had painted it. A deliveryman brought me flowers. No card." She leaned forward. "Do you know that in all my years on this earth no one has ever bought me flowers? No one. Ever."

She wiped the tears from her eyes. "But this was the kicker. They were the exact same flowers I had painted. Almost an identical match. I didn't paint roses, Dan. Roses are the traditional Valentine's Day flowers but I didn't get roses. And the colors? Even if someone had seen that painting, and went out to buy me flowers, they could never have gotten it totally right. But these were."

Dan sat back in his chair and his hands fell off the table. "Whoa. That's amazing."

"So how can I deny any more that God loves me and cares about me? Given all the evidence and realizing how bad I've messed up in my life...He's been there, waiting."

"You decided to accept that gift?"

"What did Pastor Andrew say on Sunday? That following God is telling Him you'll do whatever, wherever, whenever. That terrifies me. But He's already at work. I might as well trust Him."

Dan's face lit up with a grin. "Skye, you really mean it? You've recognized you're a sinner and need a Savior?"

"That was the easy part."

"You accept that Jesus died and rose again for your sins?"

She nodded. "And yes, I've decided I don't need to be Thomas...God's shown me Himself in plenty of ways for me to believe. It was the choice to give up my will to His that was hard. And I expect it will continue to be for a long time. He will help me with that, won't He?"

Dan nodded. His starry eyes swam. "Yeah, Skye. He'll help you. He already has. Welcome to the family."

"I'm glad you asked me to coffee, as I longed to share that with you but couldn't find a time to do so."

"Me too. We'll call it a divine appointment." He glanced at his phone. "Speaking of, I should probably head back to church to work on my message for Sunday."

She placed a hand on his arm. "Wait. How was your Valentine's Day, Dan? I thought about you and as much as I understood how, prayed for you."

A tear fell from the stars to travel down his cheek. "Yeah, well, it was rough, but you know, God showed up when I needed Him to as well. I was a traditionalist when I was younger and had even proposed on that date. Figured I wouldn't forget the date and that it would be important not to. I was right. It was...and I haven't forgotten."

"Good memory?"

"The best kind of memory, but it brings up a world of hurt too not having her by my side to celebrate and remember." He rose and zipped up his coat. "I really do need to go. And Skye, I really am thrilled with your news and look forward to seeing that painting someday."

Skye watched him go and sat to sip her chai. Her heart was heavy with Dan's brief revelation. The depth of his pain reached out to her. She finished her drink and headed back into the cold. For once in a long time, she had an image in her mind that she wanted to paint.

~*~

Once the kids were down for a nap, Skye picked up her brush and went to work. The object of her canvas was similar to the one that graced that magazine cover. Only this one portrayed grief and love lost. She stepped back from it when she was done and stared at the eyes that had penetrated her secrets and challenged her faith. Had she gotten it right?

She loved this painting, but it aroused sorrow within. Good art was supposed to evoke emotion, right? Feel what the artist felt. Empathize with the object of the picture. The only problem was she could never sell this one. She'd never do that to Dan. She couldn't expose his pain to the world. She picked up the canvas, took it to her bedroom, and placed it on top of the dresser. What else could she do with it?

~*~

Sunday morning came and she managed to get her kids to their classes and sat a little closer to the front this time. She didn't want to watch Dan on the big screens. Skye wanted to see him as he talked. She spied him down to the front on one side with the senior pastor and they were whispering to each other until the worship team kicked the service off.

It was still strange to her that people clapped in church. She noticed it before sitting in the back. She gripped the seat in front of her. The second song she at least had heard before. It was easy to pick up the tune, so she sang. The words made sense now and joy overwhelmed her. Before she realized it, she was sitting down with her notepad open on her phone.

Dan started to talk and she was drawn in...just like when they would go to coffee, or talk in the hall. It was like his words were written just for her. She found the book of James in the Bible on her phone and read along with him in the first chapter.

Suffering, perseverance, growing in faith. Dan started talking about losing his wife and she could hear his voice choke up as he talked about how difficult that struggle had been.

Her notes took shape.

When things are hard—
Hold on to faith, and recognize God loves you.
We can ask for His help and wisdom.
Good gifts sometimes come out of deep pain.
Faith may waver but God is always steady.

The worship team took to the stage and sang the song that had been playing in her car when she had her accident. This time the promise she heard was that God's love never fails.

Finally, a man she could count on.

And she was His.

~*~

Skye got the kids and tried to find Dan, but he was surrounded by people wanting to talk to him and have him pray for them. A surge of pride overcame her, and she shook her head and turned to leave. Why would she feel pride in his message? She held no personal stake in his life. It wasn't like she was in love with him or anything.

Or was she deceiving herself?

How else could she have painted him like she did the other day? She arrived home, and went to her room, closed the door, and stood in front of his picture.

I don't love you. I can't.

That tear looked real.

OK, so maybe I do. But you could never love me. You are so out of my league.

She sunk to her bed and wept. She grabbed a tissue, blew her nose, and went to get the kids some lunch. When she put them down for their naps, she went back to the painting.

I love him.

And there was nothing she could do about it.

~*~

Dan came home ravenous and exhausted. Eat or sleep? Eat then sleep? Or sleep then eat? He kicked off his shoes by the door, hung up his coat, and padded to the kitchen. He opened the fridge and frowned. He pulled out a plastic container of leftovers and popped it in the microwave. He'd never rest well if his stomach was pitching a fit.

He sat at the table and ate a few bites. Memories flooded his mind of the moments when he came home on a Sunday like this to a warm meal, fresh-baked apple pie, and the lavish praises of his wife who would talk to him about his message and what she got from it. They would discuss. Debate even. And for a short time, he imagined he was as good as any of the great preachers out there.

He wondered what Skye had thought. Maybe it was better not to know.

His phone beeped indicating a text message.

Great job this morning.

Skye. He texted back. *Thanks. Did it help?*

Yes.

Good. That's what I needed to hear.

Needed? You OK?

Dan looked at the screen. He didn't dare get that honest with her. *Yeah, just tired. Gonna take a nap.*

Rest well. Kids are napping too.

Will you paint?

Not today. Might take a nap myself for a change.

He closed his eyes…longing shot through him. A shared wall was all that separated him from a cure for his loneliness. But he wouldn't cross that line. He couldn't.

Rest well.

He put his dishes in the sink and dragged his weary body down the hall. Defeated by buried dreams and forlorn desires, he collapsed into bed, praying that sleep would rescue him.

~*~

He could've stayed home Monday morning. When he was married, he usually did. But the empty rooms of his apartment closed in on him and he needed to escape. He took his guitar with him.

Before he left though, he scraped the frost off Skye's car while his warmed up. At least that would be one less thing for her to worry about.

Once at the office, he dropped off his things, tuned his guitar, and headed to the sanctuary stage. He turned on only enough light so he wouldn't trip over anything. He found a stool and sat down, strapped on his guitar and let the music flow. He was so wrapped up he didn't notice when the lights outside the room turned on. It was just him, his guitar, and God.

Lord, I want what I can't have. It'd been one thing to go into ministry with Sharon as they had prepared together. But to bring any woman into this was cruel and a horrible way to start a marriage, wasn't it? He wasn't even dating someone, but he was thinking marriage. How twisted was that? Only, he'd been celibate for over a year and he missed the physical intimacy of marriage as much as he missed the friendship. Someone always in his corner. Someone who lifted him up when ministry got tough, and the attacks came.

He wasn't even dating anyone, but he couldn't even consider the option with the end result he desired. He didn't want to risk hurting someone just to 'try them out.'"

It's not your choice.

The chord he strummed was off. He paused his fingers. He kept forgetting that it wasn't all his choice. Any woman he desired had a choice as well. He definitely wouldn't let her go into a possible marriage without understanding how hard it was. Sure, he wasn't a soldier, police officer, or firefighter, but he still faced slings, and pointy arrows from well-intentioned, but at times, fire-breathing dragons.

He loved the church. He loved *this* church. Too often people forgot that he was human too. That he made mistakes. He was far from perfect. Attacks cut deep. His internal calendar was littered with scars and broken moments, where he wondered why he even stayed in this type of work.

He was part of a great church. He worked with wonderful staff and they had fun in the office. They laughed and cried together over the joys and hurts of the larger church family. The hurts sometimes outweighed the joys...at least as far as they affected his emotions.

A shadow made its way down the center aisle. As he came in to the light, he mounted the stairs to the stage and pulled up a stool.

"You did well yesterday," Andrew said.

"Thanks."

"What's got you gloomy...other than it's Monday?"

Dan gave a half grin. "Mondays aren't the problem."

"What is?"

"Me. I'm the problem."

"Care to explain?"

"I'm ready. I am finally ready to fall in love again. But I'm scared."

"What's scaring you?"

"Asking any woman to walk this path with me. You understand how hard it can be."

Andrew nodded. "You didn't know me when I was younger. I was already a pastor when I met Jennifer and fell in love. I was also too naïve to realize how challenging the journey would be. Neither of us had a clue. But here we are, twenty-two years later and still going strong, if not stronger, than we were then."

"Yeah, but I do know."

"So, you be honest about the challenges that life might hold and let God lead her. You've done enough marriage counseling to realize the challenges couples face go far beyond what we struggle with in ministry. Life is hard. Having a friend to walk through it with you makes it easier."

"I'm so lonely. I don't want to fill that longing for the wrong reasons."

"You haven't even started dating anyone. Don't you think you're jumping the gun here?"

"Date or no date, my heart doesn't differentiate."

"You're in love?"

"Yeah."

"How long have you known her?"

"Seven weeks."

"Skye?"

"Yeah. I didn't even fully realize it until she shared with me that she had come to faith. It was like the last piece of the puzzle fell into place. I was already attracted to her…but a baby Christian?"

"Have you told her how you feel?"

Dan shook his head. "I've not said anything."

"Court her."

"In this fishbowl?"

"You can be discreet, but why do you need to hide?"

"There might be more like Amy out there."

"Maybe, but you've not shown them any interest so I wouldn't worry about them."

"Until rumors start flying."

"Keep your nose clean and let them fly. They won't stick."

"Seriously? You're OK with me dating?"

"I've been waiting a long time for you to be ready. Sharon wouldn't want you to walk this path alone and I seriously don't think God does either." Andrew pulled out his phone. "How about dinner at our place later this week? Bring Skye and her kids. I would like to get to know the woman who unwittingly holds your heart."

"Are you sure about that?"

"Yeah, my daughter Anna might even be willing to help entertain the kids so we can have adult conversation…and if Skye ever needed someone to talk to about the challenges of ministry, Jennifer would be a great friend for her to have."

Dan took the guitar strap off and lowered the body of the guitar to the floor. "Thanks. Thanks for pushing, for understanding, and for being a friend."

"And for beating your pants off in racquetball. I look forward to doing it again."

"Thursday?"

"Sure, I'll reserve a court."

"Thanks." Dan slid off the stool and the two men walked out of the sanctuary together. Dan put the guitar away and opened his laptop. There was plenty of work to do and his first appointment was in an hour.

Skye. Who would've thought he'd fall for someone like her? Fuzzy pink boots and all.

NINETEEN

The best portion of a good man's life is his little, nameless,
unremembered acts of kindness and of love.
William Wordsworth

Every time Skye went to her car to head to the YMCA, she had found the windows scraped clear of ice. She suspected Dan but had no proof. It was a blessing since she was on the short side of things, scraping the front window was especially a pain. Letting the car run while she sat inside freezing burned up fuel she could barely afford.

But the flowers? Would her hunky neighbor do something like that?

Her painting was going well and her agent promised her that the work was good and the Christian publishing house was already setting up a line of cards with her name on them. It was exposure on a new level. But card buying wasn't what it used to be with so much online communication. How many people were really going to shell out the money for a card with quality art?

She submitted a Christmas series design this week, which had been eagerly accepted.

Now if only her bank account reflected these sales. Didn't she get some money up front? Where were those contracts? She had a sick feeling about it all. But who could help her figure it out? She looked up at the wall where her favorite canvas hung.

Dan. He might know. She picked up her phone

and texted him.

Do you know an attorney?

What kind?

To help me with this contract stuff.

Got it. Let me check on it and I'll get back to you.

Thanks.

Glad to help.

Within ten minutes, her phone beeped.

Roberto Rodriguez followed by a phone number.

She stared at her phone. Dare she call? She needed the truth. She dialed the number and set up the appointment.

After she hung up the phone, it rang. Caller ID indicated it was Dan again.

"Hi."

"Hey, um, Pastor Andrew and his wife Jennifer are interested in getting acquainted with you and want you to come over Friday night."

"I'd need to get a sitter."

"No. They want us to bring the kids too."

"Wait. Us?"

"Yes. Us."

"I'm confused."

He sighed. "Andrew knows we're neighbors and I've mentioned you to him. They want to meet you."

"Is this a date?"

Silence. "What if it was?"

"But I thought...?"

"What?"

"That you weren't interested in, um, dating."

"Well, things changed."

Skye wasn't sure what to say to that. Dan was interested in her as more than a neighbor and friend? She sat down, her hand placed over her heart. This can't be happening, can it? Surely she was imagining things.

"Skye, I like you and I care about you and your kids. Andrew and Jennifer want to get to know you too. No expectations."

"OK. We'll go. What time?" She jotted down the details.

"Thanks, Skye. Jennifer is a sweet woman. I think you'll like her."

"It'll be good to get out and meet some new people."

"Are we OK?"

"Yeah, we are. See ya later, Dan." Skye hung up and rose to fold the clothes on the bed. Every time she looked up she saw Dan's face. Were they OK? Yeah. She would take any time she could get with this remarkable man. He'd taught her so much. He wasn't interested in her in any other way than a friend. What did he mean by "things changed?" He wasn't interested in her romantically, was he? Nah, any good man would never want tainted goods like her.

~*~

Friday night came and there was a knock on the door. She opened it to find Dan standing there in his jacket and gloves. "Hey, I thought maybe we could ride in one car?"

"You want to do what?" She was puzzled.

"If it's not OK, that's fine."

"Doesn't that break some rule for you though?"

"It's not a rule, but a principle I try to follow to avoid me falling into temptation."

"And tonight is different how?"

"We have two little chaperones and, well, it's just different." Dan's face grew pink.

Skye tilted her head to consider him. "Fine. Did you want to drive? Since you know the way?"

"Sure." Dan ushered the kids out while she grabbed her phone and keys and followed. She came outside to once again find her car cleared off.

Dan opened the door for her and got the kids in the backseat while she at least started the engine to get it warmed up. He slid into the front seat as if he belonged there. She wasn't sure if she liked that or not.

Or if it was wishful thinking. What woman wouldn't want a man like that even pretending to be a husband and treating her like a treasure? Dreams didn't match reality in her world though.

"Did you get a hold of Roberto?"

"Yeah. I meet with him Monday after my class."

"He's a great guy. His wife Stephanie attends our Mother of Preschooler's group. Might be something you'd want to check out one of these days."

"It's Friday mornings and I'm not sure I want to give up my class for that."

"Something to think about."

"Yeah." As she didn't have enough to think about already.

They arrived at the house and Dan came around to open her car door first before helping her with the kids in the back seat. He hefted Meghan in his arms and led her and Quinn up the walk stepping behind her as he rang the bell.

A plump woman opened the door. "You must be Skye and these must be your children, Quinn and Meghan. Come in." She motioned to Dan. "You too."

Skye shepherded the kids in and Jennifer helped

the kids off with their coats as Dan took Skye's to hang it up in a hall closet.

Andrew came over with a teenage girl. "Kids, this is Anna and she's going to take you down to the play room for some fun while us adults visit."

The kids looked to Skye who gave them a nod. "Have fun. I'll be right up here if you need me." Soon the children were out of sight.

"Come sit down while I get the food on the table. There's a kid-friendly meal downstairs for the children." Jennifer led the way to the kitchen and pointed to spots for both Skye and Dan to sit.

"Are you sure there isn't anything I can do to help?" Skye asked. Dan held out the chair for her and pushed it in as she sat and went around to his own, across from hers.

"No, but thank you for asking."

"This is her thing," Andrew pulled out his own chair. "She loves to have company over and prepare a special meal."

The food was quickly on the table and Jennifer sat and stretched a hand toward Skye and another toward Dan. Andrew did likewise. "We like to hold hands when we pray at the table," she explained. All heads bowed as Andrew said a prayer over the meal.

The plates were passed around the table. Egg noodles with beef stroganoff made with tender meat. A salad with walnuts and pomegranate seeds and fresh baked bread as well as asparagus. How long had it been since she had eaten a meal like this?

How about never?

"Dan tells me you're an artist." Andrew broke the silence.

Once she finished chewing, she nodded. "Yes. I

paint, mostly acrylics, sometimes oils, or watercolor. I like to vary my mediums."

"And you got a contract with a Christian distributer?" Andrew grabbed for his glass of water.

Skye swallowed. "I'm having that looked over on Monday."

"I saw the painting you did that looked like Dan. Did he sit for that?" Jennifer asked.

"No, he didn't. I had no intention of painting him, it just sort of happened."

"But you got his eyes right," Jennifer commented.

"I hadn't even registered how unique they were." Skye stabbed her salad with a fork.

"Sounds like the Holy Spirit was working through you. It was a beautiful painting. You sold the original?" Andrew inquired.

"Yeah. It sold at a show in New York City. It was my first big sale."

"Congratulations," Jennifer offered. "That must have felt wonderful."

"It was mind-blowing and totally unexpected. I haven't gotten the check yet though, so it's still kind of hard to believe."

"So how did you and Dan meet?" Jennifer asked.

"I moved in next door," Dan offered.

"And my son decided to play hide and seek in his apartment." She glanced at Dan and saw his wink.

"That's obviously not the whole story," Andrew said.

"No. It kind of evolved from there. Dan even attended a Zumba class I taught."

Jennifer giggled. "Really, Dan? Mr. Macho Man strutting his stuff for the ladies? I bet attendance soared after that."

Dan's cheeks grew pink.

"Well, he only attended once, but some of the women have asked me when he'll return." Skye couldn't help but grin at Dan's discomfort.

"I would have returned if I hadn't bruised some ribs and twisted my knee skiing." Dan shoveled more food in his mouth.

"I was so afraid he had gotten seriously hurt on that run. One of his skis broke and he did a somersault. The silly man was laughing by the time I got to him." Skye took a bite of the main dish. "Oh, Jennifer, this is amazing. I've never tasted anything like this."

"Thank you."

"What do you think of Orchard Hill Church?" Andrew asked.

"Seriously?"

"Yeah. It's always good to hear first impressions."

"Well. I found everyone friendly. I was terrified to come. I don't remember being in church more than a handful of times in my life. It wasn't part of my upbringing. The kids instantly loved the Sunday School. I didn't know any of the songs, but I thought the music was good. I wasn't sure what to expect about anything but the message challenged me. They have every week."

"Anything you didn't like?" Andrew asked.

"Well, there was that one Sunday, but that's been resolved."

Andrew nodded. "Anything other than that?"

"Not that I can think off. Nothing that would keep me from returning."

"Why do you keep coming back?" Jennifer asked.

Skye set down her fork and took a sip of water. "I keep asking myself that same question."

"And the answer?"

"I…" *wanted an excuse to see Dan.* "I'm not sure. Just seemed like a good thing to do."

"Well, I'm glad you've been coming. What'd you think of Dan's preaching last Sunday?" Jennifer asked.

Dan's eyebrow rose as she glanced at him.

"I thought he did a great job. It was kind of like when we've had coffee, except there were five hundred people sitting across the table with me listening to him."

"Coffee? You two have been having coffee together?" Andrew asked.

"Um, yeah. Seemed a safe way to have conversation without raising expectations or gossip." Dan frowned.

"Dan's been very careful to stick to his 'principles.' Even when he watched my kids he only came as I was leaving and left right when I got home."

Jennifer's eyes widened as she looked at Dan. "You watched her kids? How did I miss this?"

"He was still on leave, hon," Andrew said. The corner of his lip quivered.

"How did he do?" Jennifer looked at her.

"Quinn and Meghan adore him. They are praying at meal times and bedtime now. They keep asking when they'll get to spend time with Mr. Dan again."

"Amazing. Was that hard, Dan?" Jennifer asked.

"Given that Sharon and I weren't able to have kids?" Dan frowned.

Jennifer nodded.

"I won't lie and say that I didn't ache inside for our losses. I was too busy to worry about it though as the kids got sick. I have a whole new respect for moms, especially single ones."

"He definitely got the royal package with the flu, washing bedding, and me getting stuck in New York City for an extra day due to a blizzard. He even got them to church." Skye gave Dan a reassuring smile.

The meal was over and Dan and Andrew took over cleaning up the kitchen while Jennifer took Skye to the living room. One wall was decorated with family photos and another had a Kincade print with beautiful matting and a frame. Someday her paintings might grace homes like this.

"So Skye. I heard you recently crossed that bridge of faith."

"It was one of those suspension ones and Dan was holding it steady for me while I asked all manner of questions."

"On firmer ground now?"

Skye nodded. "I'm not clear why I'm here though."

"Aren't you?"

"Not really. Listen, I like Dan. A lot. He's the best man I've ever met. Generous, kind, thoughtful…"

"Attractive," Jennifer added.

"Obviously. He's not in the market for a girlfriend and even if he were, there are many women better than me. I'm a divorced single woman whose background is sketchy to say the least."

"So says the artist with a critical eye. You see beauty in everyone and everything else but not in yourself?"

"Dan and I have talked. I'm struggling to understand God's goodness and love. It's all so new. But I'm no idiot. I'm not the kind of woman a pastor would date, much less marry."

"What do you think disqualifies you?"

"My history, my looks, my kids, my art…"

"Scripture says that you are a new creation when you accept Christ. If God forgives your past why wouldn't Dan?"

"He doesn't even know it all."

"Even if he did, I don't think it would matter. And what about your looks? You are an attractive woman."

"I don't dress like other people do."

"True. You have your own unique style that suits you. Why do you want to be like everyone else anyway?"

"I'm divorced."

"Doesn't that count under your history?"

"I have two kids."

"Who are adorable," Jennifer countered.

"I don't know that I could ever trust a man enough to marry him."

"Not even Dan?"

"He might be the exception." Skye sighed.

~*~

"She's bright and not afraid to tweak your nose. I like her." Andrew was washing the dishes as Dan dried them.

"There's still so much I don't know about her."

"So start finding out."

"You really think I should seriously court her?"

"Court, date, have coffee, play…yes. I think she's good for you. I don't know of any other woman, even Sharon, who could make you blush."

Dan frowned as he stacked the dried plates in the cupboard. Date Skye? Seriously consider her as a wife? Did he dare? Was he even ready? Was she?

"But how will people at church react? I mean, after the Amy debacle that's made me a little more gun-shy to be seen around any woman."

"Be discreet, but don't hide either. Stick to your principles as much as you can...except you do need to spend more time with her, without the kids."

"But some time with them all as well, I think. I'm not just courting her as a possible wife, but I would be their step-father. I don't want to mess with them. I think they've been hurt by their father in ways Skye doesn't even realize."

"Pray as you go and let God lead you. Be her friend first and let the rest come naturally."

Dan threw his towel down. "Says the man who can take his wife to bed tonight. I've been alone way too long. Letting the 'rest come naturally' could be a recipe for disaster, compromise, or both."

Andrew wiped down the sink and wrung out the rag. Leaning against the counter he stared at Dan. "There are good reasons for short engagements."

Dan nodded. "We've had our share of them, haven't we?"

Andy nodded. "Yes, and it's been a joy to see those couples grow together and serve. There are no guarantees, Dan. You understand that. Life is tough. If you don't think you could live your life without her, don't waste your time thinking about it and act. I'm not telling you to rush things, but don't expect everything has to be perfect before she becomes your wife. Even though you've been married before this is a whole new ballgame. New rules, new swings at bat. Don't waste the opportunity."

Dan nodded.

Drew patted him on the back. "Let's go join the

ladies."

~*~

The night finally ended and two sleepy kids were loaded into the car.

"I had a good time tonight, Dan. Thanks for inviting me."

"I'm glad. Sounds like the kids had fun too. Anna said she'd be willing to babysit. She's old enough to drive, which is a bonus."

"I don't have much need for a sitter."

"I'm hoping to change that."

Dan helped her into the house, each carrying one limp child. He helped her put them to bed and hung up their coats. She walked him to the door.

"Thanks again, Dan."

"It was fun. I like spending time with you," Skye said.

"Even skiing?"

"Yup. Even skiing. You're a sweet man and I have no idea why you would ever even look twice at your eccentric neighbor." She reached up on her tip toes and kissed his cheek. "But I'm glad you did. Good-night, Dan."

"Night, Skye. Sweet dreams." *I know I'll be having some.* Dan walked across the hall to his apartment and let himself in. The cold, empty space was in stark contrast to the warmth and color of Skye's apartment. But that wasn't due to her paintings. It was her.

He grinned. She'd kissed his cheek. It was a start.

TWENTY

This is awkward. Not you're awkward, but cause
we're...I'm awkward. You're gorgeous.
Wait, what?
Anna – "Frozen"

Monday morning Skye walked into the law offices and shivered. It really had been the most brutal winter as far as temperatures went. She was grateful her heat was included in her rent. And once again, her car windows were scraped clean. She was beginning to suspect her handsome neighbor, who dared to grill brats on the grill Sunday afternoon and offered her and the kids some. He also made hot dogs, which the kids eagerly devoured. The man was nuts.

"Skye O'Connell?" the receptionist asked.

"Yes."

"Mr. Rodriguez is waiting to see you, come this way."

She followed the professionally dressed woman down the hall to an office and was motioned in.

"Miss O'Connell, would you like some coffee?"

"Yes, thank you. That would be welcome."

Roberto stood and walked around his desk to greet her. "Welcome. Dan said you had some contract concerns?"

Before she could answer, the door opened and the receptionist handed them each a cup of coffee. Skye sat hers on a small table next to her chair as she sat. Mr. Rodriguez sat in the adjacent one.

"Mr. Rodriguez—"

"Roberto or Robbie is fine."

"Roberto, I think I might have gotten into some trouble when I signed up with an agent out of New York to represent my art."

"Do you have the contract?"

She pulled out the papers from her purse. "I finally got them in the mail, but can't make heads or tails of any of it."

"Do you mind if I look them over?"

"Please, go ahead."

Roberto leaned back in his chair and started scanning the documents. She saw his brow wrinkle as he concentrated and a frown marred his attractive face. A photo on the desk showed him with his wife and son. A family man. And from what Dan told her, an honorable one.

The wait seemed interminable. Finally, Roberto set the papers down. "Well, do you want the bad news or the good news first?"

"I don't care. Tell me what I've done wrong and how to fix it."

"You didn't do anything wrong. This contract is ripping you off. When you sell to someone else, they get a cut of the sale, then your agent gets a cut, and then you are paid out of what is left. It's just the way that kind of business works. However, this agent has taken a far larger cut than what is normal. Because you signed that deal in New York with that publishing company, the money goes through her first. They don't have a high markup to begin with, and you'll have to sell a lot of cards and calendars to make some significant dough. Not that you couldn't do it. Anything is possible. In my opinion, however, your agent is getting more than her fair share."

"Was that the good news or the bad news?"

"The bad. The good news is that this contract is non-negotiable for a year. After that, you can terminate it. Now for anything she sells within that year, the terms apply even years later. Any new contracts after that, she doesn't get a cut. At that point, you can find another agent or maybe you won't even need one. Here's the other piece of good news. This contract is not exclusive. You can't sell through another agent, but there is no clause in there forbidding you to find your own contracts for selling your work. She might argue that you need to go through her, but she only is paid when she finds and negotiates a contract on your behalf. If you find other buyers, you can sell to them directly without going through her. I'm surprised they allowed that loophole."

Skye leaned back in her chair. "So for now, I'm kind of stuck, and the windfall I had hoped for is probably not going to come my way."

"I'm sorry."

"What do I owe you for your time?"

"Nothing. You're not signing a contract to retain me, so no charge. If you need further advice on things like these and want me to advise you, give me a call. I'd be delighted to help." Robbie rose and handed her back the papers. "It was a pleasure to meet you, Miss O'Connell."

"Skye, please."

"Skye."

"And thank you." She took the papers, tied her coat tight, and headed back into the cold. She drove home and tried hard to warm up. She collapsed on her bed and gazed at the picture of Dan. Would she ever tire of it? She longed to call him, but he was at work. She picked up her phone and texted instead.

Met with Mr. Rodriguez

How'd it go?

He was nice. News was not good.

How are you?

Sad. Defeated.

Don't beat yourself up.

Too late, already sporting bruises.

I'm sorry.

Not your fault.

She didn't hear from him again but assumed Dan was busy at work. She gazed up at his image on the wall and recalled the kiss she'd given him Friday night. She couldn't believe her boldness in doing that, but she valued his friendship and craved time with him. The kiss left her wanting more.

Wasn't it wrong though to desire someone *that* way? Or was that temptation? Was temptation sin or the invitation?

So many things she still did not understand about this new faith.

~*~

Wednesday morning Dan sat in his usual space at the restaurant, with his usual cup of coffee and his usual breakfast. How many years had he been in the habit of meeting with these men?

Tony sat next to him and Simon and Nick were across the table.

Simon spoke of his wife's recent illness and health struggles. Nick was able to report that his wife's chronic health issues had been in remission and she even managed to attend church the previous Sunday. The first time in a long time for them to be able to worship together. Tony was struggling through sleepless nights with a new baby plus the twins.

"So Dan, guess we saved the best for last, huh? How are things in your world?" Tony elbowed him.

"I am seriously considering dating a woman."

"Anyone we know?" Simon asked.

"My neighbor, Skye O'Connell."

"The one with the pink, fuzzy boots?" Nick grinned as he raised his eyebrows.

"One and the same."

"Wow. Are you really ready for this step? What makes you think she's worth it?" Simon asked.

"I like her. She challenges me. She's come to faith in Christ. I can't stop thinking about her."

"You're in love? So soon?" Nick asked.

"I'm not sure, but I want to explore that possibility." Dan sighed. "Is it so far-fetched? I'm tired of being alone. It's not about replacing Sharon, but about finding a partner to walk this journey with."

Tony grinned. "Sounds like love to me, and we will pray that if this is God's plan for you, that you will succeed."

"Thanks, guys. I don't think winning her hand will be an easy task."

"You need a challenge," Nick said.

Dan grinned. "Maybe so."

~*~

The next morning Dan was back at the YMCA lifting weights at the bench press. A sweet red-head appeared above him. "Need a spotter?"

"Always a welcome sight." He did a few more presses and sat up. "Thanks."

"My turn?" Skye moved to take his heavier weights off and put on ones more suited for her. He towered over her petite form as she reclined on the seat and began her presses. She finished and sat up.

"Nice job. Didn't know you worked with weights."

"Not as much as I would like. It's hard to find a man who's not going to make it about more than fitness, if you get my meaning."

"Unfortunately, I do. I'm honored you trusted me."

"You've given me no cause not to."

"I am a man who still appreciates an attractive woman."

"I don't mind appreciation. At least you have control enough not to leer or make crude remarks." She wiped her forehead with the towel while he wiped down the machine.

"I would never disrespect a woman so." Dan tossed the rag into the nearby bin.

"I know. It's one of the things I like about you."

"Would you also like to get a cup of coffee before you head home and I head back to work?"

She tilted her head as she considered him and a soft smile formed on her lips. "I always enjoy a cup of coffee with my favorite neighbor."

"I'll meet you there?"

"Yeah, sounds good, Dan." She took off toward the woman's locker room and Dan struggled to not watch her go as he headed in a different direction to the men's.

~*~

He arrived at the coffee shop before her and purchased her drink. She blew in on the wind, her hair kept confined under a blue hat that contrasted beautifully with her hair. She whipped it off and strands of hair filled with static blew about. She shook her head and tried to smooth it down.

"Ugh. Winter. Remind me of why I still live in Wisconsin?" She put the knit cap back on.

"Because New York City is filled with cheats and has more snow."

"True, but it is warmer."

"Well, but you wouldn't live across the hall from your irresistible neighbor." He shoved her cup across the table to her.

Her laughter rang like Christmas chimes. Light and joyful. "Well, there is that to be sure. Where would I be without Harold?"

He faked a punch to the heart. "Harold? The older man downstairs?"

"Have I pricked the pastor's pride?"

"No, but you've wounded this man's ego."

"You? You have to be the humblest man I know."

"I don't see myself that way."

"Maybe you need to look in a different mirror."

"Explain."

"You are drop dead gorgeous, but you don't act all cocky, like women should admire you. I would suspect you consider your physical beauty to be more of a burden than a blessing."

"I didn't start looking good till after I graduated high school. I think I still see myself as that pimply kid with crooked teeth. I still remember all the insults leveled at me because of my eyes."

"Your eyes are stunning and unique. Kids made fun of you?"

Dan shrugged. "Apparently, they foretold a future of sinister evil."

"Was that why you became a pastor?"

"It's probably more of why I wear glasses rather than contacts. I became a pastor because I was convinced that's what God wanted me to do."

Skye leaned back and considered him. Dan grew uneasy under scrutiny. He fidgeted with his coffee mug.

"Why did you ask me to coffee, Dan?"

His eyes shot up to look at her. He gulped. "Because I like you. You challenge me. You don't treat me as if I'm anything special, but you also don't try to manipulate me to get something you want."

"What would I want from you?" She leaned forward, both hands around her cup.

"Attention. A date. Favors. Or more."

"As a pastor, you've had women coming on to you?"

"Not everyone always realizes I'm a pastor. I don't look like one, do I?"

"No. You don't act like one either."

"What do you mean by that?"

"You don't act high and mighty, better than those around you and you've never looked down your nose at me, but treated me as someone God cared about."

"Because you are."

"You don't try to prove yourself right. You care."

"I do care. And since I've gotten to know you over the past two months, I've come to like you more and more."

"Is that why you scrape my car windows? Invite me to coffee?"

"Yeah. Is that so bad?"

"Did you send me flowers?"

He nodded. "I missed having someone to love and knew you didn't have anyone either. I didn't expect you to figure it out."

"But don't you see? God keeps doing strange things when you're around. The only way that painting could have happened to mirror those flowers was because of Him. How could He do that without someone tuned into His Holy Spirit?"

"I love how eagerly you seek answers and grow in your faith."

"I have a million questions."

"I doubt I have that many answers."

"I love that about you. You don't pretend to have it all together, but you respect the process."

"Skye. I like you. A lot. I'm attracted to you. I've even come to like those silly pink boots. Would you be willing to explore whatever is between us?"

"What is between us? I'm not looking for a husband."

"I wasn't initially looking for a wife. I know many women, Skye, but none of them intrigue me like you do. I don't feel a spark with any of them like I do with you."

"I don't know, Dan. I have a rough background. I'm not the kind of girl a man like you should even look at twice."

"A man like me?"

"Pure. A pastor. A role-model."

"What are you saying?"

"A pastor doesn't spend time with a woman like

me."

"Who says? What makes you think that your past is an automatic deal-breaker for me?"

"It's not you, per se. It's church. Christians."

"Listen, Skye. You can make excuses if you want, but let me assure you of this. I don't live my life to please the church or other Christians. I live it to please God."

"But you have these rules…"

"Principles. Guidelines. Because, Skye, I am still a man who can be very much tempted by a beautiful woman. I set some boundaries on what I will or won't do to protect myself from gossip but also to keep myself from dishonoring God…or any woman I might be with."

"And me? You've wanted to keep from dishonoring me?"

"Of course."

"Oh. So if we dated and someone got wind of my past and started hurling the truth about that wouldn't shame you and make you run?"

"Pull out your phone."

Skye pulled it out. He took it from her hand and opened her Bible application. He opened to the book of Hosea. "Read this story later. God uses people with the roughest backgrounds to tell His story. If God used the woman at the well, the woman caught in adultery, and Gomer, who was a prostitute wife of a prophet of God, to further His purposes, I suspect He can use you if He decided you and I were a team He wanted together. If that were the case, I would gladly hitch myself to that wagon." He glanced at his watch.

"I need to get going. Saturday. Could I treat you and the kids to a matinee of the movie *Frozen*?"

She took her phone back and looked up at him as he rose to his feet. "Sure."

He bent over and kissed her cheek. Then he turned and headed back to the office. Even though it was freezing outside, he was warm all over.

Had he blown it? Had he overplayed his hand with her? It seemed that every conversation took him further than he ever intended to go because she would ask such questions. Was he moving too fast?

He strode into church, grabbed his mail, and went to his office. He sat down and it dawned on him. He had a date on Saturday. She said yes.

~*~

Friday night after Skye put the kids to bed, she went to her own room and got in her flannel jammies and snuggled in. The moon shone in her room, shedding light on her painting. She looked at the picture. Had he really moved beyond his grief to see her as more than a neighbor and friend?

A shiver caused her to wrap her blankets tighter around her. It wasn't the cold causing it, it was a wish that she wasn't alone anymore, especially during the dark, cold, lonely nights.

She'd see him tomorrow. The kids were excited about going to the movie. They were young, and she'd never taken them to the theater. Not that it was really in her budget to do that. Nor would it be any time soon.

But what was it like for Dan's wife to be loved so much? Was it ever possible that a man, especially that man, could really love her like that? Enough to overlook her past? Even reading the Scripture he suggested, well, it seemed so unreal. Thankfully, she wasn't a prostitute, nor had she ever been one. Not that anyone cared. Riley hadn't been her only partner...just the only one she married.

Regrets didn't help though, did they? Could she regret a marriage that gave her such beautiful children? She only wished...well, if wishes were fishes she'd be drowning in the ocean. She threw back the blankets and grabbed her robe. She padded to the living room and turned on a light near a blank canvas set up for tomorrow. She pulled out her brushes and paints and went to work. A lonely heart needed help expressing itself.

~*~

The phone rang, awakening her from the spot she collapsed to on the sofa. It had been where Dan slept when he stayed with the children. She imagined snuggling up to him. Wanted. Loved. The kids were playing on the floor, but watched her stretch and answer the phone.

"'ello?" her scratchy voice answered.

"Good morning. I was wondering if you and the kids would like to join me for some special pancakes...I was thinking of adding chocolate chips to the mix. Think they would like that?" The timbre of his voice resonated in her heart.

"Kids." She pulled the phone away to talk to them. "Dan wants to know if you would like some chocolate chip pancakes at his place this morning."

The kids started jumping up and down, screaming "Yes!"

Skye smiled as she spoke into the phone once

again. "Did you hear that?"

Laughter greeted her. "How soon can you get here?"

"I don't know. I probably need to scrape off my car and the journey is quite long." She couldn't help but grin at her fake excuse.

Dan laughed. "Your car windows are scraped already."

"Hmmm. Thank you. Fifteen minutes? We need to get dressed."

"Bummer. Pancakes taste much better in PJ's."

"Fine, maybe the kids can keep theirs on, but I am not coming to your house in my ratty pajamas."

"Ratty pajamas, huh?"

"Stop it."

"Stop what?"

"See ya in fifteen."

"I can hardly wait."

She hung up the phone and strode to her room to grab some clothes before locking herself in the bathroom to freshen up. Dan confused her. The consummate gentleman was showing interest in her and, flirting? He didn't do things like that unless it was intentional. She liked this side of her neighbor. He was definitely learning how to have some fun in life.

Maybe it was now her turn to try that fun thing too.

TWENTY-ONE

Love is our true destiny.
We do not find the meaning of life by ourselves alone —
we find it with another.
Thomas Merton

Dan hefted Meghan in his arms as they traversed the busy parking lot at the theater. Skye held Quinn's hand and kept up with him. Dan paid for the tickets and stood in line for popcorn and soda. Not that the kids could really eat much after stuffing themselves with chocolate chip pancakes earlier. He wished Skye would have felt free enough to come to breakfast in her pajamas as well, but even he had changed into his jeans before they arrived.

"Dan?" Meghan asked as she settled into a chair in the theater.

"Yeah?" He inclined his head her way.

"You gonna be my daddy?"

Dan's eyes shot to Skye's. She was biting her lip. "You already have a daddy, sweetheart. No one can really take his place. Why do you ask?"

"Because I don't like my daddy. He's not nice to Mommy or us."

"You've mentioned that before, but he's not around right now," Dan said.

Skye nodded in confirmation.

"He always comes back," Meghan complained.

"Maybe you need to pray for him. I suspect he doesn't know Jesus, does he?"

Quinn piped up, "He uses His name a lot, but I think that's a bad thing."

Dan nodded and let out a deep breath. "Possibly. Pray for him. Pray that he learns to love God and can be a better daddy."

"But he'd live with Mommy again, right? I don't want that. We like you better." Meghan snuggled up to him and his heart melted.

"No one can predict the future. Pray that God gets a hold of his heart, and trust that God loves you and your mommy very much."

"And you love us too." Quinn grinned and nodded, full of confidence in his statement.

"Absolutely." Dan watched Skye blush as he caught her gaze.

"Popcorn?" She offered the kids as the lights dimmed.

~*~

When the movie finished, Dan helped the kids pick up all their containers to toss. He escorted them out to the bathrooms and to the car for home.

"Thank you for taking us," Skye shyly offered.

"My pleasure."

Meghan twirled like a princess as Quinn reached to pick his nose.

"Stop that, Quinn," Skye admonished.

"But Christoff said that's what men do," Quinn protested.

Dan chuckled but stopped when Skye shot a reproving glance his way. He sent a wink to Quinn.

Both kids drifted to sleep in the car. Dan carried Quinn up as Skye struggled to manage Meghan. He placed Quinn in bed, pulled off his shoes and coat, and tucked the little boy under the covers. He stood by as Skye finished with Meghan. They walked out of the room together and Dan assisted Skye in getting her coat off. Touching her briefly sent shockwaves to his soul. He pulled back and glanced away to see a fresh canvas painted with a close up of an eye.

His eye if he wasn't mistaken.

He walked over to it as if in a daze. He studied the intricacies of the painting, the detail, and the emotion it conveyed. Shaking his head, he continued to stare. "How…?"

Skye came to stand beside him. She shrugged. "I don't know. Your eyes are fascinating."

"But it's like you're exposing my soul."

Silence hung between them. He wasn't sure how he felt about the painting. Naked. The sorrow and pain that he thought he'd buried, emerged full force as he gazed at the image before him. Skye's gentle hand wiped away an excaping tear.

"I didn't paint it to hurt you."

He shook his head and stepped away. "Yeah…but it did anyway." He hesitated a moment and reached for her hand, taking it in his. His thumb drew a small circle inside her wrist. He frowned but met her silvery eyes, softened with grief over the pain she'd unintentionally caused. "I guess it's a testament to how good you really are." He dropped her hand and walked out the door to his own apartment.

Tossing his coat aside, he slumped down in his favorite chair. A dark shadow hovered over his soul and he didn't know how to shake it. Had Sharon ever understood him the way the artist across the hall did? All his carefully constructed defenses crumbled at the image she had captured with a brush, paint, and her imagination. *God, how does she worm her way into my very soul like that? And what does it mean that she affects me so deeply? I long for her—to be with her, to be a part of her days and yes, even her nights. Lord, help me.*

He slumped over in silent petition to the King for the agony in his soul. He finished, and finally wandered to the kitchen to pull out a can from the cupboard. Is this what he was reduced to? Canned soup for dinner? He shook his head and put the can back. He grabbed some brats out of the freezer and threw them in the microwave to thaw. Putting his coat back on, he headed to the porch and started up his grill. The heat was welcome. He put the lid down as the unit heated up inside. Nothing like the comfort of a good ol' German bratwurst, as his father used to say.

Once the brats were cooking on the grill, he went inside to slice an onion and thaw some frozen buns he kept on hand. The rest he tossed in the fridge. He grabbed a bag of potato chips off the top of the fridge and opened it. Summer, football games, picnics...so many memories wrapped up in food.

He chuckled as he pulled the brats off the grill. It was the one food Sharon never enjoyed, so he only made them when she was gone. Now, he could have them whenever he wanted. And for all that, he still couldn't eat apple pie. He closed up the grill, cutting off the fuel so that it would burn out quickly. He sat down at the table longing for a good German lager, but he gave up drinking any alcohol when he went into ministry, not wanting to risk being an unintentional stumbling block to anyone. Still, he could sure go for one right now. Ah, those lovely "principles" that Skye chided him for. He poured a glass of ice water and sat down to eat, thankful for food, a warm place to live and yes, even for a spunky red-head next door who saw too deeply into his soul.

He'd need to do something about her…

~*~

Skye stared at the painting after Dan left. Her own tears flowed freely. What good was art if it hurt someone? Or was Dan correct and she was so good that her paintings brought out deep emotions in the person viewing it?

A text came to her phone later that evening.

Can I take you out to dinner Friday night?

Dan. He wanted to actually date her? How long had it been since anyone had shown her any kind of attention like that? Too long. Her fingers got busy.

Yes. I would like that.

6:30 OK?

That will be fine.

Wonderful. Keep painting.

Keep painting? He would encourage her that way after the way she hurt him? She pulled the offending canvas off its stand and took it to her room. She placed it on the wall next to the other one of Dan. The one she'd never shown anyone. Not all art needed to be sold, did it?

She still had bills to pay though. Not selling her art meant not paying rent. Or having gas for her car. *Lord, what am I to do?*

~*~

Sunday morning rose bright, clear, and bitterly

cold. She debated even trying to go to church. She longed be there though. To worship, to learn, to perhaps catch a glimpse of Dan in his element. She really did have it bad for this man.

The week dragged on. She caught glimpses of Dan at the YMCA, but he either didn't see her or was keeping his distance. She longed to sit down for a cup of coffee. See how he was doing. How badly had she wounded him?

She finally dragged out her phone. *I'm such a chicken*, she chided herself.

How is your week going?

His response was an hour later, making her wonder if he was angry with her.

Busy. Lots of meetings and counseling appointments. Looking forward to Friday night.

Me too.

Painting lots?

Some. Nothing spectacular.

Don't be so critical. You're an inspired artist.

Not if it hurts people.

Not all pain is bad, Skye. Sometimes we need to experience it to move past it.

I'm sorry I hurt you.

Forgiven, but you really have nothing to apologize for. Gotta go. Another appointment. Have a great afternoon.

You too.

She set the phone aside and headed back to her easel. Abandoning her paints, she decided to attempt something in charcoal. It wasn't a medium she used often, but today seemed a good day to play with something different. The bleak winter outside called for expression on paper.

~*~

Friday was finally here and Dan dressed in a suit, forgoing the tie. He looked in the mirror, trying to see into his own eyes. Not an easy thing to do. What would Skye see in them tonight? Attraction? Desire...perhaps love?

What did he want her to see? He glanced away afraid of the answer. She obviously picked up on strong emotions and his moods better than even he did. The last thing he wanted to do was scare her off. He chuckled at the remembrance of how Andrew told him how Skye stood up to Amy. Scaring this petite spitfire would be the least of his worries. Letting temptation and desire overrule common sense? Now that was a legitimate concern. In many ways, he'd been a widower for far too long.

He hoped to rectify that soon.

He knocked on her door at six-thirty sharp and when she opened it he was stunned at the beauty before him. She had accentuated her sapphire blue dress with understated silver jewelry. A strand of twisted silver with no pendant and simple silver hoop earrings peeked out from her hair. He noticed a few weeks back that she stopped wearing the silver stud on her eyebrow and the small hoop on her lip. The effect was to give her a soft and almost exotic look rather than that of a...well, he couldn't think of the word and it wasn't worth the effort.

"Dan?"

He shook his head. "I'm sorry. You stunned me. You look lovely, Skye."

"I'm not too dressed up?"

"No. Perfect. We're going to DeLuca's Cucina. A

friend from church owns the place. You do like Italian, right?"

"Who doesn't?" She gave him a soft smile as he helped her with her coat. She pulled on her gloves and he escorted her down the stairs and out the door of the apartment complex into the frigid cold. "Where are the kids tonight?"

"My mom is having a sleepover at her house. She doesn't do that often but when I mentioned our evening out, well she was more than thrilled to take them."

Dan winked. "She likes me."

"Yeah, well, so does her daughter. You've definitely gone out of your way to prove yourself the hero time and again."

"I wasn't trying to prove anything."

"I know you weren't. It's just who you are, and I'm the grateful recipient of your care. We've upended your life."

"Yes, but in the best possible way."

"You call the flu a good thing?"

"Well, OK, that was miserable, but I've gotten the flu in the past just doing my job. It could have happened some other way than spending time with your children."

"Quinn and Meghan were terribly disappointed to learn I was going to see you tonight and they were not invited."

"I'll have to make it up to them another time." Dan was grateful she wore elegant black leather boots. As much as he would have liked to see her in strappy heels, at least her legs wouldn't be too cold for the short time they were outside.

He shut the door once she was inside and came

around to his door, sliding in with ease and starting it up. "I'm sorry it won't get very warm before we get to the restaurant."

"Totally understandable given the deep freeze Wisconsin seems to be stuck in this year."

He thought he heard her teeth chatter. "We'll be warm soon enough. I requested a spot near the fireplace."

"Sounds heavenly."

Once in the restaurant, he spied Stephanie.

"Dan. How good to see you."

"Steph, I'd like for you to meet Skye. She's a close friend of mine."

Stephanie gave a broad smile. "'Bout time you developed some new friends, Dan. Skye, it is an honor to meet you. Dan performed my wedding to Roberto."

"Roberto Rodriguez?"

"Yes, you know him?"

"He's the attorney Dan referred me to."

"Yup, that's my man. Let's get you seated by that fire."

Dan held the chair out for Skye and when she was settled in, he sat in the chair adjacent.

After placing their orders, Skye leaned forward. "Are we OK, Dan? When we last talked, you were shaken up over that painting. I don't plan to sell it. If you want, you can have it. I never wanted to hurt you. When I start a painting or drawing, I just let my brushes go. I don't always know what it will be until it's done."

"We're fine. I was shocked, that's all. Seeing that painting triggered something inside me. I would say that's the mark of a great artist. Whether a painting, song, or novel, when a piece strikes a chord like that, well, isn't that what we want as creative people? To draw out the emotion, to connect with the audience? You definitely struck a nerve with me and it was unexpected and unsettling. You can sell it. Maybe others will connect with it as well. I wouldn't deny you an income."

She sipped her water, her silver eyes considering him. "OK. I'm not sure I'll sell it, but we'll see."

"I am impressed that for not having me sit as a model, how detailed and precise your art can be."

"I don't understand that either. I never used to be able to paint like that. It's like a switch was flipped a few months back and my art has gone to new levels."

"I think God has made a lot of changes in your life recently."

"And yours as well."

Dan chuckled. "A few? He's been doing a complete overhaul. Being forced off work and facing my grief and getting help in that process has been transforming. Having a feisty neighbor with two adorable kids hasn't hurt either."

"Feisty, huh?" She allowed the waitress to place the salad in front of her.

"Shall I pray?" Dan asked as he reached for her hand. Her eyes widened as he clasped it firmly and bent his head. "Heavenly Father, thank You for this food and precious time with Skye. May our time together honor You."

Skye whispered a soft "amen."

Dan nodded as he buttered his bread. "I'm glad God planted me across the hall from you."

"I'm glad too, and the kids really do adore you, Dan."

"The feeling is mutual."

"You would make a great father."

A heaviness washed over him. He chewed his food slowly, willing tears to stay at bay. He swallowed hard and followed that with a sip of water. "It had been a fond dream."

"I'm sorry." She reached and placed a hand on his arm. Electricity shot straight to his heart. She jerked her hand back. Maybe she felt it too?

"It's not your fault."

Skye frowned. "No, but I should have known better than to bring up a painful subject."

"I'm glad I can be a positive male role model for your kids."

"You are. It's one of the things that makes you an exceptional human being, Dan."

"I'm not that special."

"To the right girl you are more than that. You are extraordinary."

"Would that girl be you?" His eyes searched hers.

A soft blush highlighted her cheeks. "Maybe."

Good. He dug into the meal.

"Dan?"

"Hmm?"

"What do you want for your future?"

"Whoa. If you would have asked me that two months ago, I would have said I didn't want one. I seriously considered ditching ministry and running away. Finding some other job and startiing over. As if I could leave my pain behind."

"It would have followed you."

"Yeah, I figured that out."

"What would you have done?"

"If I couldn't be a pastor?"

"Yeah."

"That's a great question. I never really found an answer to it. I'm sure I could do some corporate administrative work, since I do much of that within the church. Or go back to school and get a degree as a counselor and get certified. I do a lot of that as well. Or perhaps teach music, give lessons. I couldn't find my heart beating faster at any of those prospects."

"I'm glad you didn't give up completely."

"Depression sucks. I never would hurt myself, but it sure made it hard to get up in the morning and get through many days. I'm grateful I had a neighbor who didn't let me stay in the hole I tried to dig."

"Yeah, well, I'm glad you've been there for me too. It's a mutual thing. Like God understood we needed each other."

"We did. In some ways I think we still do."

"Do we?" Skye quirked an eyebrow his way.

"Well, a little thing like you would have a hard time scraping the windows of your car."

She giggled. "I always managed in the past."

"But admit, it makes your life a little easier when you're not wrangling two kids as well."

"True, especially given how cold it's been."

"See? There's proof. You need me."

"Yes, you're correct. But do you need me?"

He nodded and chewed his food. "More than you know."

She tilted her head his way but didn't press him further.

After dinner, he drove her home and escorted her to her door. She unlocked it and turned to face him. "Do your principles forbid you from entering my apartment without a chaperone?"

Dan gulped. "Not when it's a girl I'm dating."

"Is that what this was? A date?"

Dan nodded.

Skye grabbed his hand and dragged him through the door, shutting it behind her. He helped her take off her coat and hung it up. He unbuttoned his own and removed it, placing it over the back of a chair.

"Coffee?" Skye offered as she stood before him.

"No, thanks. I really enjoyed tonight."

"Me too." One hand fidgeted with her silver chain.

"I feel like a gauche teenager," Dan confessed.

"Why?"

"I really want to kiss you. Would that be OK?"

Skye smiled shyly. "I would like that."

Dan put an arm around her pulling her close. His other hand came up to caress her cheek. He bent his head and she rose on her tiptoes to meet him. Their lips brushed softly and then again more urgently. Desire exploded in Dan and he released her as if burnt.

She staggered back a step, looking at him with wide eyes. "Dan?"

"I never...I need to go. Thank you for a lovely evening, Skye."

He reached for his coat but she stayed him with a hand. "Dan? Why are you running?"

Dan released his coat and turned back to her. "Skye, I've been alone for more than a year, and you arouse feelings in me that are best experienced in marriage. If I don't go..."

"You'll dishonor me?"

"And God." He nodded. "I don't want to do anything that would hinder a real relationship between us."

"Your principles again?"

He rolled his eyes. "Yes. Listen. If I were to give

into my natural will, I'd cart you off to your bedroom right now. I don't ever want to do that to a woman I respect. You deserve to be honored, cherished, and loved by a husband."

She went to sit on the sofa. She began to unzip her boots. Watching her pull off one was torture to his already overheated body.

"Sit with me, Dan."

"I don't think that's a wise idea."

"I am capable of saying 'no.'" Skye patted the spot next to her and as if she led him by a leash he moved to sit by her. She removed her other boot. She clasped his hand and held it between her two smaller ones.

"Skye."

"Where does this end, Dan?"

"It's a first date. Do I have to have an end?"

She frowned at him. "We're talking about you, Dan. The man who puts walls up and sets rules to protect his reputation and who probably knows what his retirement account will be when he hits sixty-five. Why did you ask me out?"

Dan would have loosened a tie had he worn one. His neck tightened anyway and he tugged at his T-shirt. "You really want the truth?"

"Yes. I do."

"I wanted to date you. Court you—because I want to marry you."

Skye jumped up as if stung by a bee. "You want to what?"

"Marry you. Be your husband. Be a father to your children and any we might have together, keep you warm at night, and eat as many banana cream pies you choose to make for me."

"This is pretty sudden." She began to pace. "I

mean, you're hot. I won't deny that the desire to spend the night with you is beyond tempting, but rushing into something...that's not His plan. And I do want to honor Him. Anyway, I swore I would never marry again."

"Riley wasn't good to you."

"That's putting it mildly. The institution wasn't very attractive. But Dan, you're a pastor. I'm divorced. You can't marry someone like me."

"What do you mean, 'someone like me'? You're exactly who I want. A passionate follower of Christ. Someone who knows her dreams and reaches for them. I love your kids. I love you..."

Skye stopped and stared at him. "What. Did. You. Say?"

"I love you." Dan's heart thundered until it reverberated in his skull.

She looked lost as she stared at him and then away. Her mouth opened and closed as she tried to figure out how to respond. "You can't."

"I can't?"

"No. I'm not worthy of anyone like you."

"You make me smile. You make me want to live again, to do great things, to be a better man. You give me a chance to be a dad."

"So it's really my kids you love?"

"I adore your kids. No doubt about that. But I don't dream about them when I crawl into bed at night."

"So you lust after me."

Dan gulped. "That too."

"How can you be sure it's love?"

"If it were lust I would never be able do what I'm about to do."

"What is that?"

Dan rose to his feet pulled her into his arms and kissed her with all the love and passion bursting from within. She wrapped her arms around his neck returning his kisses in full measure. Finally, he pulled back, released her, grabbed his coat—and left.

Susan M. Baganz

TWENTY-TWO

Never be ashamed of the passion you have for each other.
It is God-ordained and something to celebrate.
Mom Acton, Feta & Freeways

Skye watched the door shut behind Dan as he practically ran from the room. Her noodle-like legs somehow managed to get her to the door to lock it. Her body tingled and longed for more of what he offered. So, this was love? Love that gave but didn't demand. Love that denied temporary pleasure for a bigger purpose.

Dan wanted to marry her. Sure, it wasn't a proposal, but what did *she* want?

Dan.

She flipped off the lights as she made her way to her room. Turning on a lamp by her bed, she slumped to the mattress and stared at the painting of Dan. The one he didn't know she had. The one she drooled over every night. Not that she needed the painted image to see him in her mind. There was no way to paint the kisses he gave her. Never had she felt the way she did when Dan touched her, much less kissed her. It was equal parts exhilarating and terrifying. Desire so strong it overwhelmed common sense.

He felt it too. And he still left.

Could she have said no? He never tested her resolve on that, and after that last kiss she wasn't sure if she would've been strong enough to deny herself the pleasure his kisses promised.

268

But she was nothing like his wife. She didn't look anything like Sharon and Skye most certainly couldn't be who Sharon had been at church. Skye had heard people talk about what a saint Dan's wife was. Skye could never live up to the shadow left by Sharon Wink.

Her kids wanted Dan as a father.

She wanted Dan in her bed.

She didn't want to be alone and struggling to provide for her family.

Marriage to Dan would give her love, a home, a complete family, a stability she couldn't achieve on her own. He had been guiding, protecting, and caring for her ever since he moved in next door. But marriage was a huge step and they both carried baggage. She carried the weight of an addiction-laden spouse who'd also been violent and was still around as a threat. He carried the specter of a wife who'd been perfect. So perfect that his grief even a year later had been palpable and threatened his career.

She wanted what he offered but her practical nature kept telling her it could never work.

She dressed for bed, climbed into the cold, lonely covers and with only the moonlight coming in the window, fell asleep staring at her painting of Dan and wishing for things she could never have.

~*~

He managed to avoid Skye yesterday. He played guitar while leading the worship team that morning, so hung backstage in between services.

Like that would work. Her red hair was like a beacon in the church as everyone stood. *Chicken! She didn't reject me outright but running away from her like I*

did? Coward. But I didn't let the temptation lead us into sin.
Yeah, some consolation that was.

Dan sat down with Nikolos at lunch on Monday.

"How are things going at home?"

"Feels like nonstop drama with Johnny. This cancer stuff has him running scared."

"He's had a rough time of it. How are things with him and Katie?"

"There's some promise there. I'm praying she can give him even more of a reason to fight this time around."

"The love of a good woman can do wonders, can't it?"

"Or the love of a good man, at least I hope that was what helped Tia turn around when she was recovering from her assault."

"Hard to believe how long ago that was now."

"Almost twenty-one months ago, and look what God has done. A wife, a baby, a home, a hit record, awards, new recording contract, ministry opportunities...my cousin struggling with cancer and living with us."

"I'm guessing the wife, child, and Johnny top the list of the things that matter most."

"Yeah, but hey, I'm glad you're back on a team. It was wonderful to listen to you singing and playing on Sunday. I've missed serving with you."

"Ditto."

"How are you doing? You appear more chipper than you were at the beginning of the year or even when you first returned from your leave of absence."

"Yeah, well, you know you mentioned that love of a good woman thing? Cupid struck me hard with a spitfire of an artist who also happens to be my neighbor."

"Skye, right? You mentioned her before. So love is in the air in that apartment building? I used to live there, on the first floor."

"Yeah, but I might have overplayed my hand."

Niko wiggled his eyebrows. "Care to share how the cool, calm pastor could have done such a thing?"

"I finally got around to taking her out on a real date, not just a quick moment to visit in a coffee shop."

"And…"

"Deluca's Cucina."

"Nice."

"And entered her apartment and asked to kiss her."

"And…"

"Niko, I was married for years. I almost hate to admit this. I loved Sharon, I really did."

"No one would ever doubt that."

"When I kissed Skye…it was like I'd never known what love or passion was before that moment."

"And?"

"I tried to leave, but she wanted to talk. She wanted to know my intentions."

"Which are?"

"Marriage. I want to marry her. I cannot imagine my life without her. I love her. I adore the kids. I can't stop dreaming about her at night or thinking about her during the day. It took every ounce of strength to walk out of there after I kissed her a second time."

"Have you talked since then?"

Dan shook his head. "No."

"Afraid?"

"Yup. I'm aware I've only known her, what, nine weeks? It feels more like nine months."

"How would you counsel someone coming to you with this kind of story?"

Dan looked at his friend and frowned. "I'd tell them to take it slow, keep strong boundaries to avoid sin…but that time is not always a factor in determining the success or failure of a marriage in the long run."

"Hard advice. But wise."

"Says the man who married quickly."

"Yeah, well, Tia and I had known each other for years before I realized I loved her."

"You were so clueless."

Niko chuckled. "Yup. I willingly admit it. I was a fool but God in His wisdom gave me the wife I needed at the right time. I couldn't imagine helping Johnny through his struggle without her by my side or Apolo to provide comfort and joy in the midst of the struggle. Dan, how would Sharon view your relationship with Skye?"

"I don't know. Would she be happy? I can't imagine Sharon would want me to be alone the rest of my life. She runs away with Jesus and I suffer alone? The fact is, it really wouldn't matter what she thought. I'm a different person than I was when I was married to her. Her death and the year since, has changed me. The real question isn't what would Sharon want for me. The better question is, what does God want for me? Is Skye the wife He wants me to have?"

"Now you get into weird stuff theologically. Did God select Skye or would any woman you are attracted to suffice as a wife? After all, arranged marriages have often fared better than ones built on feelings of love and attraction. Marriage after all is about more than that. It's a partnership with constant negotiations and irritations."

"It seems providential to me that I would move across the hall from a divorced woman with piercings, two children, and an ex who is an addict and threw a brick through my window. And she wears the silliest furry pink boots. Initially there was nothing in this smoking-hot red-head that should have made me even look at her twice other than as someone who needed Jesus."

"Did you think she was 'smoking-hot' when you first met her?"

"I thought she was cute but not my type. As if I have a 'type.'"

"She definitely didn't appear to be pastor's wife material."

"Far from it, but that's what makes her all the more perfect for me."

"Why do you say that?"

"She challenges me. She calls me on the carpet if my thinking is off. She makes me laugh. She doesn't hesitate to 'poke the bear' as it were. She's unintimidated by me as a pastor. If anything, that was a stumbling block for her."

"Is it still?"

"I don't think so. Then again, Orchard Hill is a unique church that focuses on serving in an area of spiritual giftedness. It's a blessing that the wife of a pastor isn't required to lead women's ministry or play the piano for the worship team or head up the hospitality ministry."

"Sharon could sing. Can Skye?"

Dan shrugged. "I don't really know. I'm not about to audition her as part of my checklist for the perfect wife."

"Since there is no such thing."

"I wasn't as great a husband as I thought I was either, but Sharon never said anything."

"How do you figure?"

"God's revealed that to me during my leave. There were so many things I should have done better, but Sharon never complained. She never asked or demanded things. With Skye, I think she'd be more forthcoming if I were failing her."

"And you would welcome that?"

"Yeah, I would. Sure, it pricks my pride when she's poked holes in my thinking, but she's challenged me to search, dig deeper, and really look at myself. She's not afraid to be honest about her own questions but she's also more than willing to challenge me on mine."

"You described her as a spitfire. Sounds like an apt label."

"Pray for me, Niko. That I make wise choices and that I can woo this woman. Now that I realize I love her, I am impatient to close the deal."

Niko clasped his shoulder. "Definitely praying for you. I've been in your shoes. Trust me, I understand the struggle."

"Thanks, friend."

The men spent time in prayer before they parted ways. Dan headed to the YMCA to catch a workout when he was least likely to run into Skye. He had to burn off some of his pent-up energy. And pray. Who said he couldn't do both at the same time?

~*~

"Mom, I really don't want to talk about it."

"Sweetheart, you haven't dated in years, and

Dan's a great guy. Did you kiss? Were there sparks?"

"Yes, Dan is great, we kissed, and there were earth-shattering explosions."

"So why are you so grumpy today? That canvas is filled with pent-up passion I haven't seen from you in a long time."

"Mom," she dropped her voice to a whisper. The kids were sleeping but still had big ears. "He wants to marry me."

"He proposed?"

"No. Not yet anyway. He told me he loves me and wants to build a life with me."

"That's wonderful!" Mom bounced with excitement.

"Shhh! The kids do not need to know this. I don't want to devastate them if this doesn't work out."

"Why wouldn't it work out?"

"Because I'm not good enough for him."

"I think you're perfect for him and he is exactly the kind of man you need."

"Mom, it's not just him. I would be a pastor's wife. Me? Zumba teacher, artist, and pastor's wife?"

"So? Your obligation is to your husband, not his job. The church hired him, not you. With any other career that would not be a concern. Listen, Riley was a terrible husband but he did give you two adorable kids that Dan happens to love. Give yourself and them a chance. Don't shut the door on the handsome neighbor you can't stop painting...let God lead you in this. You're not alone."

"How do I know what God wants?"

"Ask Him." Mom grabbed her coat and put it on. She gave Skye a kiss on the cheek and departed with a bounce in her step.

Skye frowned as she watched her mother leave. Locking the door, she sat at a blank canvas and prayed. "God, show me what I'm to do about Dan. I love him and yes, he fires my engines but is marrying him in Your plan for our lives? Help me know."

She opened her eyes and grabbed for her paints. All her confusion would find it's expression on that blank surface, and maybe she'd have another piece of sellable art in the process.

~*~

The next day Skye received a call from Jennifer, Pastor Andrew's wife.

"Hello, Skye?"

"Yes?"

"It's Jennifer."

"Hi. What can I do for you?"

"It might be more of what I can do for you. God has laid you on my heart since you were over for dinner and I was wondering if we could go get coffee this week?"

"Oh, um, that would be fine. I'm available tomorrow after my Zumba class at the YMCA."

"I've been wanting to try that. Is it OK if I come there for the class and we go out after?"

"I'd love to have you join us."

"Great, I will come and we'll have coffee afterwards. My treat of course."

"I'm looking forward to it."

"Great. See you tomorrow."

Skye stared at her phone as it disconnected. Could God use Jennifer to answer her prayer?

~*~

The next day Jennifer showed up for class as promised. Skye noticed that the pastor's wife was friends with many of the women in the class. Jennifer was plump but vibrant with a ready smile.

The class went by fast with the women cheering Skye on and giggling when they couldn't manage a new step. They cha cha'd and salsa'd their way to a sweat, and when it ended everyone was exhausted but happy.

Jennifer approached. "I like that you use clean, upbeat music in your class."

"Well, it is the Young Man's Christian Association, but the music choices are new for me. I figured that clean music would be more appreciated by this group than hip hop or party anthems I used to play."

"I for one am grateful. Shall we go get a quick shower before we head for our coffee?"

"I might need to get a scone as well. You ladies worked me hard this morning."

"We worked you?" Jennifer laughed. "I think it was definitely the other way around. You could dance circles around the best of those ladies."

"Only because I've been doing it longer. Many of those could easily test to become instructors."

"I can see why Dan enjoyed it when he attended."

"Beyond watching my booty shake?"

"Yes, beyond that, although I'm sure it was a pleasant bonus."

Skye smiled. She really did like Pastor Andrew's wife. "Let's get those showers."

~*~

When they settled in at the coffee shop, Skye bit into her warmed scone and groaned with pleasure.

"Good?"

"Yes. It hits the spot."

"Wonderful. I'm not going to dance around the bush. We did enough of that in class. I've been burdened to pray for you and Dan and thought maybe you needed a friend to talk to. I'd like to be your friend."

"I've not had many friends since I moved away from the inner city of Milwaukee. I left everything behind, my past however didn't stay."

"Well, maybe we can change that, at least as far as friendships go. I noticed Dan avoiding you on Sunday and guessed it could be one of two reasons. One, he is avoiding you because you had a falling out or two, he doesn't want people to realize yet how much he adores you."

"Or maybe a bit of both?"

"How so?"

"He took me on a nice date and we kissed and he told me he wanted to marry me."

"He proposed?"

"No. It was more complicated than that. I wanted to know why he would date me. What's the point?"

"How do you feel about him wanting to court and possibly marry you?"

"Dan deserves better. I'm no pastor's wife."

"If Dan weren't a pastor would you have an issue with marrying him?"

"Probably not. I mean if he were a high level corporate executive I might have an issue. I don't belong in high society. But other than that, it would be fine."

"He told you that the church hires the pastor, not the wife, right?"

"He told me it didn't matter who I was, the church wasn't marrying me."

"He's right. So what's the problem?"

"Sharon."

"Sharon? She's been dead for," her eyes looked to the ceiling as she counted, "fifteen months."

"I've heard people talk about how perfect she was. The ideal pastor's wife. That's why Amy wanted to marry Dan. She figured she would be a suitable replacement and she would've been right."

"But Dan wasn't attracted to her. He's attracted to you."

"I'm a novelty."

"I think you're more than that, Skye. You are a brilliant jewel of a princess of the King of kings. Dan sees you like God does, perfect and flawless. Yes, I know, we are all flawed and prone to sin, but what Dan sees is someone who will fill an empty spot in his heart and his bed. It's a role that only someone he adores is suited to fill if both of you are to enjoy your marriage."

"Enjoy marriage? When the sex gets old then what else is there?"

"You've enjoyed time with Dan before he ever kissed you."

"Yes."

"How?"

"Coffee here, skiing, going to the movies with the kids, pancake breakfast, working out together."

"See, there is more there. And he obviously adores your art and you've found a fabulous subject to paint, so that's a win for both of you."

Skye sighed. "I'm divorced."

"And were you a Christian then?"

"No."

"How did your husband treat you?"

"He was an addict. He was verbally abusive. He stole money from me, and once he even destroyed my work. He's been a horrible father to the kids."

"Could you see Dan doing any of those things?"

"Never."

"I guess the real issue comes down to this—do you love him?"

Skye sighed and her shoulders relaxed. "Yes. I do."

"Stop trying to be chivalrous and protecting Dan from your imagined fears. He's a wise man in many ways. He would be a faithful husband and father. Ministry is hard. It's good that you have your art. I think Dan learned some hard lessons after Sharon died too. I don't think he needs a wife like her for this next season of his life. I think he needs a woman like you to be his partner."

"Partner?"

"In many ways, yes. Marriage isn't a dictatorship. Sure, my husband is the head of our home and I submit to his authority, but I know he loves me above all else and is seeking God first in his decisions. He listens and values my opinion. When someone loves you that well, and you know that they value the relationship more than being right, it is easy to let them take the lead. It's how God designed them, and as women I think we long to be cherished, protected, provided for, and led."

"I've never experienced that."

"It can be a wonderful reality with the right man—one who seeks to honor God."

Skye shook her head. "Dan has these 'principles' he has in place to protect him and me when we would meet."

Jennifer nodded. "Andrew has those as well. Too many ministers have fallen into affairs or other troubles because they didn't keep strong boundaries on relationships with the opposite sex."

"He finally drove me in his car for our date. And entered my apartment without another adult present."

"And…?"

"He refused to do more than give me a kiss. Practically ran out the door after that."

"Good boy."

Skye laughed. "He's not a dog."

"He's trained himself well though and sometimes those things show character more than words."

"You've given me much to think and pray about."

"Think about this too, our Mother of Preschoolers group meets every other Friday morning. We'd love to have you join us. It would be a great way to connect with other women."

"I will. It might mean moving my schedule around, but we're close to a readjustment anyway. It would be nice to have more friends, but would that complicate my relationship with Dan?"

"No. Many are married, some divorced, some remarried, and a few never married, but none have set their sights on Dan as he doesn't attend except on a rare occasion as a speaker. You are used to being private. You don't need to share with them anything you don't want to. If you ever need to talk though, I'm a safe person for that. I'll be praying for you."

"Thank you, for everything. My mom is around and she is supportive, but it's nice to know someone else is there too."

"And there is Dan."

Skye smiled. "Yes, there is Dan, once I figure out what to do with him."

Jennifer chuckled as they rose to head into the frigid March weather.

~*~

Dan shoveled the walkway and cleared off Skye's car. Might be a futile endeavor if the snow kept coming down, but at least he tried and she didn't have to scrape. He headed to church, shoveled some more there before heading to his therapist's office.

"Dan, what a pleasure. It's been a while."

"Good morning, Shirley. Getting back to work has been busy."

"Why don't you fill me in and tell me why you're back in my office."

Dan recounted the past month, especially his attraction to Skye. "Am I nuts to want to marry this girl? I've never experienced anything like this, not even with Sharon. I loved my wife, although I wasn't as good a husband as I thought I was."

"Dan, you of all people understand the brevity of life. The uncertainty of anything. Marriage, babies, how long you get to spend with someone you love. Accidents, cancer, sudden death…adultery, abuse, divorce. We live in a fallen and sinful world. I've been around more years than I would like to admit to and being a woman, maybe I'm a bit of a romantic at heart. But if you love this gal and she can bring you all you say she can in a partner who will challenge and love you, who will give you a family you've longed for, who loves fitness like you do, and has already helped you out of your more rigid comfort zone—then go for it. You've grieved Sharon long enough and you've made huge strides this year. You are a different man from the one who walked into my office three months ago."

"Go for it? Really?"

"If she were to die tonight, how would you feel?"

"Cheated. Angry. Devastated."

"Not ambivalent, sad, or temporarily concerned about her kids?"

"No, it would go much deeper than that. You'd find me back here to be sure. Someone would need to scrape me off the floor."

"Pay attention to that, Dan. This isn't a passing fancy. You were faithful to your wife throughout your marriage. You've not had any desire to stray outside your marriage or even during your grieving. Women threw themselves at you and you couldn't see any of them. Then Skye came along and burst all your preconceived ideas of the kind of wife you wanted and showed herself to be what you needed."

Dan nodded. "You're right. I shouldn't spend time second-guessing what I sense God is leading me to do."

"Call and let me know how it turns out, and don't forget to invite me to the wedding."

"Thanks, Shirley."

Dan headed to the jewelry store. He had some shopping to do.

Susan M. Baganz

TWENTY-THREE

A heart as soft, a heart as kind, a heart as sound and free,
As in the whole world thou canst find,
that heart I'll give to thee.
Robert Herrick, To Anthea

Skye neglected to look through the peephole. She knew better, but lately the only people to knock on her door were her mother and Dan. Anyone else had to buzz to get in. She figured she was safe. The kids played happily in their room while she prepared some spaghetti for dinner. Sure, the sauce came in a can, but they loved her homemade meatballs simmering away in the oven. The scent even made her own mouth water.

She opened the door and immediately tried to shove it closed again. *Riley!* How did he get in? She hadn't realized he was out of jail, and her restraining order should still be in effect. She reached for her phone and hit the panic button for 911. Riley pushed his way in and slammed the door shut, bringing the kids running. Quinn and Meghan stopped and waited to see what would happen next.

Riley bent down. "Hey kids, come and give your daddy a hug. I missed you."

"You don't need to do that," Skye said to the kids. She moved into the living room and Riley stalked after her. He stopped to look at a drawing she had done of Dan, and while he was distracted she motioned for them to leave the apartment and go to Dan's.

"So, pretty boy is still catching your fancy, huh?"

"He's a friend."

"You never drew pictures of me."

"You weren't a good model. Not an image anyone would want to pay money for. I have to support myself and the children since you won't." Her hands shook as she watched the vein in his forehead throb. He was high. His hands clenched and unclenched as he stalked her. "You know you aren't supposed be here. I have a restraining order against you."

"Who's going to know? Hey," he looked around frantically, "where are my kids?"

"Hopefully safe from you."

His arm swung back. "Why you…"

~*~

Dan barely heard the knock at the door. When Quinn and Meghan spilled over the threshold, he almost suspected they were escaping punishment.

"Dad is beating up Mommy. She told us to come to you to hide." Quinn's voice shook.

Dan shut the door and knelt down to their level. "Tell me what happened."

"We were playing," Meghan stammered through her tears. Dan drew her into his arms.

"Daddy showed up and wanted to hug us. Mommy told us we didn't have to and tricked him into the living room so we could escape," Quinn explained.

"Where do you want to hide?"

"Can we hide in your bed?" Meghan asked.

"Sure." He followed the kids down the hall as he called 911 to report the incident to the police. He pulled the phone away from his mouth to address the kids. "Snuggle in. I'll close the door. OK?"

They nodded as they scrambled into the bed. He closed the bedroom door and headed down the hall.

"I need to go over there and help her," he said to the dispatcher.

"Wait until the police arrive. Domestic violence is dangerous. Do you know if he's armed?"

"I've no clue. The kids didn't mention any weapons."

"Please wait for the police."

"I can't do that. I'm in the apartment across the hall. Her kids are hiding in my bed." He hung up and headed out the door. Taking a deep breath, he headed across the hall and listened at Skye's door. He heard a smack and Skye's exclamation of pain and furniture being toppled. He burst in through the door and quickly saw Riley towering over Skye. Dan took a few steps, grabbed the smaller man by his collar, and pulled him back.

"A man never hits a woman!" Dan bellowed.

Riley shook himself free and turned on Dan. Adrenaline pumping, Dan longed to punch the smirk off the other man's mug.

"She's my wife. I can do what I want with 'er"

"She *was* your wife. She isn't now. You've no right to come near her." His words came through gritted teeth as he fought to restrain his rage.

"I can do what I want. She can't keep my kids from me."

"You abused them. They deserve better."

Riley whipped out a knife and lunged at Dan, who managed to grab his hand and flip him over, pinning him to the floor and holding him there with his knee and the weight of his body. Riley reached up to lock his jaws onto Dan's arm, refusing to let go. Dan held firm in spite of the pain. The door flung open. Police entered with guns drawn, quickly restrained Riley, and dragged him out to the squad car. An officer stayed to take their statements.

"Dan?"

"Bruce, hey, thanks for getting here so quickly."

"Need that bite attended to?"

"I can probably handle it."

Skye stepped forward and forced him to sit at the table. "No. I'll take care of it." She left the room and got a first aid kit. When she returned, she motioned to a chair. "Have a seat, Officer."

"Officer Bruce Ziegler, this is Skye O'Connell. This is her apartment and Riley O'Connell was the man your partner hauled out of here."

"So why are you here, Pastor Dan? And who taught you how to take down a man with a knife?"

"You did."

"Oh, yeah, right. Up to date on your tetanus?"

"Yes, Doctor Bruce." Dan chuckled as he rolled his eyes.

"Ms. O'Connell, do you need someone to take a look at that bruise? Where'd he hit you? In the eye or nose?"

"Two punches. One of each." Skye groused as she cleaned Dan's arm, sterilizing the wound and wiping away the blood before applying an antibiotic cream and gauze bandage. "There, that should hold you."

"Thanks." He rose, went to the freezer, and pulled out a frozen bag of mixed veggies. "Here, put that on the bruise."

She took the bag and gently brought it to her face, flinching as it touched her tender skin.

"He might have broken your nose. Might be good to have that checked out," Bruce suggested.

"Perfect noses are overrated," she quipped.

"Let's get down to business." Bruce began to get a statement from Skye and then Dan. A timer went off for the food as Officer Ziegler was readying to leave.

"Thanks for your help, Bruce." Dan gave the officer a pat on the shoulder.

"Yeah, next time, be more careful, Dan. You're not a super hero."

Dan nodded as the man left. He turned to Skye who was pulling out food from the oven. "Shall I go get the kids?"

She nodded. "Thanks."

"Anytime. What are neighbors for?" He slipped out the door and entered his apartment. He called for the kids. "Quinn? Meghan? It's me, Dan." There was no answer, so he strode down the hallway to his room and slowly opened the door. The kids were buried under the covers and he could barely see their faces as they clung to each other. He sat on the bed and gently touched the lump where they hid. "Hey, kiddos. It's over. Your dad is gone."

Little heads peeked out, and he gave them a grin.

"Your mom's got dinner ready. Hungry?"

The kids flung themselves into his arms and he struggled to stand under the weight of both of them. He staggered to the door as they giggled. Soon he was at Skye's door and he tapped it gently with his shoe. She opened the door slowly until she saw who it was. Dan lowered the kids to the floor and they rushed into her arms.

Skye held them close as he watched. He slowly backed out of the apartment, closing the door softly.

He went back to his own, locked the door behind him, and collapsed into his favorite chair. Leaning his head back he finally gave his heart permission to slow to a normal pace. She was safe now. That was all that mattered, right?

A rat-a-tat-tat came from the door. He dragged himself to his feet. Any energy he had earlier was now gone as exhaustion set in. He peeked through the hole to find Skye there. He unlocked and opened the door.

"Everything OK?" he asked.

"No, it's not." She stepped forward to wrap her arms around his torso and held him tight, her tears dampening his shirt.

He gently pushed hair back from her face and tilted her head up to his. "What do you need?"

"You." She thrust up on her toes and claimed his lips. He was not one to deny this woman this particular request.

Gasping for air, he pulled back. "I'm here for you whenever you need me. You know that, don't you?"

She nodded. "Come join us for dinner? Please?"

He nodded. "I'd love to." He clasped her hand as they walked back across the hall to her apartment to enjoy dinner with the family he hoped to soon claim as his own.

~*~

Skye tucked the kids in with Dan's help and then held his hand as they walked back to the living room. She pushed him down onto the couch, flopped next to him, and snuggled up to his side. "I can't believe you came to my rescue like you did. You could've been hurt."

"Well, I was hurt, but not as bad as he'd already hurt you."

She reached up to touch her swollen nose, and she could barely see through her eye now. "Yeah, well, he's done worse in the past. Words can hurt, and he's destroyed my work too. He was high again. I lose hope that he'll ever be free of his demons."

"He has a choice in that, but I understand your doubts."

"He really needs Jesus."

"I shared the gospel with him after his last arrest."

"I remember you mentioning that. How did that go?"

"About as poorly as you suspect. It is the job of the Holy Spirit to convict of sin and unrighteousness, not us."

"If he lives long enough to come to his senses."

"He's already made his choice, Skye. He can change his mind at any time, but right now, he's chosen darkness over light. Satan over God. He may not even realize that by rejecting the one he's automatically picked his side."

"It's sad."

"Yeah. But I'm glad you weren't injured worse than you were. I came as soon as I could make sure the kids were safe."

"Thanks for taking care of them."

"Any time. They mentioned that they used to hide in the closet, but he took you all by surprise tonight."

"My fault. I didn't look out the peephole."

"It's still his fault for doing what he did." Dan placed a soft kiss on the top of her head.

"You still love me even after this?"

"I'd marry you tomorrow even with your swollen

eye and broken nose if you'd have me."

"We couldn't even get a license that fast."

Dan frowned. "True. Guess that's better for you. No bride wants to walk down the aisle looking like she was in a street fight."

Skye reached over to tickle him. "You'll pay for that."

"I will?" He chuckled as he squirmed.

She turned and looked up at him and all laughter ended as he leaned down to claim her lips with his own.

Dan broke it off and slid to the carpet on his knee. "Marry me, Skye. Please put me out of my misery and say you'll be my wife so I can love you, protect you, and provide for you and the kids. I need you."

He held out a white gold ring with a star sapphire surrounded with tiny diamonds.

"Oh, Dan. This is beautiful. But are you sure?"

"Yes. I love you. Please say you'll marry me?"

Skye leaned forward, and kissed his lips and pulled back leaving him shaken. "Yes."

"Really?"

She nodded and he slid the ring on her finger. It was a perfect fit. "It's beautiful, Dan." She pulled him up to sit next to her again.

"So, um, when?"

Skye had been about to kiss him again but pulled back to give him a grin. "As soon as this bruising goes away. That should give me enough time to find a dress and for us to make our plans."

"Sooo, May?"

"Sounds good to me, but can it be small?"

"You do realize I'm a pastor at a rather large church, right?"

Susan M. Baganz

"So we need to invite everyone?"

"No. We don't, but we might need to have a reception later for everyone."

"Sounds less like a celebration and more like a gauntlet for me to run. Maybe I should rethink this." She reached for the ring.

He put his hand over hers. "No. No rethinking. No reception. Just marry me and make me the happiest pastor in town?"

"Not the world?"

He silenced her with a kiss. It took all his will to leave her that night.

TWENTY-FOUR

My beloved speaks and says to me:
"Arise, my love, my beautiful one, and come away…"
Song of Solomon 2:9

May 2013

Skye finally understood what it meant to be the beloved bride of Christ. She stood at the back of the small café at church as she waited to walk to Dan who stood with Pastor Andrew. Jennifer had agreed to be her matron of honor. Skye's mother sobbed quietly up front. Her grandfather had come from New York. Dan's parents arrived and a select group of friends he felt were close and needed to be invited. Titus, Niko and Tia Acton, Roberto and Stephanie Rodriguez, Tony and his accountability group, among others.

Quinn and Meghan were dressed to the nines and stood one on each side of her as she began her walk down the aisle to the man she had never dared to dream about. Soft guitar music accompanied her.

She came to stand before him, handing her bouquet off to Jennifer. She turned to look into Dan's gorgeous eyes and thanked the Lord for this opportunity to redeem a painful past and start anew with this man.

She swallowed hard when it came time to repeat her vows. Dan spoke his promises to her in a calm and clear voice. She never heard a word of what Andrew preached but hoped they recorded it. She would want to listen to it later when she wasn't enveloped in this haze of love and wonder.

Dan made promises to the children and they each accepted rings to wear, bringing them into the circle of their new family. Dan had even started a process of adoption, anticipating that Riley might be willing to give up parental rights if it meant he was off the hook for the money he owed her. Her ex seemed resigned to the fact that she really was no longer his.

She snapped to attention when Andrew told Dan he could kiss the bride. Dan winked at her as he drew her into his arms and kissed her gently. He whispered in her ear. "More later. Much, much more." His breath on her neck sent a shiver of anticipation down her spine.

They turned to accept the applause and congratulations of everyone around them. Jennifer wrapped her in a warm hug. "Congratulations, Skye. And welcome to the family."

Skye turned to watch her husband receive congratulations, and he glanced back at her—a warm hint of promise in his gaze.

TWENTY-FIVE

Love is really the only thing we can possess,
keep with us, and take with us.
Elisabeth Kubler-Ross

Dan shook his head in amazement as he directed his friends carrying boxes. A new wife, two children, and a new home. All within five months? Only God could bring about that kind of miracle.

Skye and Jennifer laughed in the kitchen as they unboxed pots and pans, deciding where everything should go. Quinn and Meghan were in the fenced-in backyard, playing in their new sandbox. He only hoped they obeyed his request to not dump it on each other's heads.

"Hey, Dan. Where do you want these?" Titus stood there with a hand-truck loaded with boxes labeled "Sharon."

He stared at them for a few moments. He'd not looked at those since he moved them into his apartment in January where they remained in a closet. Thankfully his moving crew didn't forget them. Dan took a shuddering breath. Tony came to stand beside him.

"It's OK to put them in the attic. They are not her. You'll always carry your love for her in your heart. The memories will be there when you're ready for them."

"Thanks. Titus, if you could put them in the attic, but not shoved in the back. Stack them where I'll be able to find them if I want."

"Sure thing." The young mechanic parked the hand-truck and grabbed the top two boxes before heading up the stairs to the attic. Tony followed with the rest.

Dan went to the sunroom Skye had designated for her painting space. He found the portrait she'd done of him and leaned it against a wall. It was the one she'd hidden from him for a long time because he looked broken and sad. He'd come so far since January, but would he ever not miss Sharon? Even with a new wife and family, the loss at times emerged as a deep ache within.

Arms wrapped around him and he lifted an arm to bring his wife to his side.

"You OK? I saw them hauling the boxes to the attic."

"Yeah. It still hurts that she's gone."

Skye lifted herself up to kiss his cheek. "I'm sorry."

"I don't understand God sometimes. But the truth is, if Sharon hadn't died, I would never have moved, or needed to take time off, or met you." He looked at his new wife. "I can't regret any of it, and it almost sounds like a betrayal to Sharon to say that I don't feel as bad that she died."

"How could you? You didn't make it happen. There's nothing to regret. You've lived the life God gave you and you've lived it well. I, for one, am grateful that Sharon trained you as well as she did. Someday I'll get to thank her face to face in heaven because of how God used all of that to bring me to Him—and to you." She stepped away. "I have something to show you. Think of it as a wedding present, just a little late because it took time to get it matted and framed." She pulled out a brown wrapped package and placed it on the worktable.

"Go ahead, Dan. Open it."

A group spilled through the doorway, watching. Andrew and Jennifer, Ty, Nick, Simon, Tony, and Nikolos.

He ripped off the paper to reveal a portrait of himself. Eyes bright and laughing. He couldn't hide his own grin looking at it. He set it next to the one of his sorrow.

"That," he said, pointing to the sad portrait, "was me before you came and turned my life upside down." He then motioned to the new one as he propped it against the wall to await hanging. "This one, is me after you. You brought laughter and joy back into my life and I'm grateful. Thank you, Skye." He bent over to kiss her on the lips and everyone applauded.

Skye whispered in his ear, "I'll give you my thanks later." She kissed his cheek and sashayed through the crowd back to the kitchen. "Come on, everyone. Dan will get the grill started up for some brats, but we can't eat until the truck's unloaded. Jennifer brought her wonderful potato salad too."

Everyone turned back to their tasks and Dan glanced once again at the portrait. Yes, there would be sorrow at his loss, but there were good memories too, and now was the time to make more of them with his new family and old friends. He might not understand it all but he could grab for the joy that was there in this moment. God was good and proved it over and over to him. He strode outside to get the grill warmed up. Bratwurst in Wisconsin was always a good idea.

ACKNOWLEDGEMENTS

It would be impossible to thank everyone who has helped me on my journey, so I apologize in advance for those I will miss. It doesn't mean you are any less valuable and thankfully God keeps better track of those things than I do and His "well done, good and faithful servant" has more merit than any thanks written here.

So here it goes. Special thanks to:

Doris Pollard Wichern – another early reader and one of my most faithful cheerleaders in this writing adventure.

Lisa Lickel – thanks for being such a wonderful mentor, friend and shoulder to cry on when the publishing process throws me those curve balls. I don't think I would have ever taken that first step in this journey to publication without your gentle push.

Andrea Boeshaar – my carpooling buddy, friend, prayer partner, "critter" and encourager. I'm blessed to know you!

Beth Ziarnik – for your love and prayers on my journey.

David Mundt – for praying for me as I wrote this and being a beta reader and giving me valuable feedback as an Adult Ministries Pastor. Thanks for believing in me.

Ken Nabi– for your support and believing in me and the calling God has on my life. Thank you for praying for me as I wrote this novel and tried to shine a realistic light on the bride of Christ.

Julie Cosgrove – for being a beta-reader of this story and giving me valuable input.

Community Church Fond du Lac – for being an inspiration for Orchard Hill. We're not perfect—but I've seen great things in our church family and I'm proud to be associated with you all.

Sally Shupe – my faithful editor. Thank you for finding all those silly errors!

Nicola Martinez – who supports my writing while allowing me the joy of helping others on their journey to publication. I'm grateful for our friendship.

BIOGRAPHY

Susan M. Baganz chases after three Hobbits, and is a native of Wisconsin. She is an editor with Pelican Book Group's imprint Prism Book Group, specializing in bringing great romance novels and novellas to publication. Susan writes adventurous historical and contemporary romances with a biblical world-view.

Susan speaks, teaches, and encourages others to follow God in being all He has created them to be. With her seminary degree in counseling psychology, a background in the field of mental health, and years serving in church ministry, she understands the complexities and pain of life as well as its craziness. She serves behind-the-scenes in various capacities at her church as well as serving on the board of her local American Christian Fiction Writer's (ACFW) chapter. Her favorite pastimes are lazy...snuggling with her dog while reading a good book, or sitting with a friend chatting over a cup of spiced chai latte.

You can learn more by following her blog at susanbaganz.com, her Twitter feed @susanbaganz or her fan page, facebook.com/susanmbaganz

Thank you

We appreciate you reading this Prism title. For other Christian fiction and clean-and-wholesome stories, please visit our on-line bookstore at www.prismbookgroup.com.

For questions or more information, contact us at customer@pelicanbookgroup.com.

Prism is an imprint of
Pelican Book Group
www.PelicanBookGroup.com

Connect with Us
www.facebook.com/Pelicanbookgroup
www.twitter.com/pelicanbookgrp

To receive news and specials, subscribe to our bulletin
http://pelink.us/bulletin

May God's glory shine through
this inspirational work of fiction.

AMDG

You Can Help!

At Pelican Book Group it is our mission to entertain readers with fiction that uplifts the Gospel. It is our privilege to spend time with you awhile as you read our stories.

We believe you can help us to bring Christ into the lives of people across the globe. And you don't have to open your wallet or even leave your house!

Here are 3 simple things you can do to help us bring illuminating fiction™ to people everywhere.

1) If you enjoyed this book, write a positive review. Post it at online retailers and websites where readers gather. And share your review with us at reviews@pelicanbookgroup.com (this does give us permission to reprint your review in whole or in part.)

2) If you enjoyed this book, recommend it to a friend in person, at a book club or on social media.

3) If you have suggestions on how we can improve or expand our selection, let us know. We value your opinion. Use the contact form on our web site or e-mail us at customer@pelicanbookgroup.com

God Can Help!

Are you in need? The Almighty can do great things for you. Holy is His Name! He has mercy in every generation. He can lift up the lowly and accomplish all things. Reach out today.

Do not fear: I am with you; do not be anxious: I am your God. I will strengthen you, I will help you, I will uphold you with my victorious right hand.

~Isaiah 41:10 (NAB)

We pray daily, and we especially pray for everyone connected to Pelican Book Group—that includes you! If you have a specific need, we welcome the opportunity to pray for you. Share your needs or praise reports at http://pelink.us/pray4us

Free Book Offer

We're looking for booklovers like you to partner with us! Join our team of influencers today and periodically receive free eBooks and exclusive offers.

For more information
Visit http://pelicanbookgroup.com/booklovers